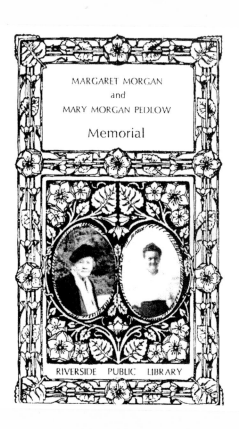

MARGARET MORGAN
and
MARY MORGAN PEDLOW

Memorial

RIVERSIDE   PUBLIC   LIBRARY

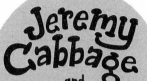

Jeremy
Cabbage
and
the Living Museum
of
Human Oddballs
and
Quadruped Delights

Jeremy Cabbage

and
the Living Museum
of
Human Oddballs
and
Quadruped Delights

DAVID ELLIOTT

Alfred A. Knopf
New York

THIS IS A BORZOI BOOK PUBLISHED BY ALFRED A. KNOPF

Published in the United States by Alfred A. Knopf, an imprint of Random House Children's Books, a division of Random House, Inc., New York.

Knopf, Borzoi Books, and the colophon are registered trademarks of Random House, Inc.

www.randomhouse.com/kids

Educators and librarians, for a variety of teaching tools, visit us at www.randomhouse.com/teachers

Library of Congress Cataloging-in-Publication Data
Elliott, David.
Jeremy Cabbage and the Living Museum of human oddballs and quadruped delights / David Elliott. — 1st ed.
     p. cm.
Summary: While searching for a loving family, orphaned Jeremy becomes entangled in a conflict between his city's arrogant and oppressive leader, the Baron von Strompié, and a group of outlandish people called the "cloons."
ISBN 978-0-375-84333-4 (trade) — ISBN 978-0-375-94333-1 (lib. bdg.)
[1. Orphans—Fiction. 2. Family—Fiction. 3. Adventure and adventurers—Fiction.] I. Title.
PZ7.E447Je 2008
[Fic]—dc22
2007028927

Printed in the United States of America

March 2008

10 9 8 7 6 5 4 3 2 1
First Edition

For Barbara and Eli, my only delights

[Contents]

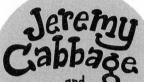

Jeremy Cabbage
and
the Living Museum
of
Human Oddballs
and
Quadruped Delights

Chapter 1

Jeremy Gets a New Mother

"He'll do," the woman said, pointing at Jeremy.

At least, Jeremy thought she had pointed at him. There was so much smoke swirling around the room it was difficult to say.

It belched out of her mouth in huge toxic clouds, just the way it did from the smokestacks of the Baron's factories in the Cudgels. It billowed from her nose and cascaded over the rubbery terrain of her upper lip. Jeremy knew it was impossible, but it even seemed that smoke was shooting out of her ears, hanging in the air around her head in thick, curling wisps, like poltergeists waiting to be sucked down into the fantastic workings of the woman's sunless insides. He coughed and found himself thinking of a story Polly had told him about three boys who had been forced to stand in a fiery furnace.

This must have been what it was like, he thought. *Exactly like this.*

Jeremy had never seen someone smoke two cigarettes at once. The woman used her tongue to roll one cigarette to the left side of her mouth as she shoved another one in on the right. The cigarettes were always in motion, like those tin ducks swimming in a line at the street fairs where Jeremy and Pickles had sometimes earned a meal doing acrobatic tricks or juggling.

He wanted to get a better look, but he couldn't bring himself to do more than sneak an occasional glance. It wasn't because of the woman's size, either, though she *was* the fattest woman he'd ever seen. Her head, the few times he got a peek at it through the haze of smoke, was as big as a watermelon. And it wasn't because of her hair, which was dyed black, black as tar, and twisted around and piled on the top and back of her head in a style Jeremy had once heard referred to as a "beehive"—in this case, a gigantic beehive, a beehive that could house all the bees that ever were.

No, it was neither of these that caused Jeremy to turn his gaze sharply to the side when Harpwitch brought him out so the woman could see him. It was the way she had first looked at him, like she was picking out an item at a store that she had to have but didn't much want.

She gave him the once-over for what must have been the hundredth time.

"Yeah," she said. "He's kinda scrawny, but he'll do."

Jeremy stepped back away from the smoke, but quick as a cobra, Harpwitch reached out a skinny arm and pulled him over to her.

"So you like our little Jeremy Cabbage, do you?" she said, pressing her bony hip into his rib cage.

"I didn't say I liked 'im," the woman replied. "I said 'he'll do.' That's different."

"Fifty piés," Harpwitch snapped.

"Twenty-five," the woman snapped back.

Jeremy watched as she raised a magnificently dimpled arm to point at a wooden sign nailed to the wall directly behind Harpwitch. He didn't have to turn around to know what the sign said.

HARPWITCH'S HOME FOR MEAN DOGS,
UGLY CATS, AND STREY CHILDREN
MEAN DOGS   ⚹25.00
UGLY CATS   ⚹15.00
STREY CHILDREN   NEGOTIABLE

He also knew that when Harpwitch lettered the sign, she had misspelled "stray," replacing the "a" with an "e."

There's no such thing as s-t-r-e-y, he told himself, as he always did whenever he thought about the sign. *That means there's no such thing as a strey child, and that means I'm not one.*

As if she had read his thoughts, Harpwitch tightened her grip on Jeremy's shoulder. He would have run, but there was no place to go. The little room that served as an office for HHMDUCSC had no windows, and both doors, the one that led to the outside and the one that led to the room directly behind the office, where Harpwitch kept the big cages that held the mean dogs, were locked. The doors at Harpwitch's were always locked. (There were no ugly cats at HHMDUCSC, or cats of any kind for that matter. Harpwitch was allergic. But she included them in the name of her establishment as a way to bring in customers. People were always looking for a tough cat to take care of the rats that roamed the streets of the Metropolis as freely as its citizens.)

"Twenty-five," the woman said again.

"*Thirty*-five," Harpwitch countered.

Harpwitch had to be careful. Jeremy was the only kid she had right now. For a moment, it seemed that she might have gone too far.

The woman narrowed her eyes and pursed her fleshy lips, but instead of protesting, she opened her cavernous mouth and coughed. Jeremy thought she was just clearing her throat, but that first cough was followed by a second, and the second by a third. Her large form took on the qualities of a giant amoeba, constantly changing its shape as the explosive coughing gained more and more control.

The smoke that had been clinging to her now surged away like the waters of the ocean surge away from the shore after an earthquake has struck its darkest depths. She quivered and lurched as if the ground were giving way under her. And still she coughed. And rasped. And barked.

It seemed that the woman would turn herself inside out from coughing. *Someone should call a doctor,* Jeremy thought. But Harpwitch didn't do so much as offer the large woman a glass of water. She knew she had her now.

"Thirty-five," she repeated. "Not a penny less."

By the time the coughing subsided, sweat was pouring from the woman's chin onto her immense bosom like an automated irrigation system gone haywire. She shoved her hand into the torn plastic bag hooked over her arm, rummaged around for a moment, and then pulled out a handkerchief.

"Done!" she gasped, using the tattered square of graying cotton to wipe away the tears the coughing fit had brought on. In her massive hands, it looked no bigger than a postage stamp.

Harpwitch released her hold on Jeremy's shoulder. Tomorrow, there would be five tiny bruises where her fingers had worked their way into his flesh.

"I'll just go upstairs and get the papers," she said, moving quickly toward the interior door. "In the meantime, Cabbage, where are your manners? Give your new mother a hug."

She reached into her pocket, produced a massive key ring, and disappeared behind the door. The huge woman jammed herself into a rickety wooden chair and, fanning her face with the handkerchief, closed her eyes. She was like a mountain of living dough.

You're not my mother, Jeremy thought. *You never will be.*

Then he closed his eyes, too. He thought of happier times, times with Polly and Pickles and all the other Parrots. He remembered the story that Polly told him about how she found him, an infant left on the street in a crate of cabbages.

"There you were," she'd begun, "naked as a baby raccoon, cooing like you couldn't imagine a better life than to be raised with a head of purple cabbage for a father and a head of green cabbage for a mother. It's a good thing I discovered you in there. You might have ended up in a pot of sauerkraut."

What came next was his favorite part, about how Polly named him after the label that was peeling away from the crate: JEREMY'S CABBAGE.

"It must have been fate," she'd concluded as she washed his face in that tiny circular pattern that always made him feel like she was rubbing in something good rather than rubbing out something bad. "After all, Jeremy is my favorite name."

The smoking woman threw a cigarette butt onto the floor, stamped it out, and before the last spark had died, lit up another. Jeremy clenched both hands into fists. It was a habit he had acquired the night of the raids.

Where is Polly now? he asked himself. *Where is Pickles? Did they end up in a place like Harpwitch's? Or worse?*

As if Jeremy had invoked Harpwitch, the door opened and she appeared, keys rattling in her pocket like a nest of beetles. In her hand were the forms that Jeremy knew would not only release him to the smoker but also free Harpwitch of any responsibility if Jeremy turned out to be sickly or, worse, a thief.

The smoking woman slammed her hands onto the arms of the wooden chair. It creaked pitifully. Jeremy was sure that it would split in two as the woman heaved herself forward and up. But the chair, though strained to the last molecule of the very glue that held it together, stayed in one piece.

Harpwitch shoved the papers toward the woman,

who stood panting and gasping from the immense effort she had just put forth. With one hand, she swabbed the handkerchief across her forehead and down her broad cheeks. With the other, she pointed at Jeremy.

"Get your things together, sonny boy," she wheezed. "Time to take you home."

Chapter 2

He Tells Her She Is Pleasingly Plump

Jeremy waited in the backseat of the car, his few possessions—two T-shirts and an extra pair of shorts—shoved into a paper bag. At one time, the bag must have held bananas. Their thick, sweet scent hung in the air and mixed with the smell of stale smoke.

He thought about opening a window, but just as he reached for the handle, the gleaming white hood of a Wisdom Wagon rounded the corner ahead of him. There was no mistaking it, either. In the dingy neighborhoods through which they prowled, the Wagons were as conspicuous as a sunstone in a pile of coal.

Jeremy wanted to put his fingers in his ears as Polly had taught him to do when the Wagons rolled through the Cudgels, but he was afraid the driver might see him. There had been troubling rumors recently, tales of rabble-rousers circulating dangerous ideas through the population of the Metropolis. The Baron didn't approve of ideas in general, but *these* ideas were causing him to keep an even more watchful eye on his citizens. The Wagon drivers were the Baron's spies; Jeremy didn't want to be reported to the PatPats for suspicious behavior.

He pressed himself into the musty upholstery of the backseat. Dust, some of it as ancient as the cosmos, rose from the colorless fabric and hung in the air around his head. He held his breath and waited.

"Charity begins at home!" the voice—a man's this time—blasted from the loudspeakers attached to the top of the Wagon. "Curiosity killed the cat!"

The huge van trolled its way down the street, slow and confident as a basking shark.

"Beggars can't be choosers!"

"Silence is golden!"

"Ignorance is bliss!"

The man's voice launched from the bell of the loud-speakers, battering the buildings' shaky foundations and lodging under the eaves, where it reverberated, again and again.

Jeremy opened his eyes. The Wagon was next to him now. He released his breath and waited for the an-nouncement. When it came—a woman's voice now—he mouthed the words along with the recording.

"These important educational messages have been brought to you free of charge through the generosity of Baron Ignatius von Strompié and his family. Thank you for casting your vote for the Baron on Election Day. And remember, What you don't know won't hurt you!"

That's a lie! Jeremy silently argued. *We didn't know the raids were coming, and look what happened.*

And that bit about Election Day? Well, as far as

Jeremy knew, there never had been an election in the Metropolis.

As the Wisdom Wagon reached the end of the block, Jeremy looked to his right and saw the smoking woman standing on the pavement in front of HHMDUCSC. From the way she was panting, Jeremy guessed that she was resting after the Herculean effort it had taken to come down the short flight of steps. Finally, she urged one foot in front of her and began to lurch unsteadily toward the car.

As she made her way, he thought about his last words with Harpwitch. Once the papers had been signed, she'd pulled him into the back room, "to say our little good-byes," she told the woman. But, of course, what she had really wanted to do was remind him about the Rule.

"Don't mess this up, Cabbage," she'd hissed. "Remember the Rule!"

Jeremy almost laughed. Remember the Rule? It would have been impossible to forget it.

There were hundreds of rules at HHMDUCSC. Rules about laughing: *Don't!* Rules about washing: *Hands: once a week. Other parts: once a month.* Even rules about dreaming: *Nightmares fine. All other dreams forbidden!* But there was one rule above all others. It was the Rule of Rules. It was *the* Rule, and it was just as true for the mean dogs as it was for the unfortunate children who found their way to Harpwitch.

Three strikes and you're out. That was it. *Three strikes and you're out,* by which Harpwitch meant you had exactly three chances for adoption. You could be returned once. It wasn't good, but it was permissible. You could be returned twice. The consequences were unimaginable, but you were given another chance. If you had the great misfortune to be returned a third time, though, look out!

Just last week, one of the dogs had been brought back by its third owner. The dog's name was Scrap. He was medium-sized, red, with a big ruff and an extravagant tail that curled over his back like a question mark. Jeremy was afraid of Scrap, as he was of all the dogs at Harpwitch's, but at least when he fed him and cleaned his cage, as Harpwitch forced him to do with all the dogs, Scrap didn't lunge on his chain and snap at him as the others did.

Though Jeremy wasn't fond of Scrap, he hated to see him come back a third time. The owner's complaint was the same as the first two had been.

"It ain't mean, like you said," complained the man, who had a stringy blond ponytail and dragon tattoos running up and down his arms. "It ain't mean at all. It don't even bite! I adopted that there dog to bite, but all it does is growl a little bit and whine. It don't foam at the mouth or nothin'! Gimme my money back!"

At first, Harpwitch tried to convince the man that perhaps he hadn't been stern enough with the dog. She even tried to hand him a pamphlet she'd written: "How to Make a Mean Dog Meaner." But when the man flexed the muscles on his arms so that the dragons looked like they were about to take flight, Harpwitch handed him his money back without another word.

"Put the dog back in its cage," she'd said to Jeremy. "The gentleman is not satisfied."

That night, Jeremy awakened to a terrible howling,

a howling that was interrupted by an even more terrible silence. The next morning, the cage was empty.

Jeremy had never been around when a kid was returned. He didn't want to be, either. He would try to forget everything else about HHMDUCSC—the sickening food, the terrible smells, and most of all, Harpwitch herself—but he would remember the Rule. He would remember the Rule the rest of his life.

The front door to the car opened, and a thick cloud of smoke rolled in. Through it, Jeremy saw a huge arm emerge and hook itself by the elbow on the steering wheel. Ever so slowly, as if she were being dragged by an enormous crane, the woman began to appear and settle into the driver's side of the car. First came her tremendous bottom, as broad and varied in its topography as a small continent. This was followed by her gargantuan back and finally by her massive head, with its colossal black beehive.

Jeremy couldn't imagine how she managed to do it. She was jammed between the steering wheel and the seat tighter than a wedge in a stump.

"I'd like to get whoever manufactured this car and wring his ding-dong neck!" she gasped. She hauled in one leg and let it settle in front of her like a dinosaur settling into a mudflat. "Why don't they make 'em for normal-sized people?"

It was amazing how clearly the woman could speak, considering the two cigarettes that were dangling between her lips.

"You probably think it's my fault, don't ya, Cole Slaw?" the woman said. "That's what I'm gonna call ya. Cole Slaw. 'Cause your last name is Cabbage. Get it?"

The woman started to say something else, but before she had a chance, she was overtaken with another coughing fit. Jeremy wondered if he should pat her on the back, but he wouldn't have been able to even if he'd tried. The car shook so violently that he had to grab hold of a seat belt to keep from bumping his head.

Finally, the coughing subsided to a wheeze. The car settled down. Jeremy let go of the seat belt.

"Like I was sayin,'" she gasped, hauling in the other leg. "You probably think I'm too ding-dong fat for this car!"

He swallowed. As of yet, he hadn't spoken one word to the woman. He certainly wasn't going to begin by telling her she was too fat.

"No, ma'am," he finally managed to say.

"No, ma'am, what?" she said.

"No, ma'am," Jeremy replied, "I don't think you are too . . . I mean . . . I think . . . I think you are *pleasingly plump!*"

The car backfired and pulled out into traffic.

Pleasingly plump! He hadn't even known he was going to say it until it was right there in his mouth.

"That's a good one, Cole Slaw!" the woman said. "That's a good one."

Jeremy wasn't sure what to make of this remark. In fact, he didn't know what to make of the woman at all. He didn't even know her name.

"By the way," she said, as if she had read his mind, "call me Tiny."

Jeremy soon realized that Tiny drove just the way she walked, lurching and weaving all over the road.

"Road hog!" she hollered, shaking her mighty fist out the window. "Sunday driver!"

He turned his attention to the throng of pedestrians making their way through the broken bottles and scraps of newspapers that littered the sidewalk. Occasionally, the wind picked up and pushed the papers over the surface of the concrete, reminding Jeremy of pictures he'd seen of devilfish skating along the ocean floor. He was hoping he might catch a glimpse of Polly. After all, stranger things had happened. But suddenly, Tiny jerked the car to the left and pulled up alongside a Wisdom Wagon that was cruising along in front of her. Now the only thing he could see was his own reflection staring back at him, like a ghostly brother lost in the glare of the Wagon's unrelenting whiteness.

"That's the way the cookie crumbles!" the voice shouted from the loudspeaker. "You win some; you lose some!"

By now, smoke completely filled the car. Jeremy's eyes began to water, and though he tried to stifle it, he coughed once or twice.

"That sounds like a smoker's cough!" Tiny said accusingly. "You don't smoke, do ya, Cole Slaw?"

What a question! He was only eleven years old!

"No, ma'am," he said.

"Well, that's good," said Tiny, lighting up a third cigarette as the car accelerated, "'cause smokin' is bad for your health!"

Chapter 3

He Is Not Afraid of Heights

Tiny stormed through the streets of the Metropolis like a general leading an army. She turned left. She turned right. At one point, she raced around the same block three times.

It was like a ride at the carnivals. Jeremy had been on one of these marvels once, just before the raids. He and Pickles had performed all morning, moving from one crowd to another, juggling and somersaulting and propelling each other through the air like human rockets. By noon, they'd earned enough to buy a trencher, a thick block of crusty bread piled with beef or pork, for which the carnival was famous.

"I'll get it," Pickles had insisted. "Some of these guys use cat meat. Stay here and sing or something. Maybe you'll earn enough to buy us a cherry slider."

Before Jeremy could respond, Pickles trotted off in the direction of the trencher stands, but not before he scooped up the coins from the red cap in which they always collected their money. When he returned, instead of their lunch, he held two tickets.

"I found 'em," he said. "On the ground. Next to one of the stands."

Jeremy wanted to take the tickets to the Lost and Found. Most of the people visiting the carnival lived in the Cudgels, as Jeremy and Pickles did. The tickets were expensive. Parents scrimped for weeks to buy a single pair. But Pickles had another point of view.

"Finders keepers," he'd insisted. "That's what the Wisdom Wagons say."

They hadn't agreed on which of the rides to try. Jeremy hoped they would choose the Wheel of Heaven, an enormous gyroscope covered with rows of lights. It floated its passengers more than ten stories above the Metropolis, then slowly spun them, as if there were no such thing as gravity. You could see all of the Metropolis from the Wheel of Heaven. He'd overheard one of the disembarking passengers say that she'd even spotted Helios, the very center of the Metropolis and the private park where the Baron had built his mansion. But when Jeremy turned to Pickles to suggest they use the tickets for the gyroscope, his friend was already in line for a different ride.

From its highest hill, nearly as high as the Wheel of Heaven, the coaster's tracks plunged almost vertically into a gaping black hole. Jeremy looked at the fiery red letters flashing over the ride: HELLCOACH. By the time he caught up, Pickles had already shoved the tickets into the vendor's callused yellow hand. They emerged twenty minutes later, on the other side of the carnival grounds, shaken to their very bones. Jeremy tried not to notice the stain that ran down the front of Pickle's ragged trousers. It was only later that Jeremy realized he never learned what had happened to the money that Pickles took for the trenchers.

That had been the day, too, that Pickles admired the bright blue jacket worn by an officer in the Junior Pat-Pats. Jeremy and Pickles had watched the pug-nosed boy bullying his way to the front of the lines all day.

"I'd like to have me one of those jackets sometime," Pickles had said.

The jacket was a wonder. There was no question about that. With its brass buttons and gold trim, it was finer than anything Jeremy or Pickles had even touched, let alone worn. But the only way Jeremy knew to get one of the jackets was by joining up, and he couldn't imagine anyone he knew doing such a thing. The Junior PatPats were even more feared than the grown-ups in the parent organization. There were stories, many stories, of JPs turning in their parents to senior officers for a chance to try on the jackets and the power that came with them.

Tiny sped on, switching from lane to lane like a performer in a car rodeo. As she accelerated, Jeremy once again considered the odds that Pickles had not been caught in the raids.

From the moment that Polly had chosen it as their hideout, Pickles had never seemed comfortable in the Licreeary. He hated its dusty aisles and the solitude it seemed to impose the moment you crawled through its windows. But to Jeremy, with its books lining the shelves, its rooms full of maps, and its orderly separation of history from science and science from stories, the Licreeary was the best hideaway in the Metropolis. It was home.

"I'm goin' out for a walk," Pickles had told Jeremy that night. "This place is givin' me the creeps. As usual!"

It was just minutes after he left that the PatPats arrived, blowing their whistles and swinging their clubs and casting their nets. Throughout the pandemonium that followed, Jeremy looked for Pickles, but he was nowhere to be seen. It was as if the boy had disappeared.

"We're almost there, Cole Slaw," Tiny announced from the front. She yanked the car to the right. The tires squealed, and Jeremy was thrown toward the middle of the seat as the back of the car fishtailed.

Even through the thick smoke that filled the car, Jeremy could see that the neighborhood through which they were zooming was very different from the street where Harpwitch's was located. There, all the buildings had been attached, their bowed fronts lined up like the tattered books on a shelf at the Licreeary. But here, the houses were separated by a hand's width of space, as if someone had come along with a giant crowbar and pried them apart.

The houses were huge, too, and made of wood rather than brick, and each was different from the next. Some had turrets that jutted accusingly toward the sky and slate roofs pitched at impossibly steep angles. Others, with their protruding fronts and small, high windows, reminded Jeremy of ships that had somehow run aground. Scattered among these larger structures sat sullen cottages, their fences with missing and broken pickets, daring anyone foolish enough to walk through their gates.

Jeremy cupped his hands against the window.

Occasionally, he saw a splotch of faded green or a smudge of pink, but it had been years, perhaps decades, since anyone had thought of painting.

Tiny jerked the car to the left in order to avoid a pothole.

"That one just about had us, Cole Slaw," she called out. "If we'd gone into that one, we woulda ended up in one of them foreign-speakin' joints."

Jeremy might have responded to this remark, but when the car swerved, his eye had caught something that nearly caused his heart to stop. Four words. Painted on the front of one of the houses: DOWN WITH THE BARON!

The impossibility of such a thing made him think he'd been mistaken. But as Tiny turned right, he had just enough time to look over his shoulder to see the bold black letters dripping down the cracked, weathered clapboards. Whoever painted them there had had no time to worry about neatness.

DOWN WITH THE BARON.

So, Jeremy thought, *the rumors are true!*

The hairs on his arms stood at attention. It was dangerous even to read such a thing. He closed his eyes.

The only time Polly had ever been really angry with him was the time she heard him repeating a rhyme Pickles had taught him.

> The Baron's digestion!
> Oh, what a wonder!
> It's the talk of both
> Wise men and fools.

When he sits on the pot
You won't hear no thunder
Just the *click-click*
Of glittering jewels.

But I've got a secret
That everyone knows;
I'll share it with you—
Mum's the word!
From the top of his head
To the tips of his toes
The Baron himself
Is a turd!

"Do you want to end up in the Choir Stall?" Polly had scolded. "Do you?"

The Choir Stall was the most notorious prison in the Metropolis. It had gotten the name from passersby, who said they could hear the prisoners inside "singing" from the other side of the high wall that surrounded it.

Jeremy never understood why Polly had been so fierce. She was very angry with Pickles, too, but he had sloughed it off with a shrug.

"It's only a song," he'd said. "I sing it all the time, and nothin's happened to me yet."

Before Jeremy had time to consider further, Tiny lifted a tremendous leg and slammed a foot down on the brake pedal as if she were squashing a bug. Jeremy shoved his feet against the front seat as the car screeched to a halt and backfired.

"Well, here we are, Cole Slaw," Tiny announced. "Home sweet home."

She opened the door and slowly swung herself around so that both feet were flat on the patched, disintegrating pavement. Her bottom, however, stayed stubbornly planted.

"Gimme a hand here, Cole Slaw!" she panted. "I'm stuck tighter than a finger in a ding-dong fizz bottle."

Jeremy hopped out of the car, thankful for his first breath of fresh air since they'd set off. Tiny held up both arms the way a baby does when it wants to be picked up. It took Jeremy a moment to realize what it was that Tiny wanted him to do. He thought about running, but the image of those four words was still stamped on his brain. For all he knew, the PatPats were watching this very moment. He wrapped his fingers around her wrists and gave a tug. His hands felt like they were sinking into soft clay.

"That little-bitty yank ain't gonna do no good!" Tiny complained. "Put some muscle into it, Cole Slaw! I can't sit in here all ding-dong day."

This time, Jeremy braced his right foot against the back door of the car.

"One," he counted, "two . . ."

On "three," he pulled on Tiny's arms as if his life depended on it. She flew out of the car with a loud pop, like one of those fake snakes in joke cans marked PEANUTS.

"Like I said," she wheezed, using Jeremy's shoulder to regain her balance, "I'd like to get whoever invented this here car and wring his ding-dong neck."

While Tiny caught her breath, Jeremy took his first look at the house. It was the largest on the block, three stories high and with so many gables it looked like it was wearing a crazy party hat. At one time or another, the house had been blue. But the color had faded so that now, with its sagging black shutters, it looked as if it were recovering from a serious accident.

On the right side, a tower rose into the air. The higher it went, the farther it leaned away from the house, as if it was considering a break for independence. At the very top of this teetering structure was a series of small square windows.

Tiny dabbed at her forehead with the same handkerchief she had used at Harpwitch's. She pointed to the windows.

"That's your room, Cole Slaw. Up there," she said. "I sure hope you're not afraid of heights."

Chapter 4

A Warning?

As she lurched her way around the front of the car toward the long sidewalk that led to the house, Tiny lit up another cigarette. Jeremy fell in behind her.

"Step on a crack, break your mother's back, eh, Cole Slaw?" she chuckled.

Since it looked as if someone had taken a sledge-hammer to the shattered squares of cement on which they were now walking, it was nearly impossible *not* to step on a crack. Clumps of wasteweed sprouted and flourished in the spaces left where large chunks of the walk were missing. But, impossible as it seemed, Jeremy did not let the toes of his worn-out sneakers cross the meandering, spidery lines.

I have a mother somewhere, he thought. *A real mother, even if I don't know who she is.*

Besides, there was Polly, and she was almost the same thing.

He stopped walking and remembered the afternoon in the Licreeary just two weeks before the raids. It was a bone-chilling day. Cold rain bucketed down and infused the air inside the Licreeary with an icy rawness impossible to ward off. The others huddled under their ragged blankets, napping or talking quietly, but Jeremy, though the cold penetrated his very blood, sat on the floor in one of the aisles, reading. It was an exciting story about a shipwrecked boy on a desert island. The boy was just about to slake his thirst by cracking open a coconut when Polly's voice brought Jeremy back to the Licreeary.

"I thought I'd find you here," she'd whispered. She hunkered down on the floor across from him. "You know what today is, don't you?" she began.

He didn't. Monday? Tuesday? Life on the streets made every day seem the same. Sometimes, it seemed silly to him even that the days had names.

"It's your birthday," Polly had said. "At least, it's the anniversary of the day I found you in those cabbages. I was practically a baby myself, and now just look at us! We're almost grown up."

Jeremy wasn't sure that he felt grown up. Not yet. But it was reassuring to hear that Polly thought he was. And he liked the idea of having a birthday. It was odd. He'd never really thought about it.

"I think a day like this deserves to be celebrated," Polly continued. "I don't have a present or a cake, but . . . well . . . I do have *this*." She reached into the pocket of her dress and pulled out a small blue candle. "At least we can make a wish."

She struck a match and held it to the candle's delicate wick. The flame sputtered for a moment as if it weren't sure it could live up to the occasion. But eventually, it seemed to gain confidence and settled into a bright, steady glow.

Together, they counted. On "three," they blew the candle out. Polly watched the gray smoke drift lazily up toward the ceiling.

"I hope you made a big wish, Jeremy," she said. "After all, big wishes stand just as much chance of coming true as small ones. Now tell me about that book."

"Cole Slaw?"

Tiny's voice broke into his memory the way a burglar bursts into the bedroom of an unsuspecting sleeper.

"What the heck are you doing back there?" she called out. "You're as slow as ding-dong molasses!"

Jeremy blinked once, realized where he was, and resumed his progress. He continued to concentrate on the cracks in the ruined sidewalk, moving sometimes to the right, sometimes to the left. Each step brought him closer and closer to the house. It lay ahead of him, unwelcome and unknown. Jeremy hated surprises. Surprises meant the raids. Surprises meant the PatPats rushing in on you like a swarm of angry hornets. Surprises meant living with Polly one moment and Harpwitch the next.

As they approached the porch, Tiny grabbed a bent metal railing and heaved herself up onto the first step. She leaned backward at a dangerous angle. Jeremy knew he should get behind her and give her a shove. But realizing where he might have to put his hands to do it, he instead stepped in front of the woman. Without saying a word, he took hold of her free hand. Her fingers wrapped around his wrist like an octopus wrapping its tentacles around an oyster.

"Now you're talkin', Cole Slaw," she panted. "Now you're talkin'."

Standing two steps above her, with his back to the house, Jeremy pulled with every bit of strength his small frame could muster. Now it was *he* who leaned at a dangerous angle. The two looked like dancers frozen in a comic ballet until eventually, Tiny slowly righted herself. At last, she was vertical. Jeremy found himself thinking about the time that he and Polly and Pickles had gone down to the shipyards to watch the masts being raised on one of the Baron's schooners.

They proceeded this way, one step at a time. Finally, Tiny scaled the last step, and both she and Jeremy stood on the porch, sweating and gasping for breath.

It was a nice porch, really. Or would have been at one time. It spanned the entire front of the house and curved gracefully around its side, like a river that had decided to follow the path of least resistance. It was the kind of porch from which, in days gone by, the wind might have carried the comforting clink of ice cubes as they tumbled from a pitcher of lemonade and the friendly *creak-creak-creak* of rocking chairs with high, comfortable backs.

But there were no rocking chairs in sight. Only boxes. Hundreds of them—some small enough to hold a single pair of shoes, others so massive as to have contained refrigerators. The entire porch, from the wall of the house to the railing, was covered with these boxes, piled topsy-turvy, five- and six-deep. The only surface of the porch they did not conceal was the space that led from the front door to the steps where Jeremy and Tiny, who was once again rummaging in her bag, were now standing.

"Excuse me, Tiny," Jeremy said. "But are you just moving in?"

Under normal circumstances, Jeremy might not have been so bold as to ask such a personal question of a stranger, but the circumstances were not normal. Besides, he'd just pulled her up a flight of steps. He had earned the right to ask a question.

"Moving in?" she asked, throwing her head to one side so that the beehive pointed to the house next door. "Cole Slaw, I was born and raised in this house. Probably kick the bucket here, too." She returned to her bag. "Now quit buggin' me with silly questions. I got to find that ding-dong key."

Jeremy inspected the boxes more closely and realized that the question *had* been silly. Anybody could see that they had been there for years, unmoved, untouched. The advertising on their tops, telling the world what they originally contained, had faded to indistinguishable smudges, and their sides, softened from exposure to the open air, bulged dangerously. Some were splitting at the corners. From one of these fissures poked a tiny hand. Its thumb was broken completely off.

Tiny found the key at last and looked up to see Jeremy staring at the hand.

"Dolls, Cole Slaw!" she said. "Doll *parts,* if you want the truth. Arms mostly. Might be a foot or two in there, too. A head, maybe. You never can tell, Cole Slaw. You never can tell."

Was Tiny a doll-maker, then?

She bent to put the key in the lock. The beehive smushed against the door. Jeremy heard the soft click of the tumblers, and suddenly, the door swung open. Tiny disappeared into the house.

Jeremy stood at the threshold, blinking, waiting for the smoke from the cigarettes to clear so his eyes could adjust from the outside light. But though he continued to stare, he could see nothing. In spite of the many windows, the inside of the house was as black as a cave.

"What are ya waitin' for, Cole Slaw?" Tiny's voice called from somewhere inside. "Your ding-dong birthday?"

A pair of eyes flared in the darkness. Jeremy's heart leapt to his throat. The eyes were red and angry, the furious eyes of a demon.

"Cole Slaw?" Tiny's voice called out again. "Get your ding-dong behind in here."

The eyes brightened. He breathed. It wasn't a demon, after all, but the tips of Tiny's cigarettes glowing in the shadows.

Once again, Jeremy thought about running. But where? He would surely get lost in the labyrinth of streets that Tiny had driven through. And the Baron's spies were certain to be crawling through the neighborhood, looking for whoever had written on the house they passed earlier. It would be only a matter of time until the PatPats found him. And that would mean only one thing: returning to Harpwitch. Even now, he could see her marking a big black "1" by his name.

He looked over at the doll's hand reaching desperately through the side of the cardboard box. Was it a warning, signaling him not to enter? Or was it waving to him, greeting him in the only way it could?

"I ain't got all day, Cole Slaw!" Tiny's voice echoed from inside.

Standing there alone, with the dangers of the Metropolis behind him and the unknown in front of him, he thought of all the stories he'd read in the Licreeary, stories of children who had been chased by giants or who had fallen under some evil curse or who had been forced to go on dangerous journeys and do impossible things in order to save someone. The children in those stories suffered terrible misfortunes, but in the end, if they were brave and if they were true, they somehow turned out all right.

"Cole Slaw?"

Clenching both hands into fists and whispering Polly's name for good luck, Jeremy took a deep breath and stepped over the threshold, disappearing like a shadow into the darkness.

Chapter 5

He Knows What to Do

Inside his sun-filled study at Helios, the Baron Ignatius Fyodor Maximus von Strompié III sat at his mahogany desk wondering what to do about this business of the cloons. His wife had been complaining again, and when the Baroness Gertrudina von Strompié was unhappy, the possibility for his own comfort was no greater than the chance of a commoner's coming into possession of a sunstone. In other words: zero.

"Send them to the Terra Nequam," she'd urged earlier that morning, referring to the ferocious no-man's-land to the west of the Metropolis and the location of the Baron's sunstone mines. "Ban them! They're unnatural! They're freaks! How can you allow them to mix with the citizens of the Metropolis? There's no place for them here among normal people!"

The Baron had never been able to understand his wife's fanatic hatred of the cloons. A day didn't go by when she didn't harangue him on the subject of their banishment.

But it wasn't that simple. The people needed the

cloons. Gertrudina would see that if she would only visit one of their establishments on the outskirts of the Metropolis. Even if he *was* the Baron, he had to have a *reason* for banishing them, didn't he? And so far, he hadn't been able to come up with one.

Of course, he hadn't tried very hard, either. He would never admit it to his wife, but in his heart of hearts, he enjoyed the cloons. Their big red noses were hilarious. And their antics—the pratfalls and the pie-throwing—cracked him up. What was so bad about that? Still, he had to admit that his wife had a point. *Everyone should stick to his own kind.* That was clear. That was common sense. *Yes, everyone should stick to his own kind!*

In the meantime, as he often reminded Gertrudina, he'd already passed the Cloon Clause—a new law requiring parents to register with the PatPats the instant their brats showed the first symptoms of *cloonodium felicitatum.* Usually, this was at about the age of ten or eleven. Until that time, the children seemed completely normal. But then the rare genetic condition began to work its mysteries on the child. The nose started to grow ridiculously round and red. The feet lengthened and broadened to enormous proportions. The personality took a sudden turn toward the outlandish.

Within a few months, the change was complete. What once had been a regular child became a full-fledged cloon. The only hope then was to get a job in one of the shows that entertained the lower classes, a prospect, as it turned out, the cloons were delighted with. In fact, peculiar though they were, the cloons, and the collection of oddballs who worked with them, freaks and social outcasts mostly, were probably the happiest citizens in the Metropolis.

"Cloons schpoons!" the Baron said aloud as he turned to the large windows that looked onto the gardens. "I'll think about it later." This, by the way, was one of the Baron's specialties—thinking about things later.

If it weren't for all these annoyances, life in the Metropolis would be perfect. And if anyone doubted it, all he had to do was look out the window of the Baron's study and gaze upon the hundreds of roses, as the Baron was doing now. But even the sight of the fountain he'd commissioned—a larger-than-life likeness of himself spitting a fine spray of water onto a group of children crouched around his knees—was not enough to calm him completely. So he did what he always did when he felt troubled: made a mental list of all the marvelous things he had done for the Metropolis. Closing all the Public Free Libraries, for example.

It was clear that the libraries had become nothing but hangouts for troublemakers. The Metropolis was much safer without them. And in case anyone was wrongheaded enough to miss the libraries, hadn't he shown how generous he could be by providing the Metropolis with the Wisdom Wagons?

As the Baron ticked off his many successes, he came at last to his most recent accomplishment, the rounding up of all the stray children. This had been the idea of the Baroness.

"Look at them!" she'd insisted, pointing out two

boys tumbling on a street corner. "Collecting change in that filthy hat. Revolting! They're multiplying, too! Like rats! Our Rosamund shouldn't have to see such things!"

The Baroness was right, of course. The number of stray children did seem to be increasing by the day, a fact that puzzled the Baron. Why didn't parents of the Metropolis take better care of their children? Look what a wonderful job he and the Baroness were doing with Rosamund. If only other people would follow their example.

"Our citizens aren't working hard enough," he'd concluded. "They should put in more time at the factories and less time at the street fairs and cloon shows. Then they could afford to look after their brats."

The next day, the Baron did two things: (1) He offered a series of rewards to anyone who could tell the police where the stray children hid at night, and (2) he passed a law increasing the mandatory hours for factory workers from ten hours a day to twelve. What he had forgotten to do was increase their wages for the extra work. Oh well, he would get to it one day.

Thinking of these things gave the Baron an idea for his Weekly Wisdom Wagon Address. He walked to his desk, pulled out the chair, and sat down. Then, with a magnificent flourish of his arm, he plucked his favorite pen from its gilt holder and at the top of a piece of parchment inscribed:

Address #577.

I have often heard it said . . . , he wrote. But immediately, he drew a heavy black line through it and started anew.

A wise man once said . . . This didn't seem to satisfy the Baron, either.

He thought for a moment, crossed out the second beginning, and wrote, *I recently said to my wife* . . .

"Ahhh," he murmured, putting the pen back to the parchment. "That's it!"

I recently said to my wife that children should be seen and not heard . . . He paused for a moment and then continued with *but some children should not even be seen.*

His concentration was disturbed by a soft, almost inaudible tapping from the other side of the oak doors that led to his study. The Baron scowled. He didn't like to be interrupted when he was working on his Weekly Address. Thinking was hard, and once his train of thought derailed, it was almost impossible to get it back on track. He knew it wasn't the Baroness because she never bothered to knock. He was equally certain it wasn't Rosamund because his daughter never visited of her own accord.

It occurred to the Baron that it had been several days since he had actually seen Rosamund. He made a mental note to ask Jack, his servant, to ask Martha, the housekeeper, to ask Jules, the upstairs valet, to ask— what was her name? Rosamund's new girl? . . . oh yes, Mary; they were always named Mary—anyway, to ask Rosamund's new girl to ask his daughter how she was.

In the meantime, the tapping grew louder. The Baron stood and struck what he considered to be a baronial pose. But the unmistakable smell of gasoline had drifted under the doors and through the keyhole, causing the Baron to sneeze in a most undignified way.

"You may enter," he said once he had composed himself.

The golden knob, handsomely engraved with the Baron's monogram, slowly turned, and the heavy doors opened with an unpleasant groan. Behind them stood a figure so pale that the Baron thought of those fish that live in slimy pools under the surface of the earth, creatures that have never seen the light of day. Two pink eyes blinked from a bald head.

The Baron stamped his foot. Finding the Chief Driver of the Wisdom Wagons in his study was like finding a fly in his bouillabaisse. It upset the natural order of things, just the way the stray children did when they appeared in the nicer neighborhoods of the Metropolis. It wasn't right.

"Wirm!" he bellowed. "You?"

"Yes, Your Royalish and Most Excellent Baronage," rasped the man. He slithered into the room, keeping his eyes focused on the floor in front of him. "It is I. Your humble servant, Jeriah Wirm."

He wore an orange-and-brown-striped turtleneck, which, from the way his head wobbled from side to side, seemed to be doing him the service of keeping his neck erect.

The Baron marched to the front of his desk. "Look around you, Wirm!" he fumed. "What do you see?"

With great effort, the bald, pale man lifted his head and glanced upward.

"I'll *tell* you what you see!" the Baron continued. "You see the study of an important man doing important work."

"Yes, Your Regaling Highness," Wirm whispered. "It's just that . . ."

"It's just that what?" the Baron thundered.

You had to be tough with types like Jeriah Wirm. That's what being a baron was all about.

"I . . . I thought you'd better see *this,*" Wirm said.

With hunched shoulders and a bowed head, he slunk his way up the center of the room, while from the pocket of his trousers, he retrieved what appeared to be a photograph. Extending his hand toward the Baron, he looked his employer in the eyes for the first time since entering the room.

The Baron snatched the photograph from Wirm's soft, pallid hand and held it under the shade of a crystal lamp. The blood drained from his face so quickly it almost seemed that he had sprung a leak. Quite suddenly, he had become nearly as pale as Jeriah Wirm himself.

"Another one?" he shouted.

Wirm clucked his tongue and wagged his head. "I'm afraid so, O Noble One. Another one."

The Baron screamed until his face was the color of the grapes garnishing his dinner salad each night. The crows that always roosted in the trees outside his study took to the sky in a rush of fluttering black wings. It was as if they were thinking, *Let's get out of here! He's having one of his tantrums again.*

But the birds would have been mistaken. This was not one of the Baron's regular tantrums, like the one he'd had last week because his soup was cold. It wasn't even a super-tantrum like yesterday's, when he'd lost a game of croquet. This was a tantrum like no other.

Jeriah Wirm, standing straighter now, watched his

employer's incredible display of pique. From the way the corners of his mouth twitched, one might almost guess that he was enjoying it.

"A driver took the picture when he was out on his rounds," he explained once the Baron calmed down enough to listen.

The Baron looked at the photo again. It was a picture of a house, a house similar to many in the Metropolis, jammed up against the houses on either side and badly needing a coat of paint. But it was not the house itself that caused the Baron to kick his desk chair across the room, where it splintered as it crashed against the wall. It was the four words in bold black paint dripping down its front.

"How many does this make?" the Baron asked at last.

Wirm counted on the fingers of one hand. "Six," he said.

For a moment, the great man said nothing. When he did speak again, the blood had returned to his face, and his tone of voice was calm, gentle almost.

"You know, Wirm, I was just thinking. And do you know what I was thinking?" He chuckled in exactly the way he thought a baron should chuckle. "No, of course you don't. I was thinking that I need a new Commander General of the PatPats."

The pale man lifted his head and tilted it slightly to the left, like a dog listening to its master suggest the possibility of a walk.

"You'd like that, wouldn't you, Wirm?" the Baron continued. "You'd like to be Commander General of the Patriotic Patrol?"

With great effort, Wirm nodded.

"Are you sure, Wirm?" the Baron asked, raising his voice. "Are you sure you wouldn't like to be a lowly driver for the rest of your miserable life?"

Wirm continued to nod.

"Well, Wirm?" the Baron shouted. "Well? Which shall it be? Commander General? Or driver?"

"Commander General, O Generous One," Wirm said, continuing to nod. "Commander General."

"What are you standing here for, then, nodding like a Bobo doll?" the Baron screamed. "You know what to do, I hope!"

Wirm stopped bobbing his head. "Yes," he replied with a terrifying smile. "I know what to do."

"Well, do it, then!" the Baron shrieked. "Do it!"

As if propelled by the sheer volume of the Baron's voice, Wirm oozed backward toward the door. Eventually, he lifted a limp leg and stepped, backward still, over the threshold.

The Baron Ignatius Fyodor Maximus von Strompié III returned to the window from which earlier that morning he had so enjoyed the view.

"What a rotten morning!" he complained aloud. "First the cloons and now this!"

He sniffed, trying to regain the composure that he had unmistakably lost in front of Wirm. He noted with annoyance that his study was no longer lightly scented with the attar of roses. Instead, the smell of trouble hung in the air. Trouble and gasoline.

Chapter 6

She Looks like a Speckled Trout

In another part of the palace, Her Royal Highness Rosamund Millicent Florifica von Strompié sat at her dressing table. Behind her, a maid struggled to weave the girl's unruly red hair, thick and curly as a lamb's, into two braids.

"Let's just have pigtails today, Mary," the young Baroness said nonchalantly. She glanced upward into the mirror to see if she could gauge her servant's response. But the maid had already started the long, painful process of winding the braids in the complicated pattern that would eventually result in two tight coils resting over the girl's ears.

"Your mother left very specific instructions about your hair, Your Highness," she said.

"Oh, hang my mother!" the young Baroness responded. She stood up so suddenly that the coils, which the maid had yet to pin, unwound and fell down the girl's back. "And I've told you a thousand times, Mary. Don't call me Your Highness. It's silly. Call me Rosie."

"Yes, Your Highness," the maid replied. She placed her hands on the girl's shoulders and gently guided her back onto the velvet stool.

"I'm serious," Rosie protested. "Not a single soul calls me by name!"

Once again, the young Baroness looked at her maid's reflection in the mirror. Mary had been with her a short time, but Rosie was already very fond of her. For one thing, she didn't go tattling to her mother every time Rosie behaved like a normal girl. For another, she was kind. The last maid pulled the brush through her hair so ferociously that Rosie's scalp throbbed for hours afterward. And when she wound the braids into the bunlike coils that, according to Rosie's mother, did the best job of hiding her large ears, she pulled so hard that Rosie had complained. But her mother was unmoved. Luckily for Rosie, in addition to being a bully, the maid was also a thief. She was now in one of the factories.

The new girl hummed softly as she struggled with Rosie's hair; it was a melody Rosie didn't know. Several minutes passed.

"There!" the maid said, tucking one disobedient curl into the mass with one hand and patting the girl lightly on the cheek with the other. "Finished. You're lovely!"

"I'm not!" Rosie protested. "I look like"—she considered her reflection in the mirror—"like a speckled trout!"

The young Baroness wasn't far wrong. She was covered, from the top of her scalp to the very tips of her toes, with freckles.

These freckles were the sworn enemy of the Baroness Gertrudina, who was furious that her daughter had been born with the complexion of a parrot rather than a dove. Declaring a full-out war against them, she'd scoured Rosie's skin with everything from laundry bleach to poultices of lemon juice and chicken droppings. She'd forced her daughter to stay inside for weeks at a time in rooms where curtains had been pulled to block out every bit of sunlight. She'd allowed her to eat only white foods—potatoes and milk. At the protest of her family's physician, a certain Dr. Perfidio P. Purgatorn, she'd even consulted herbalists, toothless crones who lived in dark alleys and whose skin reeked of vetch and other plants with unpronounceable, bitter-sounding names. But the freckles were stubborn. They were as much a part of Rosie as her quick laugh and her hot temper.

"Sometimes, I think the girl sprouts them just to spite me!" the older Baroness complained to her husband. "It isn't just the freckles, either. It's her hair, too! The way she walks! Everything about her!"

"Yes," Rosie repeated as she studied her reflection in the mirror. "That's it. A speckled trout!"

The servant stood behind the young Baroness. "I like your freckles," she said plainly.

Rosie jumped up and faced the girl, who was perhaps five years older than her own ten years. "You're lying," she declared. She was disappointed. It was another thing she liked about Mary. She always told the truth.

"It's as if you've rolled through the Milky Way," the maid replied. "It's as if you're covered with stars."

In all her life, Rosie couldn't remember anyone saying such a lovely thing to her.

"Now come along, Your Celestial Highness," the maid continued, taking her by the arm. "The dance master is waiting."

The girl dug her heels into the soft carpet. "No!" she protested. "I won't!"

"Your mother was very clear about her instructions today," Mary reminded her. "She wants you ready for your birthday ball."

"That isn't for months," said Rosie, unhooking her arm from her maid's and plopping down on the floor like a rag doll. "And I don't want a birthday ball. *She* does. Besides, I hate the dance master. He's like a great whirling frog."

Before Mary knew what was happening, Rosie hopped up from the floor, grabbed her by the waist, and spun her around the room in a crazy, rollicking two-step.

"No, Mademoiselle," the young Baroness wheezed through her nose in a perfect imitation of the horrid man. "No, Mademoiselle, *I* lead. *You* follow."

The maid laughed in spite of herself. "Other girls have made friends with frogs," she said, extricating herself from Rosie's strong hands. "To their great advantage."

"I suppose you're talking about that girl who kissed a frog and he turned into a prince," Rosie replied. She took a seat on the edge of her enormous bed and kicked off her slippers. "But here's the difference. She broke a promise to that frog, and I never break promises. Besides, in the real story, the princess doesn't kiss the frog. She throws him against the wall, which isn't a bad idea when it comes to the dance master."

"Be that as it may," the young servant said, kneeling in order to slip the shoes back onto the girl's feet, "the dance master awaits. If I don't get you there soon, your mother just might get you a new maid."

This was enough for Rosie. She grabbed both of Mary's hands, pulled her up, and hopped off the bed. The thought of losing the maid was almost unbearable. Her mother would do it, too. She knew she would.

"Mary?" Rosie said, releasing the maid's hands.

"Yes?" the maid replied as she pressed the tips of Rosie's lace collar between her thumbs and forefingers. The collar had been tatted by the most skilled lace-maker in the Metropolis. Rosie had worn it fewer than fifteen minutes, and it was already beginning to curl, as if it were grinning at the joke of finding itself around the girl's freckled, ungainly neck.

"Mary." Rosie repeated the name. This time, though, it wasn't a question. "I've had five maids in the last year, and all of them have been named Mary."

For the slightest fraction of a second, the maid stopped fiddling with the collar. "Perhaps it's just a coincidence," she muttered as she resumed her work. "It's a very common name."

"That's what I thought, too, until I overheard my mother telling the Countess Langa-Nez that she always changes my maids' names"—she paused—"to Mary."

"Your mother is a very clever woman," Mary

said, suddenly turning her interest to the hem of Rosie's gown.

"Cruel, you mean," Rosie responded. "And quit fussing with my dress. You know as well as I do that it doesn't do a bit of good."

"We must hurry, Your Highness," Mary said, taking Rosie's hand and moving her toward the door.

"I'm not taking another step until you tell me your real name."

"But—"

"I have a right to know!" Rosie declared.

The maid looked toward the window, hiding her face from Rosie's view. She was remembering the deliberate cruelty with which the older Baroness had instructed her.

"Above all," Gertrudina had concluded after a long list of do's and don'ts, "you are not now, nor will you ever be, Rosamund's friend. She is a baroness. Her friends come from the highest circles. You are nothing but a common maid. That's all. She will address you as Mary. There's no need for her to know your real name, whatever it is."

The young maid turned back to Rosie, who, true to her word, had not moved a muscle. She patted Rosie's hand affectionately.

"Telling you my real name would put us both in danger," the maid said. "What if you were to slip in front of your mother?"

Rosie hadn't thought of this, but she understood instantly what the maid was suggesting. If Rosie were to accidentally call the maid by her real name in her mother's presence, Mary would be dismissed for breaking the rules the older Baroness had imposed—dismissed or worse.

"Tell me the first letter, then," the girl replied. "Surely no harm can come from that."

"One day, perhaps," the maid said as she whisked the girl out the door with a gentle but firm hand. "But for now, the frog awaits."

Chapter 7

It Wasn't Lost on Him

"Cole Slaw? Did you find it yet?"

Though Tiny was in the next room, her voice was muted, as if she were on another floor of the ramshackle house.

"Not yet," Jeremy called out. He was sitting on the edge of a wooden crate directly beneath a bare, flyspecked bulb. It flickered over his head like a bad idea.

"Well, keep lookin', Cole Slaw. You just got to find it. It's in a—"

"A big red envelope!" Jeremy called back. He sighed heavily.

Careful not to jostle the haphazard stacks of boxes that surrounded him, he hopped down from his perch into the only open area of the room, a three-foot square of wooden floor. Shaky towers of boxes rose to the ceiling, stacked in the same wobbly minarets that filled every available space in Tiny's house until its interior was a web of twisting, narrow pathways. They confirmed what the boxes on the porch had hinted at. Tiny was an incurable pack rat.

"Waste not, want not," she'd declared on their first day together, two weeks earlier. "That's what that loudmouth on the Wisdom Wagon is always shoutin', and I believe 'im, Cole Slaw. I save everything! You never can tell when you might need a spare thumbtack or the odd spoon."

Jeremy could understand saving thumbtacks and spoons, even when they were bent beyond use. But what about the bags of bottle caps or the shoe boxes full of dust?

"There might be something in that dust that I didn't see when I was sweepin' up," she'd explained. "A paper clip or one of them twisty things you tie things with."

But Tiny's obsessive saving had backfired. Now, amidst the hundreds of boxes and bags and crates and cartons, she couldn't find the one thing she desperately needed: the deed to her house, the piece of paper that proved it was legally hers.

Jeremy took a black crayon from his pocket and marked an X on the side of the box he'd just sifted through. Its collection of rubber bands, string, thimbles, candle nubs, mismatched socks, seed packets, candy wrappers, Popsicle sticks, newspaper clippings, frayed shoelaces, and a lone bowling pin had been one of the easier ones.

He was deciding which box to inspect next when Tiny appeared at the end of the path that opened into the space where he was working. That was one of the things about the maze that Jeremy couldn't get used to. It muffled sound so that the woman could materialize without so much as a single echo of her broken-down slippers slapping against the bare floor.

Her massive shoulders pressed against the cardboard that rose on either side of her. Jeremy noted again that if she were an inch wider, she wouldn't be able to navigate the maze. As usual, a cigarette dangled from either side of her mouth.

"Like I told you before, Cole Slaw," she said, frantically looking up at the piles, "if we don't find that ding-dong deed, the Baron's gonna take away my house. I never even heard of no Squatters' Law."

Tiny was referring to one of the Baron's lesser-known pieces of legislation. It required all home owners to produce documents proving ownership. If they couldn't, if the papers had been lost or destroyed in a fire, the Baron declared that the property belonged to him.

"If he takes away *my* house," Tiny continued, bobbing the beehive to emphasize her point, "he takes away *your* house. Get what I'm gettin' at, Cole Slaw?"

Jeremy knew exactly what she was getting at. If the deed could not be found, Tiny would have to leave the house and live with her sister. And her sister, she'd explained every day since his arrival, was not the kind of woman who would welcome one extra mouth to feed, let alone two. In other words, if he didn't find the deed, he would find himself back at Harpwitch's.

"I adopted you to help me find that ding-dong deed," Tiny said, turning sideways to allow her shoulders some freedom from the pressing cardboard.

Jeremy watched with apprehension as ashes from

her flaring cigarettes floated to the floor. It wasn't lost on him that many of the boxes were filled with old paper—receipts, religious flyers, pages torn from books, empty cereal boxes. Paper was flammable. It *burned*. One errant spark and the house would turn into a bonfire the likes of which would rival the great conflagrations of history. He'd planned a route of escape from every room. But he knew this was foolish. The boxes had long ago covered the windows, casting the rooms into an eternal dusk and preventing their use as a means of exit. The only way out was down one of the dark, twisting alleys.

Tiny stepped into the space, turned around, and shuffled back down the path she had come from. "That deed is somewhere in this house, Cole Slaw," she said as if he were standing directly in front of her. "And you better find it!"

Jeremy watched her massive form disappear into the shadows of the passageway. The matter of the deed was troublesome. He didn't want to go back to HHMDUCSC under any circumstances. On the other hand, Tiny had been curiously uncommunicative about what life would be like when the deed was found. If it was true that she had adopted him only to help her find the deed, once it was in her hands, what then?

For the moment, it was best not to think about it, but it nagged at him and caused him to feel unsure about what he would do if he actually were to find the document. In the meantime, there was nothing to do but keep looking.

He moved the rickety wooden ladder Tiny had

provided to get to the tops of the piles and tested it against the next stack. He hoisted his weight onto the first rung. It felt steady enough. He began to climb.

When he reached the top, he discovered that the pile was crowned with a small green box that hadn't been visible from the bottom. Though the box wasn't large, it was jammed up tight against the ceiling. Getting it down without upsetting the precarious balance of the entire stack would be tricky. If he pulled too hard, the whole thing could go tumbling down and he might be buried in an avalanche of Tiny's junk.

Keeping one hand wrapped tightly around the ladder, Jeremy tested the box with the other. It was completely wedged between the carton beneath it and the moldering ceiling. But he kept at it, cupping his hand first around one corner and then another, until the box grudgingly began to give way. Soon enough, it was safely tucked under his arm.

He began his descent and tried to guess what the box had originally contained. A pair of boots, he thought. Or a vase, maybe. But he'd learned from experience that whatever its contents had been, there was no way of knowing what now lay hidden beneath its lid. Yesterday, he had carelessly flung aside the lid of a carton on which Tiny had scrawled MOUSETRAPS. There had been no warning that the mummified corpses of the mice they had trapped were still lodged under their deadly metal snappers.

Stepping onto the relative security of the floor, he placed the small box on the crate he used as a workbench. He took a deep breath and closed his eyes. Preparing himself for anything—snakeskins, beetle carcasses, rabbits' feet—he slowly lifted the cover from the box and peeked at its contents through half-opened eyes.

"Cotton balls!" he whispered with relief.

The soft white mounds spilled over the sides of the box and onto the floor; it was as if Tiny had somehow managed to trap a cloud. But from the heft of the box, he knew that it held something more than the white tufts of cotton.

He began to remove the nappy white spheres one at a time, dropping them around his feet until it looked as if he had been caught in a blizzard. Eventually, a form began to reveal itself—a narrow cylinder, slightly larger at one end than the other. Jeremy recognized the object instantly.

"A spyglass!" he shouted.

He lifted the telescope from the box and held it horizontally in the palms of his outstretched hands. It had the feel of an ancient thing, but there wasn't a single scratch on its silver and brass barrel. Using his thumbs, he slowly rotated the instrument. It glowed softly in the dim light.

Cautiously, Jeremy extended the eyepiece until the telescope was three times its original length. Holding the far end with his left hand and the eyepiece with his right, he brought it to his eye and pointed it toward a stray ticket stub that had escaped from one of the boxes and fallen to the floor. He was expecting the lens to be cracked or, at least, clouded. But to his surprise, the perforated edge of the ticket stub came into sharp focus in the very center of a perfect circle of light.

Wrapping the fingers of one hand tightly around his discovery, he climbed back up the ladder. Though there was little to see in the room, he used the telescope to examine every square inch of the lit area. It seemed to capture the light and hold it, so that he was even able to see individual specks of dust that had fallen between some of the floorboards. It was a remarkable instrument.

He scrambled back down the ladder and carefully tucked the telescope into the elastic band of his shorts. Tiny told him that he could keep anything in the boxes he found, but what need did he have of dead mice or broken cups or empty wooden spools? The telescope, though, was a different matter. He realized it from the moment he made out its elegant form, lying as solemn and still as an Egyptian mummy in its bed of cotton. The telescope would help him find Polly.

Chapter 8

A Thread of Light

Later that evening, after a peculiar dinner that Tiny called Goo Bucket, Jeremy stepped across the threshold into his room at the top of the turret. It was almost a cell, really, but it was relatively clean and it was private and it was his, at least for the moment. It was also the only room in Tiny's house that wasn't crammed with her worthless collections. She was too large to climb the narrow stairs that led there.

Though the room was small, it was pleasant, perfectly square, with a window in the middle of each of the four walls. From the moment he'd entered it, it reminded Jeremy of a story Polly told him when he was very young. Later, he read it himself from his favorite book at the Licreeary.

A powerful king lived in a great palace. The palace was in a sunny land, but beneath it lay a dark secret—a labyrinth whose twisting passages turned onto each other so diabolically that whoever entered it could never find his way out or escape the jaws of the Minotaur, a creature half man and half bull with a mighty appetite for human flesh.

In Jeremy's imagination, his room in the turret was like the palace, sitting atop the writhing corridors of the maze Tiny had constructed below. Of course, it wasn't fair to say that Tiny herself was a monster, but it was impossible for Jeremy not to make the connection between the creature of the story and the gigantic woman roaming the arteries of the unsolvable puzzle beneath his room. Tiny wasn't cruel, but he would never describe her as motherly, either.

Today, however, Jeremy wasn't thinking of the story of the Minotaur, but instead of the miners in the Terra Nequam, men and women forced to spend all their daylight hours underground, like moles, working in the Baron's sunstone mines.

He sat on the edge of his cot.

I'm coming out of the mines, he told himself. *And just like the miners, I'm bringing up a treasure that has been hidden for years.*

He was referring, of course, to the telescope, but he knew he was much luckier than the miners. The mines were dangerous places, filled with noxious underground gases and given to mysterious explosions and subterranean avalanches.

Part of Jeremy knew that the chance of his using the telescope to spy Polly walking on the street or stepping out the door of a strange house was against all odds. But Jeremy also knew that life wasn't always rational.

If life were rational, he reasoned, *I never would have been left in a box of cabbages. If life were rational, there would be no such places as Harpwitch's Home for Mean*

Dogs, Ugly Cats, and Strey Children. If life were rational, I would not be spending day after day sifting through boxes of old string and disintegrating recipes and mice skeletons.

He removed the telescope from his waistband. Then, holding the eyepiece with one hand and cupping the rounded barrel with the other, he cautiously extended the instrument. It was like a mighty dragon leaving its cave.

He held his breath, listening for the gratifying click that would tell him the spyglass had reached its fullest length. Careful not to let his fingertips smudge the soft, ancient gleam of its surface, he lifted it to his eye and pointed it to the window that faced directly north. It framed a view of neighborhoods very much like the one in which he was living. But now he could pinpoint each house, watch the comings and goings of its inhabitants, and if luck were with him, maybe even find Polly or one of the Parrots. Once again, he thought of the story of the Minotaur.

The tale ended when a hero named Theseus volunteered to enter the labyrinth. Theseus found the monster and ended his reign of terror once and for all. He had succeeded with the help of the king's daughter, Ariadne. She had given him a ball of thread to unwind so that he could follow it to find his way out.

The telescope is like Ariadne's thread, Jeremy thought. *Except it's a thread of light.*

That evening and each evening after, he sat at the windows until the telescope could no longer extract a single particle of light from the polluted darkness of the Metropolis night. He was already becoming acquainted with some of the residents to the north—the old woman with the cane, the little red-haired girl who played hopscotch by herself hour after hour, the frightening man who muttered to himself as he counted the number of steps it took him to reach the door of his house from the curb.

To the east was more of the same, but Jeremy also knew that this was the direction that led to the center of the Metropolis. Once, at noon, when the sun was at its highest, Jeremy snuck up to his room to see if the telescope could reach as far as Helios. He watched in wonder as a glint of light, brighter than a sunstone, sparked within the circle framed by the lens. This, he knew, was the sun reflecting off the gilded roof of the Baron's palace.

To the south lay a kind of wasteland. Boarded-up buildings surrounded what must have been a park at one time. Neglected, it had metamorphosed into a field of thorns, overgrown with wasteweed and littered with the rusting parts of metal objects no longer recognizable in their decay. One of the structures facing this desert reminded Jeremy of the Licreeary and made him feel homesick for the cheerful times he had spent there with Polly and the others.

But it was to the west where Jeremy trained the telescope most often, for it was to the west where the house with the graffiti sat in the middle of its block like a rebellious general.

DOWN WITH THE BARON. Four words. By themselves, none of them extraordinary. But strung together, they were as dangerous as dynamite. Each time Jeremy raised the telescope to study them further, goose bumps popped out on his arms. And yet, he could not stop himself. He was drawn to them the way animals are sometimes drawn to music, and he spent hours examining each of the letters besmirching the front of the abandoned house.

As he had noticed on that first day, their author had been in a hurry; the black paint dripped as if the pigment were trying to escape from such a perilous endeavor. But with the aid of the telescope, Jeremy saw, too, how naturally each of the letters had been formed. He didn't know what to call the subtle curlicues that finished off some of the finely executed lines, but he understood that whoever had written the words was also an artist of sorts.

As for the message itself, Jeremy didn't know what to believe. It did seem to him that the Baron lived in luxury while the rest of the Metropolis starved. *On the other hand,* Jeremy thought, *he is a baron, and barons are used to palaces and rich foods and fine clothes.* At any rate, while Jeremy wasn't sure that he entirely agreed with whoever had written the words, part of him admired the bravery and conviction it had taken to do it, and he wondered if he would ever feel so strongly about something.

And so the time passed at Tiny's, the daylight hours with Tiny haranguing him to search through the boxes and the evenings with the telescope helping him to search through the world surrounding Tiny's house.

In the meantime, the large woman was growing more desperate. She now smoked *three* cigarettes at once. Worse, she couldn't let Jeremy alone. She sometimes spent the entire day with him, accusing him of carelessness or not working hard enough. She herself never lifted a finger, except to light another cigarette.

"Did you find it yet, Cole Slaw? Try that box over there. No! Not that one. The other one. Are you sure you looked through every single box in that stack? What was the use of my shelling out thirty-five piés for you? I paid good money so that you'd find that ding-dong deed!"

He was working in a small room now. Its walls were lined with shelves, though of course Jeremy hadn't known that until he had dismantled some of the towers pressed directly against the room's perimeter. He'd just finished a box marked SARDINES. To his surprise, it was crammed with can after can of the unlucky fish, the expiration dates more than ten years passed and all the keys broken off and missing. But the next box he picked up, about the size of a shoe box, was unmarked and surprisingly light; in fact, Jeremy thought that it was empty.

He shook the box gently. There was no rattle, and nothing bumped against the underside of the lid, but he could hear something slide lightly over the bottom and hit the interior walls, something that might be an envelope. Pearls of sweat popped out on his forehead; the hair on the back of his neck stood up. He looked behind him. Tiny had shuffled out of the room to find another pack of cigarettes.

Slowly, he lifted the corner of the box and peeked inside. At first, he saw nothing. But as his eyes adjusted to the dim world inside the box, a color began to define itself against the nondescript cardboard bottom. As if it were materializing for his benefit alone, the color began to take shape. There was no mistaking it! A square red envelope lay in the bottom of the box as peacefully as that fellow who had slept for a hundred years.

What happened next, Jeremy could never explain. He snatched the envelope from its hiding place and deftly tucked it under his shirt. He even threw the empty box behind one of the towers lest it spark Tiny's memory about where she had hidden the envelope. When she shambled back into the room, three cigarettes dangling from her down-turned mouth, he didn't say a word.

He spent the rest of the day answering Tiny's questions and suffering in silence her complaints about his work. But when Jeremy entered his room that evening, he took the envelope from his shirt and placed it in the center of the bed.

The envelope presented him with a terrible dilemma. If he gave it to Tiny, as part of him knew he must, he would have fulfilled his function and Tiny might return him to HHMDUCSC. On the other hand, if he kept the envelope a secret, Tiny would have to forfeit the house to the Baron, and as she had told him many, many times, he would have no place to live, a situation that would also mean a return to Harpwitch.

Jeremy went over and over the problem the envelope presented until the architecture of his mind began to seem very much like the labyrinth of the story. There was no escape; all paths led to Harpwitch's Home for

Mean Dogs, Ugly Cats, and Strey Children. Try as he might, he simply could not find the ball of thread that would show him the way out.

Throughout the evening, Jeremy distracted himself with the telescope. There was a full moon, and he could see almost as clearly as in the daylight hours, but the red envelope lay heavily on his conscience. Though he fought the urge, his thoughts returned to it again and again like a school of fish that struggle upstream to return to the place they were hatched. Jeremy finally tucked the envelope under the thin mattress. No further in his deliberations than when he began, he crawled under the gray coverlet and fell into a fitful sleep.

Was it the dreams that had awakened him? Dreams of a fierce game of tug-of-war with Jeremy on one end of the rope and Tiny and Harpwitch and the Baron on the other. Dreams of Polly roaming the labyrinth, calling for him. Dreams of the raids and Pickles.

He awoke with a start, sitting straight up in bed. He checked for the envelope. It was there, under the mattress, just where he had hidden it. It was only then that he noticed the powerful scent wafting through the western window, the one that faced the house with the graffiti. He recognized the sharp smell instantly.

"Gasoline!" he said aloud.

Chapter 9

A Famished Beast

Gasoline!

He hopped out of bed and stepped toward the western window. Sure enough, the smell of gasoline grew stronger, carried on a breeze that was picking up and rattling the sill in its frame.

Heavy with sleep, he looked from the window to the landscape below. The moon, round and blemished as one of Tiny's dinner plates, cast its cold, silvery light on the houses. To Jeremy, they seemed like images in an old-fashioned photograph rather than real structures filled with living and breathing people.

Even with his naked eye, he could see something moving in and out of the shadows cast by the moonlight around the house with the graffiti.

"A cat," he whispered.

But no, it was much, much bigger than a cat, though from this distance, it was difficult to know what was substance and what was shade. He reached for the telescope, as silent and powerful as a relic from an ancient religion. With the surety of a sea captain, he extended it and raised it to his eye.

He'd just brought the graffiti house into focus when the circle of his lens was filled with a flash of orange so bright that he very nearly lost his hold on the telescope. When he recovered, he didn't need it to see the thin line of flames lapping at the foundation of the house. He watched in horror as, quicker than a frog's tongue, it darted up the rotting timbers and slithered like a ravenous serpent through the windows. The house exploded in a magnificent and terrifying fandango of smoke and fire.

"Fire!" Jeremy shouted. "Fire!"

But he was so high up that he doubted even the keenest ears could have heard him. Frozen as if hypnotized by the beauty and sinuous activity of the flames, he continued to yell with all the force his lungs could muster.

"Fire! Fire! Fire!"

Perhaps it was Jeremy's warning shouts, after all, or perhaps it was the monster roar of the flames that awakened the houses on either side of the inferno. Whatever the cause, lights clicked on in both buildings. It was a good thing, too, because now Jeremy saw with horrific clarity what was about to happen.

Sparks from the house were shooting high into the air in an eerie fountain of black smoke and burning ash. For a moment, the glowing embers hung like stars suspended in the heated atmosphere. But then, with spooky accuracy, they began to drift back toward the earth. First one. Then another. Then another. They landed on the roofs of the neighboring houses like malevolent angels, inviting these structures, too, to become their partners in the fiery dance.

Jeremy understood at once the mortal danger he and Tiny were in. He shoved the telescope into his shorts and ran to the door, returning only to snatch the red envelope from its hiding place under the mattress. Later, he couldn't remember his feet touching the floor as he raced down the steps and through the dark, twisting alleys of the house to the space where Tiny lay snoring. She was like a mountain someone had modestly wrapped in nightclothes.

"Tiny!" Jeremy shouted. "Tiny! Wake up!"

But the sleeping woman slumbered on, oblivious to the danger that was approaching with every shallow breath.

Jeremy cupped his hands and shouted directly into her ear. "Tiny! Wake up!"

Still no response.

Jeremy was desperate; closing his eyes, he stuck his hand directly into the woman's towering hairdo, now flattened against the pillow. Even in his desperation, he was surprised at how hollow the beehive was. It was like an empty piñata. Jeremy wiggled his fingers, frantically searching for something to take hold of. He found it at last, a strand of hair that seemed to stand straight up from the middle of the huge woman's scalp. He wrapped his fingers around it and gave a mighty yank.

"TINY!"

That did the trick. She sat up so fast that Jeremy hadn't had time to let go of her hair.

"What the heck are you doing, Cole Slaw?" she roared. "Trying to murder me?"

"We've got to get out!" Jeremy gasped. "There's a—"

"Let go of my ding-dong hair!" the woman shouted. "Did you find the deed? Is that it?"

"No . . . I mean . . . yes . . . I mean . . . there's a fire, Tiny! A big fire! It's heading straight for us!"

By now, a thick, acrid smell was winding its way through the passageways, overpowering the odor of stale cigarette smoke that clung to every object in Tiny's house.

"Fire?" Tiny repeated, as if hearing the word for the first time in her life. "Fire?"

The smoke, now visible, grew stronger and blacker; the terrifying meaning of the word hit her all at once.

"FIRE!" she shouted, hopping out of bed like a person half her age and one-quarter her bulk. "Out of my way, Cole Slaw!"

With an arm thick as a ham hock, she knocked Jeremy into one of the towers, nearly bringing it down upon both of them, and sprinted toward the door. Jeremy righted himself and wasted no time following her.

By the time they reached the outside, the entire neighborhood was in flames. The fire was jumping from house to house as if it were playing a game with itself. Though the residents had called the Fire Academy, no engines had arrived, nor could Jeremy hear the plaintive wail of sirens to indicate they were coming. The only sound, in fact, was the angry bellow of the flames satisfying their enormous appetite.

In the end, Tiny's house was consumed with all the others. Jeremy's turret was the last to go; it broke away from the main structure as if fainting from the heat.

For a moment or two, his room seemed suspended in midair, a glowing skeleton of joists and beams. But then, as if it understood the futility of resisting, it collapsed all at once onto the pile of burning rubble.

Tiny watched the spectacle without the slightest show of emotion. She simply stared at the flames as if hypnotized, barefoot and silent, the hem of her enormous nightdress flapping indelicately in the breeze. Ironically, Jeremy realized, it was the first time he had seen her without her cigarettes.

Ultimately, nothing remained. The neighborhood was transformed into a moonscape of cinder and ash. Some of the residents were wailing; their cries of anguish mingled in a clangorous chorus of despair over the hiss of the smoldering rubble. Others were like Tiny, silent as stone. Still others were using sticks to poke around the edges of the ashes, hoping to salvage something from the terrible destruction.

Jeremy took the red envelope from his pocket and handed it to Tiny.

"I . . . I found it," he said.

Tiny looked at him as if he were a stranger. Then she burst out laughing.

"Oh, that's a good one, Cole Slaw," she said, gasping for breath. Tears rolled down her cheeks in quantities that seemed to Jeremy enough to have quenched the fire itself. "That's a ding-dong good one!"

When Jeremy later recalled the incident, it was with a terror that he had not felt during the conflagration itself. He sometimes thought that it had been like a great, famished beast, roaring and devouring everything in its path. Other times, he remembered it as a spider, hatching hundreds of little spiders, each as ravenous and fast-moving as the parent.

But the real horror Jeremy felt came not from the fire and its terrible destructive power, but from the memory of what he had seen through the telescope just before the graffiti house had burst into flame. It was something he had not told a soul—the bald man, speeding away from the house in a Wisdom Wagon, so pale that he might have been made from the very skin of the moon.

Chapter 10

Someone Might as Well Say It

"I want to get up!"

Rosie curled her hands into fists and pounded the thick mattress of her canopied bed. It was, perhaps, the hundredth variation of the sentiment that the young Baroness had uttered that morning. But no matter how many times she complained, Mary's response was always the same.

"Your mother says you are to stay in bed until you feel better."

"I feel fine, and she knows it! In fact, I feel perfect! Watch this!" The girl crossed her eyes, scrunched up her nose, and wagged her head from side to side. "Would a sick person do *that*?" she wanted to know.

But the maid's instructions from Baroness Gertrudina had been absolutely clear: "Keep her in bed until I say that she may get up."

Mary placed her hand on Rosie's bespeckled forehead, not to check the girl's temperature—she knew the girl wasn't ill—but to push back the ringlets that spilled down and danced over her eyes in an unruly red mop.

"Perhaps you shouldn't have kicked the dance master," she chided.

"But he *pinched* me!" Rosie shoved the covers away from her and held out her freckled arm. The spot she pointed to could as easily have been a smudge of dirt as the bruise that Rosie insisted it was. "I can't help it if I stepped on his foot. It's my mother's fault for trying to make me a dancer. He should have pinched *her*! Anyway, I didn't kick him. Not hard."

The maid took a sudden interest in a large, leatherbound book that was resting on the corner of the bed.

"He's still limping, you know," she forced herself to say sternly.

"Please . . . Pippa!"

Rosie locked her eyes on to the maid's face, the way a cat locks its eyes on to an unsuspecting robin. But nothing. The response she was hoping for—a quick twitch of the maid's eyebrow, perhaps, or a sudden, involuntary gasp—didn't occur. In fact, the maid hadn't done so much as bat an eye.

"Rats!" Rosie muttered, picking up a pen from her bedside table and crossing *Pippa* off the list she kept there.

This list consisted of all the names Rosie had ever heard. Whenever she thought her maid might be expecting it least, she addressed her by one of these names, certain that she would eventually hit upon the right one. Then, according to Rosie's plan, the maid would be caught off guard and give herself away. So far, the only result was that the list was much shorter. She'd held out hope for Pippa, too.

"Rats! Rats! Rats!" the girl declared.

Rosie hadn't forgotten the danger that Mary talked of when the subject of her real name first came up, but she'd convinced herself that if she did discover the name, she would never be so careless as to make a slip of the tongue in front of the older Baroness.

"I'll be like one of those kids who speak a lot of languages," she explained. "They never make mistakes. When someone in the room speaks Kelch, the kid speaks Kelch. But if a Petrish speaker comes into the room, the kid automatically slips into Petrish. I'll be just like those kids. When my mother is here, I'll call you Mary, but when she's not here, I'll call you . . . Babette? . . . Beryl? . . . Beulah?"

"Don't forget what happened to Rumpelstiltskin," the maid responded.

"What?"

"When the miller's daughter guessed his name, he stamped himself into a fit and disappeared."

"But *you* would never do that," Rosie responded. She took Mary's hand into her own and squeezed it affectionately. "You won't ever leave me, will you, Mabel? . . . Maisie? . . . Marigold?"

Rosie stood on the bed and began to hop on one foot. Before the maid could protest, the girl cut her off.

"My mother said I had to stay in bed," she declared. "She didn't say I had to lie down. Watch this!"

In spite of the firmness of the mattress—the Baroness Gertrudina did not believe in soft beds—the girl bounced so high that she was able to accomplish a complete flip. She landed perfectly, planting her sturdy feet squarely in the middle of the bed.

"Not bad," she said, more to herself than to her

companion. And then, before the maid could stop her, she repeated the entire sequence. Backward.

Mary marveled once again at Rosie's acrobatics. They were remarkable, especially for someone who'd never taken a lesson. But like so many of Rosie's talents, any form of gymnastics, from backflips to the simplest forward roll, was forbidden. In fact, the Baroness Gertrudina's latest theory was that exertion was the cause of the freckles. Even the dancing instructions she was forcing upon the girl were kept to the simple steps necessary to execute a light waltz. Any dance that Rosie might have enjoyed, a rollicking biserka, for instance, was absolutely prohibited.

Rosie flopped onto the mattress, stretched out full length, and propped her head on her hands. Nestled as she was in a tangle of shiny golden comforters, she appeared to the maid, whose affection for her young charge grew daily, like a piebald angel lazing on a bank of silky clouds.

"Tell me the story," Rosie said after a moment.

"Again?"

The maid opened the book she'd picked up earlier and ran a thumb along its gilded edges.

"What if I were to read to you from . . ."

"No!" Rosie shouted. "Not that! I'll go crazy! *The Exalted History of the Family von Strompié*?! It's total claptrap! My father made the whole thing up. Every last word! No! I want to hear *the* story. I'll start!"

She sat up and crossed her legs. Clearing her throat, she began.

"Once upon a time, in a land not far from this one,

there was a group of lost children. They had no parents but lived all together in an abandoned building full of books. The vines that covered the building had already begun to conceal its name, carved into the stone lintel over the door. The only letters left were l-i-c . . . r-e-e . . . a-r-y, so the children called their home the Licreeary."

Rosie copied the maid's inflection exactly, letting her voice rise and fall at all the same places.

"Though they were often hungry," she continued, "the children were not totally miserable because they were taken care of by a girl named—"

The sound of sharp heels marching along a marble floor echoed in the hall outside the girl's room.

"My mother!"

In an instant, the knob on the gilded door began to turn. Rosie dashed back under the covers and rested her head on the pillow. She looked for all the world as if she had just awakened from a heavy sleep.

The Baroness Gertrudina charged into the room like one of the dust storms that assaulted the Metropolis from the Terra Nequam deserts. The maid shivered.

"Good afternoon, Madam," she said. She lowered her eyes to the floor and curtsied.

The Baroness inspected the maid a moment before speaking.

"And how is our little patient?" she asked with something that might have been called a smile if the cruelty present in her lips had not shone through so transparently.

"I believe she may be better, Madam," the maid answered.

"Nonsense!" the Baroness hissed. "Can't you see how flushed she is?"

There was no denying it. Rosie's cheeks were the color of radishes from her earlier acrobatic exertions.

"Remove those blankets at once, you stupid girl," the Baroness commanded. "What are you trying to do? Roast the silly thing? By tomorrow, there won't be a centimeter of fair skin on her!"

The maid turned to fold the comforters back, hoping that Rosie's wrinkled nightdress would not belie the girl's romping. She needn't have worried. The Baroness had already swept out of the room as unexpectedly as she had entered.

"She won't be back," Rosie said, sitting up. "She can only bear to see me once a day."

"Now, Rosie . . ." The maid sat on the bed and put her hands on the girl's shoulders.

"We both know it's true," Rosie said. "Someone might as well say it. But here's the thing. As long as I have you, I don't care." She threw her arms around Mary's neck.

"Now," Rosie said, releasing her arms, "let's go on with the story."

"All right," the maid responded. "Where were we?"

"The children were hungry but not totally miserable because . . ."

The maid picked up the story, taking Rosie's hands as she did so. ". . . because they were taken care of by a girl named . . ."

She hesitated for the tiniest fraction of a second, just the amount of time Truth needs to find its way into the world.

"Polly!" Rosie shouted.

"That's right," the maid said. She stood and turned her head toward the curtained windows. "They were taken care of by a girl named Polly."

"No! That's not what I mean!" Rosie threw the blankets aside. "And you know it. I mean it's *you. You* are Polly!"

When the maid looked back, her sudden smile radiated throughout the dim room as surely as if someone had lit the chandelier that hung over Rosie's bed.

"What a clever thing you are!" she laughed as she pulled the girl affectionately to her. "Especially for a speckled trout!"

Chapter 11

Abandoned

The Baron Ignatius Fyodor Maximus von Strompié III paced back and forth in his study. Every sixth or seventh step, he kicked the leg of his desk. The Baron hated to wait. He was an important man with important things on his mind. How could he possibly do the work of running the Metropolis if he was forced to spend half his life waiting?

Just last week, he'd had to fire one of the kitchen servants because when he asked her for a glass of milk, it took her a full minute to retrieve it from the kitchen two floors below. The nerve! Didn't she know that when he wanted milk, he wanted it *now*?

"What were you doing, anyway?" he'd asked her as he snatched the glass from her hands. "Milking the cow?" (Later, he congratulated himself on the searing quality of this witticism.)

Then, when he told her to pack her things, the woman had the impertinence to protest. She'd worked at Helios ever since she was a little girl, she told him through ridiculous crocodile tears. She had no place else to go! And was that *his* fault? he'd wanted to know. He had to make an example of her, of course. It was his deeply rooted belief that this was one of the most important parts of *being* a baron—making examples of others.

Stopping in front of the desk, he pulled a gold watch out of the silk-lined pocket of his vest. He watched distractedly as the minute hand bumped around the face with an infuriating sluggishness. One minute to ten.

"Where is he?" the Baron asked aloud, though there was no living thing to hear him except the brown rat hiding in the shelves that lined the paneled walls.

Just as the watch chimed the final stroke of ten, a light rapping fell upon the door. The Baron ran behind his desk and flung himself into the new chair, a copy of the one he had kicked across the room days earlier. He picked up a sheaf of papers on which he had been playing tic-tac-toe and shuffled them with a ferocity that conveyed the impression that he was just finishing up some monstrous piece of governmental work.

"Enter!" he called out in his most baronial voice.

At the other end of the study, the door inched open and the spectral figure of Jeriah Wirm appeared. Wirm entered just as he had before, casting his eyes downward and slinking his way toward the desk in a manner suggesting his body contained neither muscle nor bone. But the Baron was expecting him this time. The shock of seeing the pallid, lowly creature in the grandeur of his study was not so alarming to his delicate sensibilities.

"You're late, Wirm!" he tried to shout, but his voice unexpectedly cracked. It sounded as if he were yodeling, which ruined entirely the effect he was striving for—that of a very important man, gravely inconvenienced.

"But our appointment was for ten, was it not, Most Majestically High One?" Wirm whispered.

"When I say ten o'clock," the Baron responded, this time taking care to modulate his voice so there would be no repeat of the yodeling, "I mean the *first* stroke of ten, Wirm. Not the last! You have kept me waiting for nine strokes of the clock. Nine strokes!"

The Chief of the Wisdom Wagons halted his slithering advance. He bowed so low that the top of his bald head nearly grazed the carpet.

"I see that I have greatly disturbed your schedule," he rasped. "Allow me to return at a time more convenient for your punctually perfect self. Tomorrow, perhaps, or next week. . . ."

He lifted his limp foot and took a small step backward, meaning, it seemed, to follow his own suggestion. But the Baron jumped up from his desk.

"Stop!" he cried out, his voice cracking a second time. "Er . . . I mean . . . *I'll* be the one who decides what's been disturbed and what hasn't! Not *you*, Wirm. Now, have you succeeded?"

"See for yourself, O Nobleness!" Wirm half whispered.

Like a conjurer, he produced a photograph from the pocket of his trousers. Without moving forward, he held the snapshot outward in fingers as colorless and soft as maggots.

Trying not to run, the Baron rounded the corner

of his desk. It wouldn't do to have Wirm think him anxious. With tremendous restraint, he slowed and drummed his fingers along the desk's gleaming mahogany surface. Unfortunately, in doing so, he knocked an inkwell off its perch. A miniature blue tsunami surged across the papers he had been fidgeting with earlier. Leaving the mess behind him, the Baron practically sprinted to where Wirm stood. He plucked the photograph from the smaller man's fingers and turned back toward the crystal lamp.

The Baron cleared his throat, extended the photograph toward the light, and then glanced back at Wirm, as if to say, *This had better be good.* He turned his attention to the picture.

Opening his eyes to their widest, he furrowed his brow and tilted his head first to the left and then to the right. Squinting now, as if he were having difficulty bringing the photo into focus, he moved it back and forth away from his face, peering first at arm's length and then suddenly hauling it forward to just an inch away from the tip of his bulbous nose. Next, he turned the photograph over and stared, blinking, at its back. Finally, he threw it onto the desk, where it landed, image side up, in a tidal pool of blue ink.

"What is the meaning of this?" the Baron roared. "That is a photograph of nothing!"

"Ah, yes," Wirm replied. "A photograph of nothing."

The Baron snatched the picture up from the desk and once more held it under the light. Ink dripped from its back onto his hand-sewn boots.

"Is this some kind of joke, Wirm?" he bellowed. "Is

this some kind of miserable pale man's humor? Because if it is, Wirm, if it is . . ."

"It is a picture of nothing, Sire," Wirm continued, "because nothing is all that is left."

Once more, the Baron brought the photograph close to his eyes. A tiny blue stain wicked its way outward onto the starched front of his silk shirt. Now that Wirm had told him what to look for, he could begin to see it. Nothing. Ashes. A photograph of nothing but ashes. Slowly, a smile began to etch itself into the puffy flesh of his lower face.

"Splendid, Wirm!" he shouted. "Absolutely first-rate!" He actually hopped in his delight.

"I must inform Your Observant Holiness," Wirm whispered, bowing again from the waist and sweeping his arms into an X in front of him, "that the fire spread to other houses throughout the neighborhood."

But the Baron met this news with something akin to joy.

"Good!" he responded merrily. "It should have! People have no business living in a neighborhood where such things are written. Now they won't have to worry about it. You have done them a favor, Wirm. I congratulate you!"

Wirm bowed a third time, though this time with just a nod of his head. The Baron came closer to the pale man until he was near enough to whisper in his ear. He gave the photograph a single shake. Ink splattered onto the wall.

"But what about *this* house, Wirm?" he asked. "Was the culprit inside?"

Wirm cleared his throat in a way that made it seem he might be choking. "I'm afraid, O Magnificent Being," he finally mouthed so softly that the Baron had to lean in even closer, "that the house was like the others."

"A-ban-doned?" The Baron's voice rose with each syllable.

"Abandoned," Wirm repeated.

The Baron screamed until his face turned the color of tomatoes when they drop from the vine and lie rotting in the dirt. Using both hands, he bulldozed the entire contents of his desk's surface onto the floor, streaking the spilled ink along the mahogany surface and smearing it onto the sleeves of his shirt. Screaming still, he snatched a pillow from the back of an embroidered chair and ripped it in half. Its feathery entrails exploded into the air.

Jeriah Wirm stood as still as one of the figures in the painting that the Baron had now pulled from the wall and was shoving his foot through. Minutes later, the Baron Ignatius Fyodor Maximus von Strompié III stood panting and sweating in front of his servant.

"Wirm," he wheezed, brushing away a feather that clung to the ink on his chin. "This is *my* Metropolis! Do you hear me? I make the rules! I pass the laws! *Me!* I'm telling you now, Wirm, if you know what's good for you, you'll find who is doing this, and when you do, well, leave *that* to me! The Choir Stall is ready and waiting."

"And once I discover the identity of the guilty party?" Wirm inquired. Already, he was backing his way toward the door.

"The PatPats, Wirm. Commander General. You have my word on it."

"Leave it to me, Royal One," Wirm whispered.

The heavy latch of the door clicked behind him, and the Baron was once more alone in his study. Even the rat had disappeared into the dark hole from which it had entered earlier that morning.

Chapter 12

He Says Hello to Orville

"So . . . the bad penny returns." Harpwitch looked up at Jeremy without the least sign of surprise. "I thought it would."

Keeping a tight grip on the torn collar of Jeremy's shirt, the PatPat dug his thumb into the tender spot between the boy's shoulder blades.

"Caught him sneaking around one of the old neighborhoods," the man snarled.

"I wasn't sneaking," Jeremy protested. The sickening taste of the air at HHMDUCSC rolled over his tongue.

"He had *this* tucked in his shorts." The PatPat used the hand that was not holding Jeremy to produce the telescope. "Stole it, no doubt."

"Ah, thievery," Harpwitch replied. The word was as natural in her mouth as her own yellow teeth. "Now, that's more like it."

With a hand practiced at holding that which did not belong to her, she took the telescope from the Pat-Pat, automatically appraising it as she estimated its heft. She would get a pretty penny for it.

Jeremy lunged for the brass and silver instrument.

The PatPat lifted him off the floor and dangled him like a rabbit.

"I didn't steal it!" Jeremy shouted. "It's mine!"

After the fire, he had tried to give the telescope to Tiny. It was just before she left to go to her sister's. But the huge woman had only shrugged.

"Keep it, Cole Slaw," she'd said as they stood side by side on the street in front of a smoldering pile of rubble. "I got no use for it now." With that, she lit a cigarette, jammed herself into her car, and drove off. "See ya round like a ding-dong doughnut, Cole Slaw!" she'd called out the window. The last Jeremy saw of her, she was shaking a fist at an old woman she had run off the road.

Harpwitch reached deep into her pocket and pulled out the key ring. Using just the tips of her long, thin fingers, she selected a brass key no bigger than the pointed nail on her index finger. With this, she unlocked a drawer in her desk and placed the telescope deep within it.

"You'd best leave the little rat here, Officer," she said. "I'll make sure the spyglass gets returned to its rightful owner."

"*I'm* the rightful owner!" Jeremy shouted. The drawer locked with a sharp click. "And I'm not a rat!"

Once the roar of the PatPat's quadricycle faded into the distance, Harpwitch turned to Jeremy with eyes as cold and focused as a rattlesnake's.

"That's *one,* Cabbage," she said.

If life at HHMDUCSC had been difficult before, the weeks that followed were agonizing. Harpwitch had somehow managed to get a whole new supply of dogs and, following the advice in her own pamphlet, was in the process of turning them into vicious, lunging brutes. But it wasn't the care of these savage creatures that increased Jeremy's suffering, and it wasn't even the new restrictions that Harpwitch had levied since his return—the smaller portions at mealtimes, for example, or the shortened hours set aside for sleep. It was the loss of the telescope.

Jeremy had not been able to rid himself of the notion that the telescope would lead him to Polly. He clung to it like a drowning sailor clings to a piece of driftwood, believing, in spite of the odds, that it would carry him safely to shore. It was this belief that helped him survive the daily humiliations and torments Harpwitch inflicted upon him. He would get that telescope back if it was the last thing he did.

I'll study her until I know her better than she knows herself, he vowed. *One day, she'll make a mistake with those keys. When she does, I'll be ready.*

Whereas before he had tried to avoid the woman's presence, he now sought it out. He thought of a million little questions to pester her with and invented troubles that would require her attention.

"Excuse me, Miss Harpwitch, but I can't find the mop."

"Excuse me, Miss Harpwitch, but I think one of the dogs has the mange."

"Excuse me, Miss Harpwitch . . ."

"Excuse me, Miss Harpwitch . . ."

"Excuse me, Miss Harpwitch . . ."

With each of these interruptions, Jeremy knew that he risked a cuff on the neck or a boxing on the ears. But the sting left by each blow dissipated when he remembered why he had put himself in the position to receive it: He was watching every move she made.

His primary fear, of course, was that he would run out of time, that she would sell the instrument before he could retrieve it. But so far, he was certain that the telescope was still in her possession. If she'd already turned a profit on it, she would have let him know. Harpwitch was not the type to waste an opportunity for cruelty.

As the days passed, Jeremy's knowledge of the woman grew. It was both surprising and comforting to learn she was not as invincible as he once thought her. She had digestive problems; not all the bad smells at HHMDUCSC were coming from the dogs. There were other weaknesses, too; the hearing in her left ear was not as good as in her right, and she had a mysterious allergy that sometimes caused a purple rash to spread across her forehead like a field of wilted tulips.

But of the many subtle vulnerabilities Jeremy discovered, none was so telling as the one that popped up every time a fistful of piés was about to change hands between her and a customer. A hiccup. It was as predictable as the announcement at the end of the Wisdom Wagons' messages, and Jeremy secretly smiled to himself every time he heard it. A single hiccup, high-pitched and short, like a squeak from a member of the weasel family. It always happened at the same moment, just when the customer pulled the wad of piés—meant to pay for whatever cheerless service Harpwitch had offered—from its hiding place, deep in a pocket or inside a sock.

Harpwitch did her best to disguise this gastric alarm as a cough or a sneeze, but there was no hiding it, and Jeremy soon developed a theory about what that hiccup meant.

It's panic, he told himself. *Panic, pure and simple.*

He could see it flash behind her eyes just as the hiccup made its way through her sharp teeth out into the air.

She's terrified! Jeremy told himself. *Once she sees the money, she's afraid she won't be able to get her hands on it, that the customer will somehow change his mind. She can't control herself. She hiccups!*

Jeremy knew that it wasn't because the horrid woman needed the piés, either. He'd spied stacks of them, more than he had ever seen in his life, in a wooden box she kept under the desk. It was simply that once she'd laid eyes on someone else's money, she couldn't rest until it had become hers. It was as if her palms had come into contact with the blistering oil of wasteweed leaf and the piés were the only balm that could soothe them.

To test this theory, Jeremy tried to get the hiccup to manifest itself. For days, he made it his life's work to startle it out of Harpwitch. One time, he knocked over the bucket of filthy water with which he mopped the office each day. The next afternoon, he allowed one of the dogs to escape from its cage and run loose in the office. But no. Though Harpwitch was furious—and Jeremy paid for her fury with the edge of her hand— the hiccup stayed put, cowering somewhere in its den, deep in the dark spirals of Harpwitch's intestines. It was only the sight of someone else's money that did it.

If a customer only knew it, when he heard that hiccup, he could pretend to put the piés back where they came from and Harpwitch would be reduced to a sniveling beggar.

Though he had no idea how he was going to make use of this information, Jeremy stored it with something close to glee. He was like an inventor who gathers his tools without knowing what his imagination will produce, taking delight in the inventory itself.

But his observations were interrupted one day about two weeks after his return. He was just about to water the most frightening of the dogs, a huge pinkish brute named Lucifer, when he heard Harpwitch calling him to the office.

"Ah, here's our little Cabbage now," she wheedled as he presented himself.

She pushed him in front of a man and woman who together would not have weighed as much as one of Tiny's feet. They were dressed in black, the man in a suit and the woman in a dress that hung on her frame like a tent whose poles had collapsed.

Less than ten minutes later, Jeremy found himself on a bus jammed between this peculiar couple, whose name he learned was Parsepin. Mr. and Mrs. Aldo Parsepin. This time, there had been no good-bye from Harpwitch. She'd merely held up two fingers.

Neither Parsepin spoke a word to Jeremy, but he was able to deduce from their bickering that he was to act as a companion to someone named Orville. Apparently, Orville had not been feeling up to par, and it would be Jeremy's responsibility to cheer him and restore him to his former self.

But who exactly was Orville? The Parsepins' son seemed to be the only logical answer, but when, during a pause in their sniping conversation, Jeremy finally found the courage to ask, Mr. Parsepin looked down at him as if he had asked the answer to two plus two.

"Did you hear that, Matilda?" Mr. Parsepin said to his wife. "He asked who Orville was."

Mrs. Parsepin sniffed in a way that indicated her olfactory nerve had been deeply offended. "Who is Orville, indeed!" she muttered.

Was it Jeremy's imagination, or did she actually jab him with her elbow?

The trio finally descended from the bus into a neighborhood not so different from Tiny's except that the houses were farther apart and seemed to be in slightly better repair. The paint on the facades was less faded, the fences surrounding them less sagging. Cautiously, Jeremy inspected the front of each house to see if whoever had visited Tiny's neighborhood had left the same message here, but the only words he saw were on the KEEP OUT signs that almost everyone had planted in their dusty front yards.

The Parsepins scurried down the block like two black beetles and, in a few minutes, scuttled up to a house that was no different from those surrounding it. They abandoned Jeremy on the porch and ran down a long central corridor as if they had been shot from a cannon.

"Orville, we're home!" Mr. Parsepin cried out as he turned into a room to the left.

"Orville darling, we've brought you a playmate!" Mrs. Parsepin said, jockeying her husband for first place.

Jeremy listened for the ring of footsteps on the wooden floors or the timbre of a young voice returning the greeting, but he was met with silence. Perhaps Orville was sicker than he had understood. But before he could consider if this might be so or not, Aldo Parsepin returned, grabbed him by the elbow, and propelled him down the hall into the room where Matilda stood fretting over a large wooden table.

The drapes in the room had been pulled, but as Jeremy got closer, he could see that in the middle of the table sat a goldfish bowl and, in the goldfish bowl, a rather large goldfish, gasping for breath and listing heavily to one side.

"Say hello to Orville, boy!" Mr. Parsepin commanded.

Chapter 13

Congratulations, Cabbage!

"He killed Orville!" Matilda Parsepin shrieked. She pointed an accusing finger at Jeremy.

It was later that day, and Aldo and Matilda Parsepin stood once again in the outer office of HHMDUCSC.

"We want our money back!" Aldo Parsepin demanded. "You didn't tell us he was the murdering type!"

"Homicide, Cabbage?" Harpwitch asked, raising an eyebrow. "Impressive."

"It was a goldfish!" Jeremy protested. "And I didn't do anything. Orville was already sick."

"Liar!" Matilda Parsepin yelled hysterically. "Assassin!"

Aldo Parsepin slammed a bony fist onto the counter. "We should charge *you* for the funeral expenses," he said to Harpwitch.

Less than a minute later, the Parsepins were scrambling down the steps. Their black figures faded into the twilight of the Metropolis like shadows. Harpwitch had not returned their money. Instead, she'd threatened to take them to court, mentioning one of the Baron's most recent laws. The Businessperson's Bill of Rights, he'd called it. Its main point was that the customer is always wrong. But what sent the Parsepins flying was her mentioning that she was a personal acquaintance of the von Strompié family and was frequently under the employ of the Baron himself, something that Jeremy had often suspected. After all, he'd reasoned, Harpwitch had not come across that box of piés by simply selling dogs and children.

Like all the residents of the Metropolis, Aldo and Matilda Parsepin knew what happened when one had a disagreement with the Baron or any of his cronies. Lonely as their home may be without Orville, it was preferable to a cell in the Choir Stall.

Harpwitch stood on the doorstep and watched the Parsepins disappear into the waning light. When she was satisfied that they were gone for good, she turned to Jeremy.

"Congratulations, Cabbage!" she said, pulling the door closed behind her. "That's *two*!"

The next morning, Jeremy was sweeping the steps that led to the front entrance. It had been a dreadful night, full of terrifying nightmares. Scrap had been in them. And the fire. And, of all people, Pickles. What was his friend doing in such terrible dreams? It was this question that Jeremy was trying to answer when he heard the voice behind him.

"Excuse me, young man. We seek an establishment with the unfortunate name of Harpwitch's Home for Mean Dogs."

It was a woman's voice, high, absurdly high, like a

voice of a man when he is imitating a woman. And oddly muffled. As if she were speaking through a towel. He turned to see who it might be. The wooden handle of his broom cracked sharply against the hard stone of the step as it fell.

"Oh dear, Bo," the speaker said to her companion. "He's dropped his broom. We've frightened him."

"Yes, Ba," replied the man. "I'm afraid we have." He picked up the broom and held it out to Jeremy. "Here you are, son."

His voice was as low as the woman's was high; it vibrated gently against Jeremy's skin, like the lowest note of a bass violin.

Jeremy blinked, rubbed his eyes, and then blinked again. He wondered if he was seeing one of the mirages for which the Terra Nequam was famous. Against the grays and blacks of the Metropolis, the couple looked as unlikely as orchids in a desert.

The woman's dress was the color of cherries, and over the ripe crimson, orange ruffles flounced from her neck to her knees like the petals of an absurdly happy flower. The man's purple jacket was a shocking contrast to his yellow-and-green-striped trousers, and the cravat he had tied around his neck nearly blinded Jeremy with its iridescent pink and blue polka dots. Though both were sporting white gloves, they were holding hands. But it was what they were wearing over their heads that had caused Jeremy to drop his broom.

"We're terribly sorry about these bags," the woman apologized through the hole that had been cut for her mouth.

"It's difficult to explain at the moment," the man joined in.

Jeremy couldn't help himself; he grinned. "That's all right," he managed to say.

Polly had often told him to be ready for anything. "It's one of the great secrets of life," she always added after this advice. But she didn't mean what most people meant when they said such a thing—be ready for anything bad, for it's bound to happen. No, Polly had meant the opposite. "Be ready for anything *good,* Jeremy, so that when it shows up on your doorstep, you can allow it to come in."

Well, the couple had shown up on his doorstep, literally, and Jeremy *was* ready, though for what, he couldn't guess. He only knew that he was overtaken with an uncontrollable urge to laugh, and not *at* them, either, but *because* of them. Because they dared to defy the drab, predictable world of the Metropolis, and because they seemed so kind. The man had even picked up his broom and called him "son."

If Polly were here, Jeremy thought, *she would be ready. I will be, too.*

He heard the door open behind him, then the unmistakable grind of Harpwitch's voice.

"Yes? Can I be of some assistance?"

"I do hope so," said the man through the hole in his bag. "We are hoping to adopt a child."

Seconds passed. For their part, the couple seemed willing to stand there forever, holding hands and staring out at Jeremy from the holes that had been cut for their eyes. He saw that someone had taken the trouble to paint eyelashes on both the upper and lower edges of the holes. Two red circles, the size of apples, appeared where cheeks would have been.

Harpwitch cleared her throat. "Children are hard to come by these days," she said at last.

Jeremy knew instantly what Harpwitch meant by this remark. Her unerring instinct for greed had guided her to realize that the man and woman were desperate and that they had the means to pay. But the man was unfazed.

"We know that, Madam," he replied as he turned toward his companion.

"They're expensive," Harpwitch said matter-of-factly. "*Very* expensive." Her hand lit on the top of Jeremy's head like a bird of prey.

"We are prepared," the woman replied. She patted the enormous handbag she carried, ruffled like her dress but in alternating bands of chartreuse and turquoise.

Harpwitch sighed heavily, and though Jeremy couldn't see her, he knew exactly the expression she was arranging her face into. He also knew that it was every bit as much of a mask as the bags the man and woman were wearing.

"Little Jeremy here is the only child I have right now," she said. "It would break my heart to part with him."

What a great actress she would have made, Jeremy thought.

"He's a good boy, then?" the woman asked. A pair of bright eyes sparkled in the darkness under the bag.

"Why don't you answer that question yourself, Jeremy darling?" Harpwitch said. She flexed her fingers slightly so that the tips of her nails dug lightly into Jeremy's scalp. "Are you a *good* boy, would you say?"

"I—I try to be," he stammered.

"That's all that any of us can do, isn't it?" the brightly dressed woman said.

He looked down and bit his lower lip to keep from crying out. It was the shoes the couple were wearing. They were gigantic! Twice the size, at least, of normal shoes.

"Certainly, no one should ever expect more than that," the man continued. "Don't you agree, Jeremy?"

Though Jeremy continued to be amazed at the size of the couple's shoes, he felt something stir deep within his chest. For the first time since he'd been separated from Polly, someone had used his name with kindness.

Harpwitch spoke before Jeremy could reply. This time, there was no pretending.

"The price is set by the law of supply and demand. Supply is low. Demand is high. Two thousand piés!"

Jeremy jerked his head around to stare at Harpwitch. Surely his ears had played a trick on him. Two thousand piés? No one in the Metropolis had that kind of money. No one but the Baron and his friends.

"You heard me, Cabbage," Harpwitch said, completely ignoring whatever response the couple might be having under their bags. "You didn't know a little street grunt like you was worth so much, did you?"

Jeremy felt his heart sink. Why was it that

Harpwitch had decided to lose her mind at just this moment? As curious as this man and woman were, surely they were preferable to life at HHMDUCSC. He liked their crazy clothes and he liked their crazy shoes. He liked the way they held hands and the way they glanced at each other through the bags. And most of all, he liked the way the man had said his name, as reassuring, almost, as Polly's hand on his shoulder.

Yes, they *were* wearing bags over their faces. But which was better? Jeremy asked himself. The cheerfully painted eyes and cheeks? Or the jarring reality of Harpwitch's stonelike expression with its impenetrable eyes and harsh, hawkish nose?

But the fiend had asked an unimaginable amount of money. Cruel to the end, she had made it impossible. He turned back to look at the couple. He could feel them returning his gaze through the bags.

"Two thousand piés," Harpwitch repeated. "Take it or leave it."

"Cash?" the man said. "Or will a check do?"

Harpwitch was immediately sorry that she hadn't asked three thousand, or four, but if the strange couple was stupid enough to agree to the unheard-of price she had thrown out in a moment of devilish inspiration, she wasn't about to give them time to change their minds. She set about preparing the paperwork.

She hadn't counted on Jeremy's having an inspiration of his own.

He waited until they had moved into the outer office to settle the deal. He knew it would come. It had to. And it did. Right on time. The brightly dressed woman reached into her purse and produced a neatly folded stack of piés. Jeremy turned to Harpwitch. There was the flash in her eyes; she was at her weakest now.

"I want my telescope," he said.

The hiccup nearly knocked her backward.

"What?"

"I think you heard me, Miss Harpwitch. I want the telescope."

"Have you lost your mind, Cabbage?" she whispered through her teeth. She hiccuped again.

"I won't go without it," he said, raising his voice to be sure that the man and woman could hear. "The choice is yours, Miss Harpwitch. What will it be? The telescope? Or the two thousand piés? Look at them, Miss Harpwitch. Look at them."

The woman fanned the piés under Harpwitch's nose, giving her the opportunity not only to see the money, but to smell it, too.

Fury sucked the color from the horrible woman's face; she hiccuped again.

"Cabbage," she hissed, "if you know what's good for you, you'll . . ."

"What's all this about a telescope?" the man asked, stepping forward.

"She stole something from me," Jeremy said. "I want it back."

Harpwitch was hiccuping so violently that she could barely speak.

"But, Jeremy," she sputtered, making an attempt, however late, to return to the part she had played earlier. "I no longer have the telescope."

"I don't believe you, Miss Harpwitch," Jeremy said. "I think it's still in that drawer."

"Jeremy darling, don't be unreasonable. I told you, I don't—"

The man took another step. Jeremy hadn't realized quite how tall he was.

"Perhaps you'd better open the drawer so that Jeremy can see for himself," he said. This time, his voice did not sound like a bass violin. It was more like the first rumblings of an earthquake.

Harpwitch yanked the keys from her pocket and shook them at Jeremy, like a voodoo witch with a rattle.

"I warn you, Jeremy Cabbage," she snarled. "You will rue this day for the rest of your life!"

Jeremy took the keys from Harpwitch and opened the drawer. The telescope was there, just as he knew it would be. He removed it with both hands and focused, just for the sheer impertinence of it, on Harpwitch's nose, which, he noticed with satisfaction, was twitching with rage. If anything, sleeping in the darkness of the drawer had sharpened the telescope's incredible power.

"We can go now," he said.

The woman handed Harpwitch the money. As the three of them—Jeremy and the eccentric couple—reached the door, Harpwitch called out after them.

"What do you want a child for, anyway?" she asked. "They're trouble. All of them!"

The couple turned so quickly that she instinctively tightened her grip on the hard roll of cash she'd already buttoned into the pocket of her dress.

"Why does anyone want a child?" the man asked. "To love, of course."

"Are you ready, Jeremy?" his companion asked.

Jeremy nodded.

He turned his back to Harpwitch and paused for a moment, allowing the realization to wash over him that this was the first occasion since he had fallen under her control that he did not fear a surprising pinch on the back of the neck or the sting of a belt biting into his calves. For a moment, he wondered if his knees were going to buckle from utter happiness.

Chapter 14

But Who Was He Blaming?

HHMDUCSC was behind them now, its bad smells and its bad intentions and its bad memories fading with each step. With Bo's hand resting protectively on his shoulder and the telescope tucked securely into the waistband of his shorts, Jeremy felt safe for the first time since the PatPats had delivered him to Harpwitch after the raids. As for Bo and Ba, they seemed to understand that there are times when silence is as comforting as good conversation. Except for the *slap-slap slap-slap* of the couple's enormous shoes on the pavement, the odd trio moved down the sidewalk without a sound.

Jeremy used the time to think about those last moments with Harpwitch, recalling her face with unmitigated delight when he'd asked for the telescope. He even squeaked out a hiccup to remind himself of the way the spasms had pinched the air when they attacked his old tormentor, transforming her into some kind of preposterous jack-in-the-box.

But better even than the memory of the hiccups

was what had happened when Bo responded to the wicked woman's question about their reasons for wanting a child. *To love, of course,* he'd said. The effect those four potent syllables had on the poisonous atmosphere in the office was instantaneous. They'd cleansed it, scouring, temporarily, the misery that hung in the air like the spores of an invisible fungus. They'd all felt it, of course, but none of them more than Harpwitch, who, to Jeremy's great astonishment, suddenly looked both very, very old and very, very young. It was as if the power of the words had momentarily relieved her of the heavy burden of her own cruelty. Without it, she was as bewildered as a blind woman who has just been given the gift of sight.

Jeremy allowed the words to work on him, too. *To love, of course,* he repeated to himself as he walked down the street. *To love.*

Eventually, the threesome arrived at the side of a canary-colored car that in its cheery, gleaming exterior looked as out of place on the drab Metropolis street as the noonday sun might at twilight. It was minuscule, hardly bigger than one of the Bang'ems that Jeremy had seen at the street fairs. A large silver horn, half as big as the car itself, was mounted on its tiny hood.

"Here we are!" Ba said, gesturing with her gloved hand toward the door that, Jeremy noted, popped open of its own accord. "You first, Jeremy."

Jeremy couldn't believe she meant he should actually get *in* the car. It seemed impossible. But as he put his foot on the running board and ducked his head under the low yellow roof, he saw that the car was amazingly roomy. In a matter of seconds, all three were comfortably tucked into the front seat, Bo behind the steering wheel, Ba on the passenger's side, and Jeremy between them.

"Home, Lemondrop!" Bo said. He patted the shining black dashboard of the automobile as if it were a beloved cocker spaniel.

With a loud *hooooo-ahhhhh!* the car started, raced its engine, and pulled out into the deserted street. One of Bo's arms lay comfortably on the seatback behind Jeremy. The other was propped on the padded armrest of the front door. Lemondrop seemed to be driving herself!

"She's just like a pony," Ba said, pulling a ball of fuzzy pink yarn and a pair of wooden knitting needles from her bag. "She always knows the way home."

After the rough-and-tumble ride of Tiny's jalopy, Jeremy was amazed at how easily Lemondrop navigated the crumbling concrete of the Metropolis's streets. On the long journey home, she made just one mistake, turning right when she should have turned left.

"She's a tiny bit dyslexic," Ba whispered, patting Jeremy's shoulder lightly. "None of us is perfect."

Only once did Jeremy feel uncomfortable. Lemondrop had stopped at a crosswalk, allowing a man dressed in a filthy, torn coat and ragged trousers to cross the street. But as the man approached the car, he suddenly lurched toward them, as if he meant to open one of Lemondrop's doors. The man's face was lined with deep furrows, and a dark void showed where a tooth should have been. He rolled his eyes wildly. Jeremy was sure he heard him cursing the Baron under his breath.

Jeremy shivered, remembering the dangers that had lurked on every corner when he was on the streets. But the man wasn't dangerous, just poor and hungry and ill. Jeremy was as surprised as he when Bo reached into his pocket and handed him a fistful of silver coins through Lemondrop's window.

"Be careful what you say, friend," Bo advised the man, modulating his deep voice so as not to frighten him. "In the Metropolis, even the potholes have ears."

The man blinked, bewildered at this unexpected act of goodwill. As Lemondrop pulled away, Jeremy watched in the rearview mirror as the man slowly moved to the other side of the street, a bit straighter, or so it seemed to Jeremy, than when he had approached the car.

The difficulties of his life before the raids led Jeremy to recall also its pleasures—the freedom to roam wherever he might, the long nights reading in the Licreeary, the camaraderie he enjoyed with Pickles and the other Parrots, but most of all, what he felt for Polly. The ache, as familiar now as his own heartbeat, returned to him.

Don't worry, Polly, he said to himself, rubbing the telescope as if it were the magic lamp he'd read about one late night in the Licreeary. *Don't worry. I'll find you. I'll find you no matter where you are.*

On and on, Lemondrop drove. Through neighborhoods like Tiny's. Through neighborhoods like the Cudgels. Through large grids of crumbling buildings and through parks that at one time had been the site of spirited games of batterball but were abandoned now to the debris that each day seemed to generate a bit more of itself, like a dark volcano forming on the floor of a polluted sea.

When they came to the factories, Lemondrop closed her windows. The smokestacks were belching black smoke into the sky. It seemed to Jeremy that they were venting Hell itself.

"The Baron," Ba said, nodding toward the factories.

Jeremy wondered if they were going to drive right to the Terra Nequam, but as they approached one of the heavily guarded gates that led out of the Metropolis, Lemondrop slowed down and turned right.

"Almost there, Jeremy," Bo said through his bag.

Suddenly, the street widened, and the buildings on either side seemed in slightly better repair than in the neighborhoods through which they had driven. There was more life on the street, too. Jeremy even saw a couple walking arm in arm. He also couldn't help but notice that the soot, which elsewhere in the Metropolis clung to every struggling blade of glass and settled on every eyelash and lodged itself under every fingernail, was just the tiniest bit less black.

"Luckily, the wind usually blows the filth from the factories away from us," Ba said.

"Yes, lucky for us," Bo added, "but unlucky, I'm afraid, for the rest of the Metropolis." His voice sounded angry—angry and accusatory. But who was he blaming?

Without warning, Lemondrop pulled over and, with another loud *hooooo-ahhhhh,* came to a screeching halt. They'd stopped in front of a building the likes of which Jeremy had never seen. All the buildings on the street were large, but this one dwarfed the others in its size and its grandeur. It was made of a whitish stone, and clean—or, at least, clean for the Metropolis—wide steps led to a long, narrow porch, the roof of which was supported by four thick columns.

At the Licreeary, Jeremy had read about museums, with their high ceilings and their shining wide halls and their glass cases filled with all the treasures of the world. He had never been to a museum, of course. In fact, as far as he knew, there were none in the Metropolis.

But if there were, Jeremy decided as he looked past Bo and toward the building's grand facade, *they would look like this.*

Lemondrop's door popped open—Jeremy was already used to her independence—and Bo, Ba, and finally Jeremy got out.

Now that he could see the building fully, Jeremy noticed the large banner that was tied with sturdy rope to the two outermost columns. The banner fluttered and snapped in the breeze, waving to him.

A LIVING MUSEUM AND MORAL EXHIBITION OF HUMAN ODDBALLS AND QUADRUPED DELIGHTS, he read.

"At last," Ba sighed. "Home sweet home."

Chapter 15

Are You Coulrophobic?

As Jeremy looked on, the huge double doors to the building swung open. A boy appeared. He was taller than Jeremy, older, too, perhaps fourteen or fifteen. He was dressed grandly, in a tuxedo and a top hat, which he'd cocked so far to the left Jeremy wondered how it managed to stay on his head. Jeremy blinked. Beside the boy stood an enormous pink pig; she must have weighed five hundred pounds. Both boy and pig began to descend the stairs.

"Your welcoming party has arrived," said Bo, waving to the boy.

As the boy got closer, Jeremy could see that his tuxedo was shabbier than it had first seemed, the cuffs of the pants frayed, the wide silk lapels threadbare and patched. Nonetheless, Jeremy was suddenly aware of his own simple T-shirt and shorts.

The boy and his porcine companion, who wore a scarf checked in various shades of pink around her neck and a shining brass ring through her nose, were now at the bottom of the steps.

"Jeremy," Bo said, gesturing toward the welcoming party, "I'd like you to meet Toby. Toby, this is Jeremy."

Before Jeremy could extend his hand, Toby grabbed it and shook it with such hearty conviction that Jeremy felt it all the way to the top of his head.

"Glad to meet ya," Toby said.

With the same rough enthusiasm with which he had shaken Jeremy's hand, he now gave Jeremy a hearty slap on the back, propelling him forward.

"We're gonna be great pals. I know it!" Toby continued, jumping up to where Jeremy now stood. "This here's Letitia," he said. He tilted his head toward the pig and clucked his tongue. "Where are your manners, Letty? I taught ya better than that. I know I did. Now, say hello to Jeremy."

Jeremy looked down at the colossal animal and hoped that the way she expressed her friendship wasn't as exuberant as her master's. Fortunately, Letitia only grunted as, with great dignity, she bent her front legs and lowered her impressive head, giving the distinct impression that all five hundred of her pounds had curtsied.

"Letitia here can spell better than most humans," Toby announced proudly. "And she can cipher, too. Letitia, what's two times three?"

Jeremy listened in wonder as the great pig produced six very precise grunts.

"Letitia is a sapient pig, Jeremy," Bo said by way of explanation.

"Sapient!" A man's voice, higher than Bo's but with

the same musical resonance, resounded through the air behind them.

It had been a morning of great surprises. Bo and Ba appearing like a human bouquet on Harpwitch's doorstep. His own bravery in getting the telescope back. Lemondrop. The tuxedoed boy and his pig. But none was so great as what Jeremy discovered when he turned to see who had spoken.

It was a man, a bald man, dressed identically to the woman who stood beside him, in a white caftan and sandals. But it was neither the man's baldness nor the couple's peculiar clothes that caused Jeremy's jaw to drop. It was their color. Every part of the man and the woman not covered by the robes—their hands and fingers, their faces and necks, their arms, their legs, their feet, and in the case of the man, his entire head—was a shimmering, brilliant blue.

"Sapient," the blue man repeated. "S-A-P-I-E-N-T. Adjective. Wise and discerning."

Before Jeremy could respond, the man continued. "Oh, but my manners are deplorable. Appalling! Abominable! Insufferable and intolerable!"

As if to clear the air of the words with which he had cluttered it, he made an extravagant sweeping gesture with his arm.

"Please allow me the joyful jubilation," he went on, "the precise and pulsating pleasure, the great, gracious, gripping, gargantuan gratification of introducing myself."

Jeremy was struck speechless by the torrent of words pouring forth from the blue man, but even if he'd wanted to say something, there was no opportunity.

"My appellation, if you will . . . ," the man continued. "My moniker, if you won't . . . my name, if you must . . . is Alexander. However, my friends, my pals, my chums, my intimates, my buddies, comrades, and amigos, which you most certainly will be principal, preeminent, paramount, and primary among, are free to use my sobriquet . . . my cognomen . . . my diminutive . . . in short, young sir, my nickname, Lexi."

Jeremy wasn't sure, but he thought perhaps the man had told him that his name was Alexander but that Jeremy should call him Lexi.

"Don't worry, Jeremy," Ba whispered into his ear as Lexi bowed from the waist. "He doesn't always speak like that. He's just showing off at the moment. He'll calm down once he knows you."

The top of Lexi's head was now directly in front of Jeremy's eyes, and he could see that the blue of his skin wasn't completely solid but was instead composed of an intricate pattern arranged in swirls, columns, and rows. Without warning, Lexi righted himself and presented his companion.

"And this lovely example of the feminine race is my spouse," he announced.

Jeremy waited for a moment before turning toward the woman to whom Lexi had gestured. Surely the man was not done speaking. Lexi's blue lips, however, for the moment at least, seemed to be sealed. But just as Jeremy opened his mouth to say hello, he started up again.

"Yes! My companion!" he exclaimed, raising the index finger of his right hand over his head. "My consort. My escort. My marriage partner. My better half. My helpmate. My rib. That is to say, dear boy, my wife, Connie."

Connie went from peacock blue to a deep purple. Jeremy guessed that she was blushing.

"Don't be put off by his highfalutin ways," she said. Her broad smile exposed a row of straight white teeth that heightened the lovely aqua of her lips and cheeks. She extended her hand, then seemed to change her mind and instead threw her arms around Jeremy. "Ah, what the heck," she said. "You're family now."

"You might have heard of them?" Bo suggested. "LexiConnie: The Dazzling Dictionary Duo!"

Connie released Jeremy, who couldn't help but wonder if any of the blue had rubbed off on his neck. He wasn't proud of what he said next, but it was the only thing he could think of to say.

"You're—you're blue!" he stammered.

Connie held out an arm as if she meant that Jeremy should take a closer look.

"Yes, but sadly, not by birth," she explained. "I think it would be lovely to be naturally blue, don't you? Indigo, perhaps, or cerulean."

"But . . . but . . . ," Jeremy started.

"Tattoos!" Connie said.

"Between us," Lexi added, "we cover every word in the English language. Or perhaps it's more correct to say *they* cover us." He looked into Jeremy's eyes and raised an eyebrow. "Every *square inch* of us."

"Feel free to check it out," Connie said, offering her arm once more.

Jeremy took Connie's wrist and brought his nose to within an inch of her arm. As his eyes adjusted to the short distance, he began to see them. Word after word after word in alphabetical order, each with its definition, tattooed in the tiniest letters, in columns that ran up and down the length of Connie's arm, disappearing, finally, like a highway into the horizon, up and into the sleeve of her caftan.

"I'm A through L," Lexi announced proudly. "It's all there, from 'aardvark' to 'lysis.' The A's start here." He tapped the top of his head. "The B's and C's run from nose to shoulders. D's, E's, and F's? Chest and back, naturally. The G's, the H's, and the I's are here, around my waist. Now, J's are *really* interesting." He put his hand on his bottom. "They're—"

"I'm M through Z," Connie interrupted. " 'Ma'am' to 'zymurgy.' The arm you're looking at covers the S's."

"Salad," Jeremy read. "Salamander. Salami. Salary."

"Between us, there isn't a word we don't have tattooed . . . somewhere," Lexi proclaimed. Once again, he raised an eyebrow.

Jeremy looked up from Connie's arm. Bo and Ba stood smiling before him, as cheerful as the giant-sized jars of candy that Jeremy had longed for at the street fairs. Toby, his hat clinging mysteriously to the side of his head, and his intelligent porcine friend stood next to them now. They were smiling, too, if it could be said that a pig can smile. Finally, he turned his gaze back to Lexi and Connie, as blue as the expanse of the Ocean Occidental he had traced with his finger on maps at the Licreeary. Overhead, the banner flapped in the breeze. He thought maybe he was beginning to understand.

"Is . . . a Living Museum some kind of circus?" he asked.

The others applauded.

"Kind of, yes," Bo answered, smiling broadly. "We're entertainers."

"Toby and Letitia have a very popular act," Ba added, putting her arm around Toby's shoulders. "They've been with us since . . ." She stopped herself and began again. "Well, for a while. So have Lexi and Connie."

And were there others? Jeremy wanted to know.

"Many others," Bo said. "Melchior, Madame Josephine, Radu . . ."

"Gravitas," Toby added.

"We mustn't forget Sylvana just because she's visiting her sister in the Petropolis," Ba said.

"That's right," Connie chimed in. "Or Watkins."

"And every single one of us has a talent," Lexi proudly proclaimed. "A special ability. A gift. A faculty. A facility. An endowment. A genius. An aptitude. A strength. A capacity. A capability. A skill, a knack, a bent, or a flair. We're special. That's why we're here."

"And you?" Jeremy turned to Bo and Ba.

An awkward silence seemed to fall on the group. Lexi and Connie suddenly busied themselves, looking up words in each other's ears. Toby seemed to find something of great interest in the sky, and even Letitia turned her back to the gathering and sat—rather delicately, Jeremy noticed, for a pig her size—facing the steps.

Bo cleared his throat. For the first time since they had met, there was something about Bo that made Jeremy feel the man was uncomfortable. Perhaps it was the way he cleared his throat. Perhaps it was how softly he spoke.

"I suppose it's time?" he said, looking at Ba.

"Yes," she answered, taking his gloved hand. "Go ahead, dear. I'm sure it will be fine."

"Jeremy," Bo began, "we'd like to remove these silly bags now. But before we do . . . before we do, well, there's something we need to know."

"We don't want to be nosy," Ba continued, nervously picking at a ruffle close to her neck. "After all, this is your first day with us, and if you'd rather not tell us, that's all right. It's just that we feel it would be better if . . ."

"Ask me anything," Jeremy said. "Anything you like."

He was resolved that whatever Bo and Ba wanted to know, he would do his best to tell them. They had rescued him from Harpwitch. They had helped him to retrieve the telescope. They had treated him with kindness. Besides, what did he have to hide?

"Really," he said. "It's all right. I don't mind. I don't mind at all."

"Okay, then," Ba continued. "If you're sure it's all right."

"I'm sure," Jeremy responded. He glanced toward Lexi. "Absolutely and positively," he added.

Bo bent down so that he could look directly into Jeremy's eyes. "Are you . . . ," Bo began to ask. "Are you . . . coulrophobic?"

Jeremy wondered if something had gone wrong with his ears. He had learned a great many words living with Polly in the Licreeary. That was what the Licreeary was about, wasn't it? Words. But try as he might, he had no idea what Bo had asked him. What was it he had said? Coal-ra . . . ? Koolrra . . . ? He wanted to show the kindly couple how clever he was, but he simply didn't know what Bo was talking about.

"Coulrophobia." It was Connie's voice this time. She was reading from the bridge of Lexi's nose. "C-O-U-L-R-O-P-H-O-B-I-A. Noun. An unnatural fear—"

"—of clowns," Bo said quietly.

Clowns? That same uncontrollable urge to laugh that Jeremy had experienced when he had first seen Bo and Ba suddenly returned. *Clowns! Of course!* That explained the clothes and the shoes and even Lemondrop. She was a clown car!

Wait till Polly finds out! he thought. *She won't believe it! I've been adopted by clowns!* He was practically giddy.

"It's all right," he finally managed to say. "It's fine. I'm not coulro . . . coulrophobic!"

Bo and Ba pulled off the bags that hid their faces.

Once again, in spite of himself, Jeremy's jaw dropped. Bo's nose was the shape and color of a pomegranate! Two circles covered his cheeks, just as they had on the bag, except now they were yellow, and a fringe of hair, the same color as his nose, circled the back of his head. His blue and yellow eyebrows, arched in an expression of perpetual surprise, looked as if they had been painted on to his broad white forehead. Beneath them, two eyes, the color of onyx, twinkled merrily. Ba looked almost exactly like her companion, but her nose, though just as red, was not nearly so round. She had a full head of hair, too, which bounced and flopped around her face like hundreds of springs.

Jeremy could only stare, his mouth opening and closing just the way Orville's had before he floated to the surface of the bowl. He knew he had to say something. All of them—Lexi and Connie, Toby, Bo and Ba, even Letitia—were watching him.

"It's okay!" he managed to blurt out. "I . . . I *like* clowns."

This led to an explosion of cheers and laughter and general mayhem. Lexi picked up Jeremy and carried him around on his shoulders, but not before Toby had delivered a powerful but friendly whack on the back, shouting, "I *knew* we'd be pals!" Letitia trotted in impromptu circles around the entire group.

All of them were laughing now, and each burst of laughter was more rollicking than the last. Eventually, the celebrants calmed themselves, gasping for breath, and Lexi put Jeremy down.

"There is one thing, Jeremy dear," Ba said, wiping tears, either of laughter or of joy, from her eyes. "You see, we're not *exactly* clowns."

Not exactly clowns? What could she mean?

"But your clothes!" Jeremy protested. "And your shoes! And Lemondrop! And your—"

Thank goodness Bo came to his aid. He had been about to say *and your noses,* which struck him somehow as impolite.

"We *look* like clowns," said Bo.

"And we *act* like clowns," Ba continued.

"But the truth, dear boy," Bo said, "the truth is . . . we're . . . we're cloons!"

Chapter 16

Any Fool Could Do It

"Cloons?"

The Baroness Gertrudina von Strompié turned her back to her husband and set about straightening the folds in the heavy drapes that hung at the windows in his study. She moved from panel to panel, yanking at the pleats until her fingers ached.

"Cloons?" she said again, disguising the impatience in her voice with a tone an octave above her usual contralto. "You must be joking! At Rosamund's birthday ball?"

"Why not?" the Baron asked.

He picked up a puzzle he kept on his desk. Two sections of steel chain. The object was to twist the links just so until they separated; it was simple. Though he had owned the puzzle for months, the Baron had never solved it.

"Must you play with toys?" Gertrudina asked.

"This is not a toy!" the Baron declared. He emphasized his point by giving the puzzle an exasperated yank. "I'd like to see the kid who could solve it. Besides, it helps me relax."

And the Baron *needed* to relax. The demands placed on him were tremendous. Yesterday, for example, he had passed a new law making it illegal to have an accent in the Metropolis. The Gobbledygook Provision, he'd called it.

The Baroness dropped it. She wished, though, he would get this business of the graffiti settled. It was causing him to be uncharacteristically stubborn. She had to be careful.

"I thought you were thinking of sending the cloons to the Terra Nequam."

"*You* were, you mean," argued the Baron. He stared quizzically at the point where the links of chain interlocked. "Not *me.*"

"Not *I,*" the Baroness corrected.

"Not I. Not me. What difference does it make?"

He jerked at the ends of the puzzle.

Gertrudina clutched the drape so fiercely that she nearly caused the filigreed rod supporting it to jump from its bracket and come crashing to the floor.

"But surely you can see that inviting the cloons to perform at Rosamund's ball is sending the wrong message to our citizens," she protested. "You must set an example for them. I was hoping to have the Metropolian Opera perform."

"The opera!" the Baron grunted as he tugged at the chain with increasing frustration. "Everybody ends up dead in operas, sprawled all over the stage like . . . like . . . upholstered footstools. It doesn't seem the right kind of thing for a girl's birthday party."

"Birthday *ball,*" the Baroness corrected again. "How

many times must I say it? It's a ball. Not a . . . not a . . . *party.*" She said this word as if she'd been forced to take a large bite of an unripe persimmon. "And do I have to remind you," she continued through clenched teeth, "that Rosamund is not just any girl? She is a young baroness. In spite of her looks."

"I don't see anything wrong with the way she looks."

"When was the last time you saw her?" she countered. "Last week? Two weeks ago?"

"I'm"—*clank*—"a busy"—*clink*—"man!"

"Well, if you *had* seen her, you would have noticed that the freckles are getting worse." Real distress entered her voice now. "No matter what I do, she seems to get less and less like a baroness and more and more like . . . like one of those stray children."

"Maybe it's the influence of that maid," the Baron suggested, resting momentarily from his exertions with the chain. "Fire her. I'll send her to the mines."

The Baroness had already considered this possibility. But the maid was so superior, in both her work and her general intelligence, to any of the others who had waited on Rosamund that she couldn't bear to get rid of her. In fact, the Baroness had even found herself thinking the impossible—this maid, with her natural charm and her quick wit, was more like a baroness than her own daughter.

"No," she responded. "No, that wouldn't be wise just now. Perhaps later. Now, let's come to some agreement on the cloons."

"Oh, have the bleeping opera if you want!" he

shouted. He raised his arm and flung the toy across the room. "But we're having the cloons, too!"

"But—"

"No! I've made up my mind! If it will make you feel any better, I'll find a reason to get rid of them. But after the ball."

This was the concession the Baroness had been waiting for. She had been winning arguments with her husband since the day they met. She wasn't about to start losing now.

"Promise me," she demanded. "Promise that after the ball, you'll find a way to send the cloons to the mines."

"Oh, all right! I promise! I'll do it!" the Baron said.

"Very well," she answered. "We'll have both the cloons and the opera. The freaks can perform early in the day, before any of the important guests arrive. After that, they go! Once and for good!"

Before her husband could protest, she opened the door and exited.

With relief, the Baron heard the door click shut. Why did his wife torture him so? Couldn't she see that he had important work to do?

He wondered if it had been wise to marry a woman with such refined tastes. Well, it was too late to think about that. Besides, he had much more pressing matters on his mind.

He trudged across the room and picked up the puzzle. Unsolvable as it was, it was still less mysterious than the graffiti, which was appearing everywhere now and with increasing frequency. On houses. On fences. Even on the stone walls surrounding Helios itself. He had lost count of how many times Wirm had reported that another instance had been discovered. It was always the same. Always in that peculiar black lettering. DOWN WITH THE BARON.

That's why he had been so insistent that the cloons perform. It wasn't for Rosamund. It was for *him*! Trouble was coming. He could feel it. He needed relief. And those puzzles weren't going to bring it. Gertrudina was right, of course. (She was *always* right.) The cloons were freaks, but just now, he needed to laugh. Yes, he would keep his promise to his wife. He would drum up some reason and send the cloons off to the Terra Nequam. But this one last time, he would enjoy himself.

He gave the chain a halfhearted yank, but its two parts remained as they were, linked.

I think I'll have the PatPats arrest the manufacturer of this stupid thing, he decided. *It's false advertising. The directions said any fool could do it.*

Meanwhile, just outside the entrance to his dark hidey-hole in the basement of Helios, Jeriah Wirm lifted his leg and stamped his foot on the damp stone floor. He brought a pale hand to his ear and listened until he was satisfied that the skittering inside had stopped.

"Yes, run, my darlings," he muttered as he stepped into the room. "Run while you can. When I'm Commander General, the first thing I'll do is get a cat. A big cat!"

He poked around on the trestle he had set up for a table, his fingers nimbly palpating the various familiar objects—a dented tin plate, a twisted fork and spoon, a cup whose rim was chipped. When he found the candle, jammed like a cork into an old bottle, he reached into his pocket and found the large box of matches that was always there.

With a practiced hand, he lit the candle, its wick sputtering once or twice before the flame rose to reveal the mosaic of photographs that had been pinned to the wall. These were the photographs that Wirm had shown the Baron, the ones he'd taken at the site of the incidents. The photos were remarkable in their sameness. DOWN WITH THE BARON! DOWN WITH THE BARON! DOWN WITH THE BARON! Always in an identical hand.

But these were not the photographs that Wirm had come to study. From the pocket of his jacket, he pulled a handful of other photos. Their edges curled around his finger and thumb as if they were loath to be seen by the likes of Jeriah Wirm. These were the pictures that Wirm had *not* shown the Baron.

"No sense telling him *everything,*" Wirm lisped.

He dealt the photos onto the table. Like the photos on the wall, these, too, were similar, but they depicted no words, no writing of any kind. In fact, the untrained eye might have seen them as failures since the surface of each rectangle was nothing but a shining gray blank.

But these were no mistakes. A more careful inspection revealed a vague tracing on each one, the outline of a shoe print, the same shoe print that Wirm had discovered at each of the graffiti sites. It was not the human footprints that Wirm was interested in, though; it was the line of hieroglyphics that encircled them. Animal tracks.

Without removing his eyes from the photographs, Wirm reached for the magnifying glass that lay next to the misshapen cutlery. He brought the lens to his eye. Like a cyclops, he bent over each picture, tracing the image of the track with the tip of his pointed fingernail. Even in the flickering light, there could be no doubt: Whoever was writing the rebellious slogan was accompanied by some kind of animal. The tracks were curious, like a child's drawing of a tulip with a leaf protruding on either side of the base.

"What are you, my beastie?" Wirm asked aloud. "You're not a dog, no. Nor a cat. A kangaroodle, perhaps? A creature from the Terra Nequam? What are you?"

Of course, he might have asked the Baron's permission to enter one of the closed libraries where he could do some research on the tracks, but that posed too many problems. For one thing, the Baron would be suspicious about what he was doing there. For another, Wirm loathed the big buildings filled with books. The towering shelves made him feel even smaller than he was, and the bright colors on the volumes' spines accentuated his awful paleness. Still, if what he found in the library could have solved his problem, Wirm might have overcome his revulsion, except for one sticky detail. He wouldn't have been able to find the book he needed. Jeriah Wirm, like many of the citizens of the Metropolis, had never been taught to read.

"Never mind," he chuckled as he put the magnifying glass down and gathered up the photos. "Never mind. I'll find you. I'll find you, and when I do, it will be the Choir Stall for you and Commander Generalship for me."

He blew out the candle and immediately heard the sound of a rat scuttling across the floor.

"Meow!" Wirm called out, leering in the dark. "Meow. Meow. Meow."

Chapter 17

Viragos and Vipers

"A cat, then?" Polly asked.

"Allergic," Rosie answered with a shrug.

The two girls were taking a rare stroll around the gardens, permitted by the Baroness only because the sun, with its freckle-popping rays, was behind a heavy blanket of clouds. They were supposed to be reviewing rules of etiquette from a long list set down by Rosie's mother, but the conversation had instead turned to what Rosie wanted for her birthday.

"I *would* like a puppy, though," Rosie continued. "I could teach it tricks. Like this."

She bent her knees and hopped forward in an imitation of a circus dog. Polly glanced up at the windows of the palace. It wouldn't do to have Rosie's mother see her performing such shenanigans.

"But I might as well forget about it," Rosie continued, resuming her place alongside Polly. "*She* would never allow it. 'A dog?'" She lowered her voice, mimicking her mother's tone and intonation. "'A dog, you say? Might I remind you that Helios is a palace! Not a kennel!'"

Polly tried not to laugh. It wasn't right to encourage Rosie in these antics, but the way she had flared her nostrils and lifted her shoulders was a perfect caricature of her mother.

Rosie's performance was cut short by a commotion just on the other side of the trees through which their path wound. Boys' voices raised in what appeared to be a race toward the palace. Flashes of blue darted in and out of the sunlit spaces between the trunks—a squadron of Junior PatPats, on their way to make their weekly report to the Baron.

"Creeps!" Rosie called out after them.

Polly remained silent, not even making an attempt to chide Rosie for her name-calling. A shiver of revulsion made its way up and down her spine as the boys ran into the palace.

They're like a pack of well-dressed wolves, she thought.

The wolves had barely reached the palace door when three silver clangs of a bell rang through the air. This was the signal indicating it was time for another of the endless lessons the older Baroness had arranged for her daughter. The list went on and on: The Diction of the Cultured, for which the girl was forced to hold her nose while she practiced rolling her R's. (Polly had laughed until her face was wet with tears at hearing Rosie chant over and over again, "Rice with raisins is relished in Rangoon.") Posture and Grace. Table Manners for the Well Bred. ("When dining at official functions, real ladies only give the *appearance* of eating.") How an Aristocrat Accepts a Gift.

The classes were taught by variations of the

amphibious dance master, each one more horrible than the last. Parasites all, they were getting fat on Rosie's mother's desperate need to transform her daughter into something the girl would never be. In fact, in spite of the masters' promises to the contrary, it was apparent to the entire throng that not one of them was having the slightest effect on Rosie. If anything, her high spirits and tomfoolery were increasing.

The bell rang a second time. Rosie pretended not to hear and picked up a woollyworm that had inched its way onto the gravel path. She placed it under her nose. The caterpillar, black with orange stripes, clung to her upper lip, giving the impression that the girl had suddenly sprouted a mustache.

"Don't make me go!" Rosie begged. "Pleeeeease!"

Polly gently removed the caterpillar and placed it in the grass.

"Your mother is in quite a mood this morning," she said. "If that bell rings one more time, both of us will pay."

Rosie herself didn't mind punishment. She was used to it. But she couldn't stand to see the Baroness take her hand to Polly. She turned and began to drag her feet toward the palace. She'd taken no more than two steps when she stopped in her tracks. A short figure in a blue turban waddled toward them.

"Oh no!" Rosie whispered. "It's *her*!"

Signora Calvina Porchini was by far the worst of the viragos and vipers the Baroness had employed to instruct her daughter. Her nose was so turned up that it might rightly have been called a snout, and she wore the turban to hide the fact that she was practically bald. With her special talent for nastiness, it was only natural that her area of expertise was the one that Rosie hated most: Keeping Servants in Their Place.

"Yoooo-hoooo!" Signora Porchini cried out in a disagreeable falsetto. "Little Baronesssssss! It is I! Your favorite tutorrrrr! Yoo-hoooooooo."

As if she were keeping off flies, the signora twirled a filthy white handkerchief in the air over her head. The handkerchief, stained in clashing hues of purple and red, doubled as a napkin to protect her mighty bosom from the multitude of stains it would otherwise have received from the jelly cakes she constantly jammed in her mouth.

"Yoooo-hooo. Little Baronessssss. Time for your lessssonnnnnn!"

Polly took Rosie's hand.

"Ah, little Baroness, there you are!" croaked Porchini as soon as the two girls were in easy earshot. She curtsied like some preposterous drunken chicken, holding her arms out to her side, wobbling first to the right and then to the left. "Today is your lucky day," she clucked as she righted herself. "Yes, my royal bonbon. Today, you'll learn how to deal with a sassy cook."

It wasn't clear to Polly if Porchini had pinched the air to demonstrate what was in store for the cook or if she had snatched an unsuspecting gnat from the swarm that seemed to be in her attendance. In either case, the effect was chilling.

"To the kitchen!" Porchini squealed. She licked her lips and turned on her heel.

Polly watched helplessly as Rosie dragged along behind Porchini. Before the two turned the corner, Rosie looked back. With her index finger, she pushed her nose up into a snout and mimicked the unstable curtsy the short, turbaned woman had previously executed. Polly disguised her burst of laughter with a fit of coughing, hanging well behind until the signora and her unwilling tutee had disappeared. Then she walked to the back of the palace, careful to enter through the door Gertrudina had instructed her to use when she was not in Rosie's company.

With a quick step, she made her way through the unlit corridor to the dark, narrow stairs used by all the servants. At the top, she turned left and entered her room, next to Rosie's, where she kicked off the slippers that the Baroness made her wear—a full size too small—and walked over to the spot that had become her favorite: a broad window seat that looked beyond the kitchen gardens to the expanse of park at the back of the palace. Next, she dropped to the floor the cushion that ran the length of the seat. She preferred the natural, smooth feel of the wide oak casing to the imported velvet that, as the Baroness never failed to point out, had cost more than Polly could hope to earn in a lifetime of service at Helios. Finally, she sat, settling in with one foot down and the other tucked under her.

She looked about her and sighed. "I must be crazy," she said aloud.

The silk tapestries, the high ceilings, the luxurious bedclothes. These did little to comfort her. She missed her old room at the Licreeary.

It wasn't a room at all, really, she told herself. *Just a little section of floor in one of the back aisles.*

But she had collected her favorite books there, and each night, after the Parrots had settled in, she would lie on her thin blanket, light a candle, and choose from the stacks of volumes she'd lovingly piled around her. Then she would read, sometimes until morning. Stories of glass mountains, of golden keys, of boys turning into ravens, and of strong, brave girls who risked their lives to find their destinies. So far, the only book she'd discovered at Helios was *The Exalted History of the Family von Strompié.* Yes, she yearned for her room.

More than that, though, she yearned for Jeremy. From the very beginning, she'd felt a special connection to the boy. *It was his laugh,* she told herself. *The way he was laughing in that crate of cabbages, as if it were the funniest thing imaginable.* And as the years passed, it had become clear to her that the rough life of the streets would never taint his natural optimism or tarnish his unwavering goodness.

She recalled the evening a few months earlier at the Licreeary. There had been very little to eat that night, only a loaf of stale bread and a couple of rotting pears. The Parrots sat in a circle in the crumbling lobby, their eyes wide with hunger, their stomachs growling, each of them wondering how that single loaf of bread and two wormy pears were going to feed the lot of them.

It was Jeremy who'd answered their question. He pointed at the moldy bread. "Pass me some of that goose," he'd shouted, as if he had been sitting at a banquet table. What a show he had put on! Oohing and aahing, smacking his lips and licking his fingers with the greatest gusto imaginable as he shoved a crumb into his mouth. Eventually, the others couldn't help themselves; one by one, they joined in the charade, competing to see who could put on the most convincing show. That night, instead of lying awake, listening to the sound of their gnawing hunger, they fell asleep reliving their pantomime. And all because of Jeremy.

Polly shifted her weight. Would she ever hear that laugh again? The last time she saw him, he was being carried off over the shoulder of a PatPat, like a bag of potatoes on its way to the marketplace. She'd cried out his name, but in the awful din of the raids, he hadn't heard. Where was he now? For the hundredth time, she made a silent pledge that she would find him, find him just as she had that day so many years ago.

A slight breeze swept in through the open window. It wasn't quite everyone who had participated in Jeremy's charade that night, she remembered. Once Pickles had realized there was no real food to eat, he'd left the circle, glowering at the bread and muttering under his breath.

Polly came to attention as she heard the creak of the door directly beneath the window where she sat. It wouldn't do to have the Baroness see her idle; if the woman thought that she had time to sit, even for a moment, she would surely add to the duties she piled on her every day. But it wasn't the Baroness. It was the Junior PatPats she and Rosie had seen earlier, five or six of them. She watched as they walked away from the door, swaggering down the very path on which Rosie and she had strolled earlier.

For the slightest fraction of a moment, Polly felt her heart stop. That boy in front! The officer with the gold braiding on his jacket! She hadn't seen his face, but there was something familiar about the way he moved, his head thrown forward, like a snake about to strike. She tried to get a better look, but it was too late. He disappeared with the others into a grove of trees.

Her heart was racing.

My mind must be playing tricks on me, she thought. *It has to be.*

For a moment, as if she had conjured him up out of her own memory, she was sure it had been Pickles.

Chapter 18

Three Cheers for Jeremy!

Jeremy's first discovery at the Living Museum was that the building that housed it, with its wide stone stairs and its grand double doors, wasn't a building at all.

He'd climbed the steps, surrounded by his new friends, including the happily grunting Letitia, feeling as if he were a prince entering a palace. But when he stepped over the threshold, rather than the frescoed ceiling he had been expecting, the sky stretched over his head with as little effort as it had on the other side of the doors. And he was able to see, not by the thousand twinkling bulbs of the grandly lit chandelier he'd imagined, but by the friendly light of the sun.

"Oh dear," Ba said, pressing her lips against her teeth. "We should have warned you."

"We're just so used to it, you see," Bo added. He sounded as if he were apologizing. "I hope you're not disappointed."

The group was huddled on a broad landing at the top of a series of wooden steps. The steps descended crazily onto a field that covered an area the size of two batterball courts. Jeremy leaned against the railing and blinked in disbelief. Except for all the activity, the scene before him might have been a splendid painting.

"Are . . . are they real?" he asked, pointing to one of the several large trees that dotted the grassy field.

Except for those at Helios, trees of any size had long ago been chopped down by citizens lucky enough to find an ax. Winter fuel was hard to come by. Those that remained were puny, twisted things. They no more resembled real trees than broken dolls resemble real babies.

Jeremy had only seen pictures of trees like the ones that grew in the field. They must have been hundreds of years old. Their dark, sturdy trunks supported branches that stretched up into the sky like a classroom of giants raising their hands.

"Beauties, ain't they?" Toby piped up. "It takes a lot of work to keep 'em healthy, too. That's one of my jobs." He gave Jeremy an enthusiastic jab in the ribs. "You can help if you want."

"It's the soot from the Baron's factories that makes it so difficult," Connie explained. "It interferes with the trees' ability to photosynthesize the light."

"Photosynthesis," Lexi announced. "P-H-O-T-O-S . . ."

"Photosynthesis," Jeremy mumbled through his amazement. "It's how plants make their own food."

"Good boy!" Bo said proudly.

Ba beamed at the others. "He's very clever, our Jeremy," she said.

"I'm not the clever one," Jeremy responded almost before Ba had finished. "It's Polly. She's the one who taught me. 'Just because our stomachs are empty doesn't mean our minds have to be.' That's what she always said."

Bo and Ba exchanged a quick glance.

"That there Polly sounds like a lulu!" Toby said. "A genuine lulu! Who is she, anyway?"

"We'll have plenty of time for questions later," Ba answered. "For now, let's give Jeremy a moment to take in his new surroundings."

But as Jeremy returned his gaze to the field, he was sure he would need more than a moment. It wasn't just the grass and trees that caused him to stand nearly dumbstruck at the top of the stairs. It was the tents scattered around the field—striped and polka-dotted, flowered and checked, some of them larger than the houses in Tiny's neighborhood. The one in the center had so many peaks its top resembled a range of small, pastel-colored mountains.

"That's the Performance Tent," Bo explained.

"And that one there, just to the left, the one with the chartreuse and pink swirls, well, that's ours," Ba added shyly.

Jeremy looked up into Ba's smiling face.

The cloon nodded. "Yes, Jeremy," she said. "It's your home now, too."

Before Jeremy could respond, Toby poked his thumb so forcefully into his shoulder that Jeremy thought for a moment he might topple over the railing.

"And see that little one right next to it? That's mine!" Toby shouted. "The one with the blue checks. Letitia likes her checks, don't you, Letty?"

The pig grunted.

It was impossible for Jeremy to take it all in. There were the animals, some grazing freely in the grass and some in elaborate gilded cages. He thought he recognized one or two of the beasts from pictures he had seen at the Licreeary, but most of them seemed to have sprung from the imagination of a great storyteller. And the people, who, like the animals, were of all sizes and colors, some of them dressed like Bo and Ba, some of them in spangles, some of them in shirts and tights in all the colors of the rainbow. Jeremy hardly knew where to look. One group was pounding tent stakes into the green earth. Another was spinning plates high over their heads on long, thin poles. Still another was piling up into great human pyramids.

"Welcome to the Living Museum!" Bo said, not without some pride in his voice. "We hope you'll be very happy here."

"Course he'll be happy," Toby asserted. He swung his arm around and let it land with a heavy thud on Jeremy's shoulder. "There can't be no question about that 'cause this is the best place in the whole Metropolis. There ain't no better people than Bo and Ba anywhere, Jeremy. Take it from Letitia and me. We oughta know. Right, Letty?"

Jeremy knew that pigs, even sapient ones, couldn't talk, but the way Letitia grunted twice almost sounded as if she'd said, *You bet.*

"Now, Toby," Ba said. She reached out to straighten the boy's top hat, which had slid so far down the side of his head that it was practically horizontal. "You'll have to let Jeremy find out for himself. You might be the tiniest bit biased."

"I know what I know," Toby responded, more to himself than to Ba. "And I ain't biased, neither. Whatever that means."

"Biased!" resounded Lexi. "B-I-A . . ." But he left off when Connie gently elbowed him in the ribs.

Even if Jeremy had known what to say, he wouldn't have been able to say it. Every ounce of his energy, every cell of his being, every nucleus of every atom of every breath he took was working to help him understand this sudden shift in his circumstances.

This must be a dream, he said to himself. *It isn't real.*

But it *was* real. After all, if the raids had been real, if Harpwitch had been real, if the fire had been real, couldn't the Living Museum be real, too? Couldn't grass be as real as weeds? Beauty as real as abomination? Kindness as real as cruelty? An image of Polly rose up in Jeremy's mind—Polly, whose goodness was the most real thing Jeremy had known.

If only she were here, he thought.

The group began to descend the stairs. Jeremy still half expected to wake up, expected to feel the sharp pinch of Harpwitch's fingers twisting his ear, pulling him back into the ferocious reality of HHMDUCSC. But the smooth, cool surface of the telescope pressing against his palm helped to steady him. So did Letitia, who walked beside him grunting with each step and taking every opportunity to nuzzle his leg with her soft, expressive snout.

When they had progressed to about halfway down, the party stopped at a landing so that Bo could point at what appeared to be a donkey. Jeremy blinked. The animal was walking a tightrope.

"That's Mazeppa," Ba explained. "She's one of our favorite acts. She's good, isn't she?"

"Cranky, too," Toby added. He gave Jeremy a resounding slap on the shoulder. "She bites. But don't you worry about Mazeppa. Or nothin' else, neither. You got me lookin' after you now, Jeremy. Me and Letitia."

Jeremy was about to respond when he spotted a man on stilts walking toward them. The man was dressed rather plainly. His long gray trousers completely covered the stilts.

"Ah," Bo said, pointing to the man. "Here's Watkins at last."

"Hurry up, Watty!" Toby called out. "Get over here and meet my new pal, Jeremy."

As Watkins made his way toward the group on the landing, he greeted each of the people he passed. In most cases, their heads barely reached his waist. Even from a distance, Jeremy could see the gentle light shining in the man's eyes.

"He's a dandy, ain't he, Jeremy?" Toby asked.

In his street-performing days, Jeremy had known many stilt-walkers, but none with such a natural, elegant gait as Watkins's. It was almost as if he were dancing.

He must have practiced for years to be able to use stilts like that, Jeremy thought.

But there was something beyond the man's elegance that set him apart from the other stilt-walkers Jeremy had known, something he couldn't quite put his finger on. Before he could figure out what it might be, the man was upon them.

"Jeremy," Bo said, resting his hand gently on the

boy's shoulder, "I'd like you to meet Watkins. Watkins, this is our Jeremy."

"I've been looking forward to this," said Watkins. He smiled in such a way that whatever nervousness Jeremy might have felt immediately evaporated.

They were ten feet from the ground, but Jeremy was looking directly into Watkins's eyes, shining gently behind a pair of wire-rimmed spectacles. Suddenly, he realized what it was about the man that he had been trying to identify. The man wasn't a stilt-walker. He was a . . . Before the word could form, Watkins snatched Jeremy off the landing and set him on his broad shoulders.

"That's it, Watty!" Toby shouted. "Give 'im a victory lap. Like you did me that first day."

This was the only encouragement the giant man needed. Holding firmly on to Jeremy's legs, he set off at a rollicking gallop around the field. Once Jeremy regained his breath, he gaped in wonder at all the sights beneath him. The trees. The animals. The people. They swirled in a kaleidoscope of color and motion. But nothing was so wondrous to the boy as what he could hear his new friends shouting.

"Three cheers for Jeremy!" they called out. "Three cheers for Jeremy Cabbage. Hip, hip, hooray! Hip, hip, hooray! Hip, hip, hooray!"

Chapter 19

Ab-so-lute-ly!

So far in his young life, Jeremy had lived in three places (four if you count the crate of cabbages): the Licreeary, Harpwitch's, and Tiny's. Each of these had been vastly different, but their interiors shared characteristics that had contributed to Jeremy's idea of what "indoors" meant: The light in each was dim, the air in each was stale, and the surfaces in each were hard. Even the Licreeary, beautiful to Jeremy though it was, had been built to keep people awake, not to lull them to sleep. That's why, when Jeremy stepped from the sunlight into the pink and chartreuse tent Ba had indicated from the landing, he gasped.

First there was the light. It filtered through the canvas walls and ceiling, dappling the interior with a brindled radiance. The tent was cleverly vented, too, so that when the breeze blew, there was a gentle fluttering throughout. Jeremy couldn't see what the floor was made of; perhaps there *was* no actual floor but simply the green grass of the field. Whatever it was, it was completely covered with soft carpets of the most brilliant colors and fanciful designs. These were arranged in no particular order and gave the impression that the pieces of a giant puzzle had been spilled out onto the floor, leaving a pattern so accidental and so pleasing that no one had bothered to pick them up.

There was almost no furniture, but around the perimeter of the tent there were tidily arranged piles of cushions, in every possible size, shape, and color. And between these, carved wooden trunks in graduated sizes were stacked into neat pyramids.

"It's beautiful," he whispered.

"We think so," Ba quietly replied.

The back half of the tent had been partitioned into private spaces with gaily painted panels, and this was where Bo and Ba led Jeremy now.

"Your room's back here," Bo said.

"Just opposite ours," Ba continued. "We do hope you like it, Jeremy dear."

Jeremy moved along with them, in a daze almost, as he tried to take in even the smallest detail, the scrolled hinges on the trunks or the subtle variations in the colors and knotting of the carpets.

Polly will want to know all about this, he thought. *She'll ask me all about it.*

His eyes came to rest on a series of full-length mirrors that stood at regular intervals against the wall. He stopped. Jeremy had never seen himself before. Not altogether. Mirrors, especially large ones like these, were rare in the Metropolis.

"Do you think I could . . . ?" he asked.

Ba started to speak, but Bo interrupted her before

she could begin. "Be our guest," he said. "That's what they're there for. Right, Toby?"

"Ab-so-lute-ly!" Toby responded. "That's what they're there for."

Jeremy walked toward the first mirror, stopping just short of the spot where he would be able to see his reflection. Closing his eyes, he counted.

"One . . . two . . . three!"

He stepped in front of the mirror and opened his eyes. Jumping jackrabbits! It couldn't be! His head was the size of a walnut! And it perched on a neck no thicker than a pencil! His fingers, on the other hand, were like the giant sausages he'd seen hanging in butchers' windows. Why hadn't someone told him? He . . . he was a monster!

His heart was pounding.

Not daring another glance, he sidestepped in front of the next mirror. This time, his head was the size and shape of a batterball, only twice as big. His ears stuck out so far that had he been able to flap them, he might have taken to the air, and his arms stretched along the sides of his body so that in the mirror, his knuckles seemed to scrape the floor.

"I—I—" Jeremy stammered.

Raucous laughter exploded into the soft atmosphere of the tent.

"These here are Whoopee Mirrors," Toby piped up, once he was able to control himself. He stepped alongside Jeremy. "See? My ears is just as big as yours. Lookee there. Bigger, even."

"I use these mirrors whenever I start taking myself

too seriously," Bo explained, wiping away the tears rolling down his cheeks.

"You should have explained that to Jeremy before," Ba scolded. "Look at the poor boy. He's as white as a slice of bread."

It was true. But now Jeremy burst out laughing, too.

"We got ya, didn't we, Jeremy?" Toby asked, giving his new friend a good-natured bump. "You should have seen your face."

"That was the problem," Jeremy answered. "I *did* see my face."

This set all three off into another round of laughter. Even Ba joined in this time.

"I guess there was no harm done," she admitted.

By now, the quartet plus pig had reached the flap of canvas that served as a door to Jeremy's room in the tent. Jeremy pushed it aside and cautiously entered. He secretly hoped that there might be another joke. But the pranks, at least for the moment, seemed to be over. The room was twice as big as his room in the tower at Tiny's. It was filled with the same wonderful light as the rest of the tent, and the floor here, too, was covered with the fabulous carpets. The only difference between this space and what he had observed in the much larger outer room was that here the panels that formed the wall were bare of any color. They were as white, as Ba had said earlier, as a slice of bread.

"We thought perhaps you'd like to choose your own colors," Bo explained. "Make it your own, if you know what I mean."

"You can even paint it yourself," Ba added. "If you'd like to, that is."

Toby gave Jeremy a friendly whack on the arm. "And don't forget! You got me to help you," he said. "Me and Letitia, that is. We're right good artists, we are. Right, Letty?"

Once again, the great pig grunted her agreement.

Ba stepped lightly over to a set of three carved trunks that were stacked against the perimeter of his room. She set the smaller two gently onto the carpet. Then she raised the lid of the large one. A pleasant scent of balmwood wafted through the room. She reached into the trunk and pulled out a pair of blue shorts and a matching striped shirt.

"Let's see if these fit," she said.

Jeremy couldn't believe she meant it. New clothes! For him!

"We didn't know what size, of course," Ba went on. She held them in the air in front of her, tilting her head to the side as she assessed their fit against Jeremy's small frame. "But it looks like they'll do. Lucky! There's a set for every day of the week. Different colors, of course."

The contents of the middle box caused Jeremy to blush: seven pairs of underwear, polka-dotted in the same colors as the shirts and shorts.

"Don't worry, Jeremy," Toby whispered. "She's got me wearin' 'em, too."

The smallest box contained shoes. Cloon shoes! Exactly like those worn by Bo and Ba.

"Just as I thought," Ba said, shaking her head as she

looked at Jeremy's feet, which were normal for a boy his age and size. "We'll work on getting some that fit. For now, you can wear these."

She pulled out a pair of sandals.

While Ba was showing Jeremy his clothes, Bo had stepped out of the room. When he returned, he was holding a small rectangular box, wooden and inlaid with an arabesque of opalescent stone.

"I was thinking," he began, "that this might provide safe storage for the spyglass."

Automatically, Jeremy's hand went to the waistband of his shorts.

"It's for Polly," Jeremy finally managed to say. "The telescope, I mean."

What he'd meant to say, of course, was that it was to help him *find* Polly, but the words just hadn't come.

Ba scurried to one side of the tent and rearranged a pile of cushions, to no particular effect, since the pile looked exactly the same when she finished as when she started. Toby started to speak, but a look from Ba shut him up.

"I think perhaps Jeremy would like to rest up a bit," she suggested. "He's had quite a morning."

One by one, the others filed out of the room. Toby nearly squeezed the breath out of him before he disappeared behind the flap, and Letitia gently nuzzled his leg.

"You let us know if you need anything," Bo added. "Anything at all."

"And that includes me and Letty, Jeremy," Toby added, popping his head back in. "Don't forget what I told ya before. I'm gonna look out after ya! I—" Toby didn't finish, disappearing quickly as if, perhaps, he had been yanked from the other side.

Alone now in the room, his room, Jeremy stood as still as if he had fallen under the spell of a powerful magic, the soft rise and fall of his chest the only motion, the rhythmic shush of his breath the only sound. He hadn't even been able to say thank you.

Eventually, he sat cross-legged on the soft carpet. He flexed and released the muscles in his legs, enjoying the feel of the plush, clean pile against his bare calves.

How was it possible, he wondered, to feel both very happy and very sad at the same time?

He placed the inlaid box from Bo in front of him and lifted the lid, half expecting music to come tinkling out. But there was no music, and Jeremy was glad of this. Inside, he saw that the box was lined with a shiny crimson fabric that someone—could it have been Ba? or Bo?—had taken the trouble to quilt in an intricate design of undulating waves. Jeremy removed the telescope from his waistband and placed it in the box.

Polly, he thought, *Bo and Ba don't even know you. They've never seen you or heard the funny way your voice goes up and down when you tell a story. They don't have any idea that your favorite flower is a daffodil or that you hate peas. But one day, they will. I promise.*

Then, with the lid of the box still opened, he stretched out on the carpet, closed his eyes, and fell fast asleep.

Chapter 20

An Announcement

To celebrate Jeremy's arrival, Bo declared an extended holiday from the busy performing schedule, and in the weeks that followed, Jeremy became acquainted with every human oddball and every quadruped delight the Living Museum had to offer.

He had tea with Madame Josephine, who curled her beard especially for him. He attended a concert, given in his honor, by Melchior and his Chorus of Singing Mice. He listened in amazement to the derring-do of Commodore Weensy, the World's Shortest Military Man. As time passed, he even began to make himself useful helping Radu—the caretaker of the creatures exhibited at the Museum—to feed the zebalo and the wowwie, and he spent many a busy afternoon with Watty, shining his collection of size 37 shoes.

Toby and Letitia were almost always by his side on these expeditions. But Bo and Ba often accompanied him, too. On the day he and Toby visited Bartolomeo and his Death-Diving Fleas, he learned that not all the delights at the Living Museum were quadruped.

"This is Wainwright," Bartolomeo, a large man with an even larger mustache, declared proudly. "My champion diver!"

He pointed to a black dot, perched on a tiny platform not six inches high. Jeremy squinted and blinked.

Is it Wainwright? he wondered. *Or a speck of dust?*

From somewhere, a drumroll sounded, and Jeremy watched in awe as the dot propelled itself from the platform into the water-filled thimble set beneath it. The minuscule splash convinced him that a daredevil insect had actually jumped.

Letitia, however, stubbornly refused to enter Bartolomeo's tent.

"Fleas and pigs just ain't friends," Toby explained, shaking his head mournfully.

Jeremy thought he understood why. He scratched for hours after leaving the Death-Diving Fleas.

After lunch one day, not long after Jeremy had met Wainwright and just when he was convinced that he had seen every marvel at the Living Museum, Bo asked if he'd like to accompany him to the Performance Tent. Jeremy had spent many hours in the tent playing hide-and-seek with Toby, but no matter how many times he pushed aside the canvas flap and entered, he was filled with the same sense of awe. The hundreds of colossal poles that held the tent up always made him feel that he was entering a sacred forest.

As he walked at Bo's side into the tent, he was surprised to see that at its very center, a narrow wooden track had been erected. The track spiraled around a center pole that reached up to the highest peak in the ceiling, some fifty feet above them.

"What is it?" he asked Bo.

Bo pointed to a metal sphere, the size of a large globe, which sat motionless at the bottom of the spiral.

Jeremy still didn't understand. He blinked. Was it his imagination, or had the ball trembled?

"Look!" he shouted. "It's moving!"

Bo nodded as the sphere shuddered and then, completely of its own volition, or so it seemed to Jeremy, began to ascend the spiral. Jeremy's eyes grew as large as coins when the ball began to roll steadily up the wooden track, as if a large magnet were pulling it toward the top.

The higher the ball moved, the narrower the track became.

"But the track is too skinny up there!" Jeremy said, craning his neck back to get a better look. "It'll never make it."

He put his fingers over his eyes, not daring to watch, but peeked through them, unable to help himself.

Up and up the sphere moved. Once, near the very tip of the spiral, it wobbled, and Jeremy gasped and shut his eyes altogether, sure that it was going to crash to the ground. But when he opened them again, the metal ball had somehow steadied itself and was continuing its ascent. It came to rest, finally, at the very top, on the small platform erected there, inches before it toppled over the edge.

Jeremy wiped away the beads of sweat that had popped out on his forehead. He looked up at Bo.

"But how did you do it?" he asked.

"Me?" Bo said. He smiled and gestured toward the ball. "Jeremy, my boy, it gives me great pleasure to introduce you to Gravitas."

Jeremy's jaw dropped as the ball opened and out stepped a cloon not much taller than himself. The cloon said nothing, but bowed gravely as Jeremy waved and applauded. Then, balletically almost, he stepped back inside and, with a flourish of his gloved hand, closed the top half over him. The ball shuddered as it had at the bottom and then began its harrowing descent.

Jeremy grabbed a pleat of Bo's trousers with one hand, not daring to let go until the sphere came safely to rest at the bottom, just where it had been when Jeremy and Bo had entered the tent. It was only then that Jeremy realized that he'd been holding his breath. Once again, he cheered and applauded. He even stamped his feet and whistled as he waited for the ball to open. But the small cloon, it seemed, was staying put.

"He's a bit shy," Bo explained.

That evening Jeremy took his place at the long plank table under the tree near the pink and chartreuse tent. Lexi, Connie, and Watty were already seated. He couldn't wait to tell Toby that he had met Gravitas, but this appeared to be one of the evenings when Toby and Letitia would be absent. He wrinkled his nose in disappointment.

Toby never explained these disappearances. If Jeremy pressed him, he said simply that he and Letitia had been "on a ramble" and changed the subject. Jeremy was thinking about these mysterious rambles when Ba set a bubbling pot in the center of the table.

"It's my own recipe," she announced, not without some pride. "I call it Snout and Hoof."

Ba had recently come to consider herself one of the greatest chefs of her day. It had taken Jeremy no time to discover that her creativity far exceeded her actual ability. Still, he joined the others in their applause. He also joined them in the tussle for the bottle of flavor-killing Fire Sauce that stood on the table.

Before anyone dared take a bite of Ba's latest creation, Bo stood.

"An announcement," he declared, his voice booming out over the others.

Lexi jumped up, spilling, Jeremy couldn't help but notice with considerable envy, a good deal of his Snout and Hoof.

"Ah," the wordsmith exclaimed. "An announcement. A proclamation. A declaration. Possibly, I daresay, a revelation."

"I think we all know what an announcement is, Lexi darling," Connie suggested to her husband, not unkindly. "Perhaps it's best to let Bo tell us what he has to say."

The blue man bowed graciously and sat down.

Bo cleared his throat once again. "I'm happy to report," he began, "that Sylvana is back from the Petropolis." This news was met with immediate applause and shouts of excitement. "She's resting from her trip tonight, but she'll be joining us, as usual, tomorrow."

Jeremy had heard a great deal about Sylvana but

had never been able to discover what her act consisted of. Whenever he asked, he was always met with the same response: "You'll see."

Now Bo turned to him.

"She'd like to meet you tomorrow morning, Jeremy," he said.

"She'll love you, dear," Ba added, heaping another ladleful of S and H into his bowl. "Just be sure to wear your helmet."

Chapter 21

There Are Two Jeremies

Jeremy had never met someone whose introduction required the wearing of a helmet. He got up early the next morning and was fully dressed by the time Toby and Letitia came to fetch him. Toby was his usual talkative self; neither he nor Jeremy mentioned the ramble.

In a matter of minutes, they were standing at the edge of the field, far from the living and performing areas. Before them, a great white X had been chalked into the grass.

"What's that for?" Jeremy wanted to know.

"Oh, that," Toby replied. "It marks the spot."

Suddenly, the air resounded with an earsplitting boom. Jeremy had heard this thundering blast several times that morning. He assumed they were explosions at one of the Baron's factories, which, as everybody knew, were nearly as dangerous as the sunstone mines. But the second the boom shook the air, Toby nodded solemnly.

"Put this on," he said.

He handed Jeremy a leather helmet as he deftly

removed his top hat and strapped an identical helmet under his chin. Letitia was already wearing hers, leather, like the boys', but checked in contrasting shades of pink. Toby had cut out holes for her large but dainty ears. She looked very cunning.

"Any second now," Toby said.

Both he and Letitia directed their gaze at a sixty-degree angle up into the vast emptiness of the sky. Jeremy had no idea what it was he was supposed to be looking for, but he followed Toby and Letitia's lead, nose in the air, squinting into the sunlight.

And then he saw it. At first, it seemed to be nothing more than a red dot, growing larger and larger as it hurtled through the air toward them. But by the time the dot had reached the pinnacle of its arc, high above the field and about halfway from the entrance to the Living Museum, it began to take a recognizable shape.

But that's impossible! Jeremy thought. *It can't be! It's a . . .*

"Yes!" the woman shouted as she hit the ground, her feet placed perfectly on either side of the X. "A perfect landing!"

She smiled broadly. Her full set of gold teeth sparkled happily in the sunlight.

"You stuck it, all right," Toby said. "So I guess we don't need *these*." He unbuckled his and Letitia's helmets and took them off as he shot the woman a knowing glance. "Not like last time."

"Now, Jeremy," the woman protested, turning to Jeremy as if she had known him all her life. "You are

Jeremy, right? Of course you are. Who else could you be?" She reached out and touched his cheek. "At any rate," she went on, "don't you listen to Toby about what happened before. It wasn't my fault. The wind blew me off course."

She was wearing overalls completely covered in spangles, which, like her helmet, were the brightest shade of red.

"This here's Sylvana," Toby said, gesturing toward the woman. "The Wuman Cannonball."

Sylvana removed her helmet. An avalanche of hair the color of winter carrots tumbled down her back and onto her shoulders.

"As I was saying, Jeremy," she continued as she stepped off the X, "it wasn't my fault. Anyway, no one got hurt."

"What about Letitia?" Toby wanted to know.

"It was very generous of her to break my fall." She bent down and gave the pig a kiss on the snout.

"Jeremy," Sylvana said, straightening up, "Bo's told me so much about you that I feel I've known you all my life. I hope it won't be any time at all before you come to think of me as your big sister. If you need anything, no matter how big, no matter how small, you just come to me."

She kissed Jeremy loudly on the cheek with the same lips, Jeremy couldn't help but thinking, that had just smooched Letitia.

"All I can say," Toby offered as the foursome began to walk back toward the tents, the three humans arm in arm and the pig leading the way, "is that it's a good thing you're one of Letitia's favorites. But you might as well know it, Sylvana—since you been gone, Jeremy is givin' you some competition in that department."

Sylvana's teeth gleamed as she pulled both boys closer.

"I'm not a bit worried," she said, giving each of them a hug. "Letitia's got plenty of love to go around. We all do. Right, Letitia?"

Letitia grunted merrily and confirmed what Jeremy was already beginning to understand. The real wonder at the Living Museum wasn't Gravitas or Watty or Wainwright or the wowwie or any of them. The real wonder was the friendship and the love he was finding there.

We're like a family, he thought. *All of us together.* And then he corrected himself. *No, not like a family. We are a family. A real family. With a mother and a father and brothers and sisters and aunts and uncles.*

His heart swelled with happiness and pride, and yet, he was also struck with a sharp pang of guilt. The most important member of his family was missing. He touched his hand to his waistband, but the telescope wasn't there. It was still resting where he'd left it that first night, nestled in the crimson lining of the wooden box.

There's been too much to do and see, he told himself. *I've been busy.*

He realized with shame that the whole morning had passed without his thinking of Polly. Worse, he was having greater and greater difficulty remembering exactly what she looked like. Her features, once as familiar to him as his own name, were becoming more and more indistinct, as if his memory of her were slowly melting. He looked up at Sylvana.

It's like there are two of me, he told himself as he walked along. *One belongs at the Living Museum and one belongs with Polly.*

Somehow, he had to bring the two together.

Chapter 22

Did He Run Out of Paint?

The next morning, Jeremy began to paint the walls of his room.

As much as he wanted to see Letitia with a paintbrush—did she hold it in her mouth? was it taped delicately to her tail?—he turned down Toby's offer of help. He asked Bo and Ba not to peek, either. Not until he was done. He even went so far as to ask Ba to leave his meals on a tray outside the door.

First, he rolled up the carpets, and in so doing, he answered the question he'd had that first day about the floor of the tent. It *was* grass. Next, he assembled his materials, gathered with Bo and Ba's help from various places around the Living Museum. Cans of paint in every conceivable color, a ladder, brushes in sizes that ranged from a single delicate zebalo hair to the big bristly things used to slap whitewash on the bleachers in the Performance Tent.

Then he stripped down to his polka-dotted under-wear, carefully folding his shirt and shorts and placing them in their trunk, which he moved, along with the cushions, just outside his door.

Finally, taking a deep breath, he dipped a medium-sized brush into a can of blue paint and began. He left his room only to answer the call of nature.

He emerged three days later, half naked and splattered from head to foot with so much paint that Ba had screamed when he snuck up behind her.

"I thought he was some wild creature from the Terra Nequam," she told Bo later.

"Blinkin' bovaloos, Jeremy!"

This was Toby, standing just inside the door of Jeremy's room, gaping with all the others at Jeremy's creation. "Why didn't you tell us? You're a regular Cassiopeia!"

Though he had mispronounced the name, Toby was referring to Cassopi, the most renowned artist in the history of the Metropolis. (Renowned, that is, until the Baron had banned him because of his departure into "modern art." "People should look like people," the Baron had snorted the first time he saw one of the great artist's portraits. "With their eyes on either side of their nose and their mouth under it.")

As genuine as Toby's enthusiasm was, however, the sentiment he'd expressed wasn't entirely accurate. Unlike Pickles, who could render anything so realistically that you felt it might come alive on the page, Jeremy had no real skill as an artist. Even Ba, who thought Jeremy was perfect in every way, would have guessed that the panels had been painted by a much younger child had she not known that it was Jeremy's hand guiding the brushes.

But what Jeremy lacked in talent, he'd more than

made up for in the energy and the feeling behind what he'd painted.

"Jeremy," Ba whispered. "I had no idea."

The panel to the left of the door showed the Li-creeary, both inside and out. Books rained from a blue sky, and from them, here and there, a princess or a stag or a woodcutter floated out. In the left foreground, there was a crate of what some might have mistaken for red and green batterballs but were in fact cabbages and, behind it, a large jar of pickles. Dominating the panel were the blue candles, hundreds of them, their flames illuminating, or so it seemed, the entire picture.

The next panel, the one directly across from the door, looked almost as if it were meant as a giant board game. Paths twisted in and out of what appeared to be boxes filled with a hodgepodge of every imaginable item—bowling pins, dolls, cups with broken handles, socks without heels or toes. There was even a box of mice. They lay on their backs, their eyes tiny X's, their forepaws pressed together as if in prayer. At the bottom left, there was a large black mound from which bees flew in and out. On the far right, a fire engulfed a large house. The fire burned its way in bright oranges and yellows across the bottom of the panel, the flames occasionally licking up into the crisscrossing paths, all of which led to the very center of the panel, where Jeremy had painted a red envelope.

The next panel was much less detailed than the other three, but it filled its audience with dread nonetheless. Its surface was the color of a bruise, a kind of purply black. Darker still were the large number 3's, which appeared randomly across the panel. At the very top, a goldfish floated on its back, like a golden prayer making its way toward Heaven.

In one corner, Jeremy had painted a telescope, but in faint outline, as if it were disappearing. And at the bottom, a red dog with a fluffy tail wandered, lost and frightened.

"Oh dear," Ba whispered, clucking her tongue and shaking her head. "Oh dear. Oh dear."

The terror and sadness instilled by this panel, though, was more than offset by the final one, the one behind Bo and Ba and the others. They turned together to see that here Jeremy had used every color available to him, even mixing some to make new ones. Oohs and aahs filled the tent.

"Hey!" Toby shouted, pointing at a figure in the front row with a top hat that was parallel, practically, to the ground. "That's me. And look, Letty! There you are, too. You're wearing your checkered helmet."

Letitia snorted her approval.

"We're all there," Sylvana exclaimed. "I'm standing right next to Bo, and behind me, well, that has to be Madame Josephine."

"And there I am, lying on my side, in front of everybody, with my head propped up on my elbow," Watty said.

"I had to make you lie down," Jeremy explained. "Otherwise, I wouldn't have been able to fit you in. I hope that's okay."

"Good job!" Watty beamed.

"Why, good gracious!" Lexi exclaimed. "I believe

you got our shade of blue just right. Perfect. Exact. Flawless. Connie my dear, you have never looked lovelier."

"You flatter me, darling," Connie replied, but it was clear from her broad smile that she was pleased with her likeness.

Radu was there and all his creatures, as was Melchior and the mice. Jeremy had even painted Bartolomeo's fleas, a fact that did not go unnoticed by Letitia, who turned her back on the painting and sat down.

Jeremy pointed to a gray ball. "Gravitas is in there," he said.

Of course, Jeremy had included himself. He wore a red shirt and a pair of shorts and was standing just left of center, in front of Bo and Ba, each of whom had a hand on his shoulder.

"But you didn't finish it, Jeremy," said Toby. He pointed to the white space, just a little bigger than the image Jeremy had painted of himself and directly adjacent to it. "What happened? Did you run out of paint?"

Jeremy shook his head.

Up to now, whenever Jeremy mentioned Polly's name, he had done so only briefly, as he had on that first day. He'd read at the Licreeary that museums always keep their best paintings in dim light, because the bright light of day would eventually fade the image beyond recognition. Somehow, he had applied this idea to Polly's memory. He had to protect it, just like museums protected their paintings. He'd been afraid that sharing too much of it might cause it to disappear altogether.

But now it came spilling out of him, like a flood

behind a burst dam. He told them everything—how she had named him, and the way she kept a jar of water by her mat, and how in the jar there was always a flower, even if it was only the tiny white blossom of a wasteweed. He told them how she kept the Parrots together and how she always found a way to laugh, no matter how dire their situation. He told them her favorite stories, especially the one about the magic purse, and how she had said, "That's how we should try to make *our* hearts, Jeremy, like the purse in that story. Never empty." And he told them about that last night in the Licreeary and the way the PatPats had swarmed down upon her like a nest of fire hornets.

When he concluded, the only sound to be heard was an occasional sniffle from Lexi.

"It's a portrait," Jeremy said, pointing to the painting. "A *family* portrait." He moved closer to the space he'd left blank, reaching out one hand as if to touch it. "But Polly is a part of my family, too."

Chapter 23

A Stray. Like Me.

"Don't you worry, Jeremy," Toby said as they worked. "Sooner or later, everyone passes through the Living Museum. Polly will, too. Right, Letty?"

The great pig grunted softly. Occasionally, Lemondrop would emit a *hoo-ahh* of pleasure as one of the boys scrubbed her trunk or polished her bumper.

Jeremy gently lifted a windshield wiper. "Toby?" he asked. "How did *you* get here?"

Toby stopped polishing a hubcap and stood up, his hat upright on his head rather than at the impossible angle to which Jeremy had become accustomed. Was it a trick of the afternoon sun, Jeremy wondered, or did Toby suddenly look much older?

"One minute Mim and Pip was here," Toby said. "The next they was gone. Just like that." He snapped his fingers in the air above his head. He spoke so softly that Jeremy wasn't even sure he was talking to him.

"Mim and Pip?" Jeremy asked.

"My mom and dad, Jeremy. That's what I called 'em. Don't ask me why. That's just who they was, Mim and Pip."

He turned his face away and wiped an imaginary smudge from Lemondrop's taillight. When he began again, there was a new quality in his voice, one that Jeremy didn't recognize.

"It was the PatPats. They took Mim and Pip away, and they never brought 'em back. Pip put up an awful fight. You should have seen him, Jeremy. He was like a tiger. But, it was no use. Mim fought, too. But them hooligans just laughed like the devils they are. I waited for Mim and Pip three days until the PatPats came back and kicked me out, out of my own house, talkin' about some kind of new law, the Squatters' Law, they called it. They just threw me right on the street."

He paused.

"I was a stray after that. Doin' what I could. You know what I mean."

Jeremy nodded. He did know what Toby meant. Letitia wagged her giant head sorrowfully from side to side.

"But I didn't have nobody to look after me," Toby continued. "Nobody like your Polly, I mean. Not until I found Letitia here." He scratched the pig on her rump. "She was just wanderin' around. Wanderin' around like me, hardly bigger 'n a batterball and so skinny that . . ." Toby didn't finish the sentence. He took a deep breath and went on. "That's when Bo and Ba found us."

Jeremy had listened to Toby's tale in the way that only another stray child could have, instinctively separating what was different from his own story while compiling the many similarities.

"Where did they take Mim and Pip?" he asked at last.

Toby shrugged and looked directly at Jeremy for the first time since he had started his tale.

"Nobody ever told me," he answered. "I never saw 'em again."

In the distance, Jeremy heard the clear silver peal of the big bell that Ba rang to let them know dinner was on the table. Toby picked up his bucket.

"I'm gonna find 'em one day, though," he said. "You wait and see if I don't."

The bell rang again. He threw his rag into the bucket and slid his hat back to its usual angle.

"Let's go get something to eat. And let's hope it ain't that Snout and Hoof. I hear that was a real humdinger."

At dinner, Jeremy was quieter than usual. In his mind's eye, he kept seeing the way Toby had shrugged his shoulders and hearing him say, *I never saw 'em again.*

Which is worse? Jeremy wondered. *Never to have known your parents, like me? Or to have known them but to have had them taken away, like Toby?*

Then he remembered what Polly had told him: "You can't measure another person's suffering, Jeremy. It's like a private ocean, with its own depths and its own changing shores. It's useless to say who has the hardest time staying afloat."

Jeremy was thinking of this when Bo stood up and gestured to Ba. From under the table, she produced a basket, which she placed in front of her. The basket seemed to be whining. What was going on?

"Jeremy," Bo said, "we have—"

But before he could finish, the basket toppled over,

and from it rolled a ball of black and white fuzz, a puppy. At least, Jeremy thought it was a puppy. He'd never seen anything quite like her. Her head was big, but her legs were short. Her ears were long and floppy, but her tail was just the tiniest stub. He couldn't see her eyes, really, because of her shaggy fur; her face seemed to be nothing but a black nose surrounded by fluff.

Eventually, the puppy stopped rolling and hopped up on her feet. First, she shook herself violently. Then she lifted her head and sniffed, twitching her nose first in this direction, then in that. Finally, as if his was the scent she was seeking, she made a beeline toward Jeremy. Though his experience at Harpwitch's had taught him to be wary of anything canine, the puppy's exuberance vanquished completely his natural caution. His face brightened. He held out his arms.

"We know she can't take Polly's place," Bo continued, "but until you find her—Polly, I mean—we thought you might like to have a little canine company."

"She just came wandering into the tent," Ba explained. "Starving, poor thing. And filthy, too. We've asked all around, and no one knows anything about her. She's—"

"A stray," Jeremy said.

He laughed as the puppy jumped into his arms. She weighed almost nothing; she was like a cloud, a squiggling cloud with a wet nose and a pink tongue.

"She was awfully dirty, Jeremy, but we gave her a bath, and, well, you can see for yourself how she turned out."

"She's a dandy!" Toby exclaimed. "A genuine, certified dandy!"

Jeremy tilted his head upward and laughed again as the puppy burrowed her muzzle into his shoulder.

"I'll call her Daffodil," he said.

By now, the little dog had managed to get both her front paws on Jeremy's shoulders and was licking him with such gusto that he allowed himself to topple backward off the bench onto the soft green grass. This gave Daffodil the opportunity she had been waiting for. She stood upright on his stomach now, two paws planted on his chest, two on his shoulders, her stubby tail wagging like a metronome on its fastest speed.

She licked his chin. His cheeks. His nose. His forehead. Anywhere, in fact, she could get her pink tongue. Jeremy closed his eyes.

"You're a stray," he whispered, holding the puppy to him. "A stray. Like me."

Chapter 24

Partners!

Three weeks after Daffodil came into Jeremy's life, Bo announced that the Living Museum would soon be re-opening for business. The place was abuzz with activity as the performers repaired their costumes, polished their equipment, and retooled their acts.

"You ain't never seen me and Letitia perform, Jeremy," Toby said one morning. "We got some rehearsing to do this afternoon. How's about if you help us out?"

After lunch, Jeremy and Daffodil followed Toby and the great pig to Toby's tent. Jeremy took a seat on the single chair in the tent as Toby disappeared and then reappeared from behind a panel. Somehow, in the matter of a few seconds, Toby had managed to change out of his everyday clothes and into the threadbare tuxedo he had worn the day of Jeremy's arrival.

"What you are about to see will amaze you!" Toby shouted as he bowed toward Jeremy and Daffodil. "A pig who can think! She can cipher! She can spell! How's she do it? Who can tell? She's a regular valerdictorian,

Ladies and Gents. A big pig with a big brain! Letitia, the Sapient Pig!"

Right on cue, Letitia appeared from behind the same panel, wearing one of her best nose rings. She gave Jeremy a regal nod of her head as she walked majestically around the perimeter of the tent, ignoring Daffodil completely, as if the puppy's excited barking were nothing more than the buzz of a pesky mosquito. She didn't stop her promenade until she reached Toby's side.

As Jeremy applauded, Toby dealt out twenty-six hand-printed cards, one for each letter of the alphabet. The letters had been formed in a very distinctive hand, one that Jeremy thought perhaps he'd seen before, though he couldn't remember where. Maybe there had been something like it in one of the books at the Licreary. The cards lay on the ground in front of Toby, letter-side up in two large concentric arcs.

"A volunteer, please!" he shouted toward the make-believe audience. "Can I get a volunteer?"

Jeremy sat solidly in his place until he realized that Toby's winking and nodding meant that *he* was the volunteer. He stood up.

"Ah, yes!" Toby exclaimed. "A young dandy of refined taste has volunteered to ask Letitia a question. Any question, sir. Any question at all."

"Er . . . okay," Jeremy muttered. He racked his brain, searching for a question. Certainly, he didn't want to begin by giving Letty a question that she might not be able to answer. "Letitia," he finally called out, "how do you spell 'Metropolis'?"

"You heard the gentleman, Letty!" Toby exclaimed. "How do you spell 'Metropolis'?"

The pig tilted her head for a moment as if she were considering whether the third syllable was an "O" or an "A." Then she walked deliberately toward the cards, following the path of the arcs, until she got to the letter "M," onto which she placed her right trotter as delicately as a ballerina touches the dance floor with the tip of her toe.

"M!" Toby shouted.

Letitia sashayed to the "E."

"E!" declared Toby.

Jeremy breathed a sigh of relief.

As Letitia went through her paces, Jeremy noticed that Toby softly clicked his thumbnail and the nail on his index finger together. But both the movement and the sound were so subtle that Jeremy couldn't decide: Was Toby signaling Letitia through these clicks, letting her know at which card she should stop? Or was Toby's fidgeting simply the jittery habit of a nervous performer?

"S!" Toby shouted. "Metropolis!"

Letitia returned to Toby's side, but not before lowering her gargantuan head toward Jeremy and glaring at Daffodil, who had paid no attention whatsoever to Letitia's demonstration of her amazing sapience. Jeremy cheered wildly and stamped his feet. Letitia bowed once more. Toby beamed.

They continued to rehearse for another hour or so. As long as Toby clicked his nails, there seemed to be no question that Letitia couldn't answer. When the rehearsal was over, Toby changed back into his T-shirt and shorts. Letitia lay down, grudgingly permitting Daffodil to curl up beside her. The little dog was apparently unable to resist the soothing rise and fall of the pig's mountainous form. It was then that Toby made Jeremy a surprising offer.

"I got it all figured out," he said. "You can be part of the act. Mine and Letitia's. We'll dress you in some of them pants with the great big legs. Ba could whip 'em up for ya in a second. You'd look good in a turban, too, I bet. Or one of them hats that looks like an upside-down flowerpot. Every time Letitia answers a question, you'll do one of them fancy jumps o' yours. Don't say ya can't, neither, 'cause I seen ya do 'em a million times. The audience'll love it."

The fancy jumps Toby was referring to were the acrobatics Jeremy had learned on the street. He'd entertained Toby with these shenanigans hundreds of times over the last months, often using Letitia as a hurdle.

"Whaddya say?" Toby asked. "You and me. Partners! All the way!"

Jeremy blinked back a tear. Their acts were the one thing that the citizens of the Living Museum did not share. They were as sacred and as independent as their own names. Toby's inviting Jeremy to join him and Letitia was a step that could only have been prompted by the boy's deepest feelings.

"I thank you, Toby," Jeremy said, once he'd regained control of his emotions. "But I . . . I mean, *we* have some plans of our own. Right, Daffy?"

Upon hearing her name, the little dog moved away from the slumbering Letitia and sprang into Jeremy's arms as easily as if she were a jackrabbit.

"Ya mean you and Daffodil?" Toby asked.

Jeremy nodded shyly.

"Ya got your own act?"

Jeremy nodded once again.

"We've been practicing. In secret. No one knows yet. Not even Bo and Ba."

For a moment, Toby's face was as blank as an empty plate. But though the older boy may have been disappointed, it took only a few seconds for the plate to crack with a tremendous smile.

"Good for you!" he said, clapping Jeremy on the back. "I'm proud of ya! You two'll be great, too. I know ya will. Now let's see this here act."

Chapter 25

They'll Be Right

Whether it was a skill he had learned out of necessity from his experience at HHMDUCSC or simply an aptitude with which he had been born, Jeremy discovered upon Daffodil's arrival that he had an uncommon talent.

Radu had been the first to detect it. He soon realized that whenever the boy visited him, the cantankerous brutes in his care quieted. The zebalo, an unpredictable creature even after years of domestication, never failed to lower his great horned head so that Jeremy could give it a rub, and once the wowwie's third eye had spotted him, the animal instantly began the high-pitched purr that indicated her complete happiness.

"You have great gift with creatures of earth," Radu told Jeremy on more than one occasion. "Very great gift."

And if Jeremy was a natural trainer, Daffodil proved to be an even more natural student. It was almost unconscious, really, the way the dog and the boy responded to each other. Even on that first night together in his room, it had taken Jeremy only an hour to teach the puppy, young as she was, to sit. In another hour, she was rolling over.

Within a week, Daffodil was anticipating Jeremy's commands so completely that it took just the softest word or the subtlest gesture and there she was, up on her hind legs revolving like a black and white tornado or jumping through a barrel hoop or sitting on a pedestal pretending to laugh at a comic strip in the *Metropolian Mistral,* the Baron's daily newspaper, which Jeremy had taught her to open and spread out with her teeth.

At first, Jeremy and Daffodil had practiced these tricks solely for their own amusement, as a way to pass the lonely hours of the night. But slowly, as their antics together grew more elaborate, an idea began to form, a bold idea.

We'll have our own act, he thought. *Why not? Just Daffodil and me. A pirate act.*

He would dress as a swaggering buccaneer, like the ones he'd seen in books at the Licreeary, the ones with names like Desperate Jack and Tortuga Tom. Daffy would be his pirate dog. Jeremy would juggle and do acrobatics, and Daffy could dance a jig on the deck of a make-believe ship.

Why not? Why not?

Thinking of Daffodil's natural gift for comedy, the act, he decided, would be funny, too.

I'll pretend to climb a mast and scan the audience with my telescope like I'm looking for ships to plunder, and Daffy can pull on the seat of my pants like she's trying to keep me on the straight and narrow.

The boy and the dog secretly rehearsed these tricks every night until the various components of their act came together like the pieces of an elaborate jigsaw puzzle.

Jeremy's instinct about Daffodil had been correct. She was a gifted comedienne. She rolled her eyes so melodramatically when she tugged at the seat of Jeremy's pants that even someone sitting in the top row of seats at the very back of the Performance Tent would be able to see her mock disapproval. Jeremy didn't even have to train her to wag her head as he swaggered about, pretending to love the life of crime. Their timing was perfect.

He didn't have their costumes yet, but he was sure that Bo and Ba would help them with these when the time came. Naturally, both he and Daffy would wear an eye patch. But more important than the costumes, to Jeremy at least, was the makeup. He would powder his face with white talcum and paint on yellow eyebrows. He would don a big red nose and a curly red wig. When he was finished, he would look exactly like a cloon, a miniature Bo. This pleased him almost as much as the act itself.

But from the very beginning, Jeremy's plan had not been entirely without self-interest. The words that Toby had uttered the day they washed Lemondrop stuck with him as surely as if they had been tattooed on his arm: *Sooner or later, everyone passes through the Living Museum. Polly will, too.*

If she does, Jeremy told himself, *I'll be ready.*

That was the real reason he would pretend to scan

the ocean with his telescope. The audience would think he was looking for treasure.

And in a way, Jeremy told himself, *they'll be right. I* will *be looking for treasure. A treasure more precious than all the sunstones the Baron can pull out of the earth. I'll be looking for Polly.*

Chapter 26

Have You Ever Been to the Terra Nequam?

The Baron Ignatius Fyodor Maximus von Strompié III jumped up from his desk and yanked the drapes shut with such force, the heavy rings connecting them to their filigreed rod clattered against each other like a mouthful of chattering teeth.

"How can I think with all that kerfuffle going on outside?" he complained, as if there were someone in the study with him, which there was not. "I ought to have those workmen arrested. They're disturbing the peace. The peace of a very important man!"

He'd been trying to write a note.

"I think I'll sic the PatPats on whoever made up the rules of spelling," he'd snarled. It was simply impossible to remember if it was "i before e except after c" or "e before i except after y." But a happier thought occurred to him: *I'm the Baron. If I don't like the rules of spelling, I'll change them.* This gave him such confidence that he finished the note and sealed it in its parchment envelope with a great glob of dripping red wax.

The note was to that boy, the one who'd helped

them during the night of the raids. The Baron distrusted the boy—he reminded him too much of himself—but the little sneak *had* made good on his promise to show them where the stray children were hiding. Of course, he hadn't done it for free. He'd insisted on being able to join the Junior PatPats—as an officer, no less, blue jacket and all. Worse, the grubby street rat had charged him a small fortune.

Still, the boy's natural gift for treachery proved to be useful in other areas—eavesdropping at the open market, for example, where he kept his little rat ears alert and his little rat eyes open for any sign of disloyalty on the part of the citizens. The boy—what was his name? something ridiculous!—always came back with a useful tidbit, too, like a weasel on a riverbank. Now the Baron had another job for him. That's what the note was about.

He moved away from the window and tried to compose himself by strolling about his study. With the swaggering gesture he used even when he was alone—after all, he'd practiced it for years when he first became the Baron, so why not enjoy it himself?—he straightened a picture here, adjusted a copy of *The Exalted History of the Family von Strompié* there. (Every book on the shelves was a copy of *The Exalted History of the Family von Strompié;* the Baron liked to give them out to his visitors.) All the while, he continued to fume about the commotion outside. He knew he would not make good on his threat to have the workmen arrested. He couldn't: They were following the orders of his wife.

The Baron stopped in front of a full-length mirror

and took in his reflection. He turned to his side so that he could see himself in profile.

That sculptor got it all wrong, he told himself, as he always did, referring to the artist from whom he'd commissioned the fountain. *My nose is not nearly so piggy as he made it. And my bottom definitely does not stick out like that.*

He reached both hands behind him and gave the bottom in question a shove inward. As he did so, the terrible groaning resumed outside, a deep lament that seemed to have originated in the very depths of the earth, which, in fact, it had. The Baron made a face and put his hands over his ears. It was giving him a headache, this groaning. It continued for several minutes, crescendoing at last into an earth-shattering, window-rattling crash.

"There goes another one!" he mumbled.

He was talking about the trees that surrounded Helios. The workmen were yanking them out like so many rotten teeth. Except, of course, that the trees were not rotten. They were perfectly healthy.

Gertrudina had explained it all to him and more than once. "Everything must be perfect for the birthday ball," she'd said. "Perfect and *new*! The trees have to go. They're *old*! I'm replacing them with replicas made of the finest plastics in the Metropolis! The flowers, too. Oh, and the grass, of course. The effect will be spectacular!"

Sometimes, it seemed to the Baron that his wife was trying to render Rosamund invisible in the splendor of the birthday party. Oh well. If his wife wanted new trees, even artificial ones, then she could have them. That's what being a baroness was all about. Getting what you want.

The uproar outside the window stopped for a moment.

The workmen must be taking a break, the Baron decided, happy not only for the momentary quiet, but for the excuse it would give him to dock their pay for loafing.

He walked away from the mirror and returned to his desk. There, he addressed the note to the boy and called for a servant to deliver it to the room the guttersnipe had rented in the Cudgels. A good place for him, too, the Baron thought. Then he turned his mind to the Big Problem. The Problem That Wouldn't Go Away. The Problem That Was Driving Him Crazy.

"I've got other things to think about besides *trees,*" he muttered.

He was right, too. The situation was desperate. Going on for months, and still not a single clue as to who was committing the outrage. Down with the Baron, indeed! Wirm assured him that he was getting closer to catching the criminal, but the Baron was becoming increasingly impatient, so impatient, in fact, that he'd come to an important decision. He had told Wirm of his plan earlier that very day.

"A reward," he began. "I'll offer a reward."

Wirm raised and then lowered an eyebrow. "Ah, yes, a reward," he hissed.

The Chief Driver had been expecting this. As with all people with limited imaginations, the Baron's solution to every problem was the application of money. But

Wirm was not about to support this idea of a reward. The people of the Metropolis often knew more than they let on. And they were desperate. A reward just might work. If it did, he would be cheated out of the Commander Generalship. He knew the Baron. Von Strompié would take credit for catching the traitor, and Wirm would be stuck as Chief Driver for the rest of his life. That couldn't happen! Not at this late date! Not after all his hard work!

Once more, he raised an eyebrow. "Of course," he remarked casually, "there is that one small difficulty."

The Baron cocked his head, waiting to hear more, but Wirm went quiet. The Baron tapped his foot, whistled, scratched his head.

"Are you going to tell me what it is, Wirm? This 'small difficulty' that you speak of?" he finally railed.

"A thousand pardons." Wirm was practically whispering.

The Baron moved closer.

"I assumed that His Mighty Intelligence had already thought of it. As he has reminded me on so many occasions, he thinks of everything." Wirm nodded his head deferentially.

It was strange, the Baron noted, how deference so often looked like insolence.

"True, Wirm! True! I *do* think of everything. That's why I'm the Baron and you . . . you are what you are. But . . . just for my own . . . amusement, let me hear what you have to say."

Slowly, as if he might be afraid it would fall off his neck, Wirm raised his head.

"Don't you see?" he hissed. "Offering a reward will call attention to the graffiti."

The Baron smirked, deciding with a certain degree of satisfaction that Jeriah Wirm was not nearly so smart as he pretended to be. Maybe it was a mistake to promise him the important job of Commander General.

"Wirm. Wirm. Wirm." The Baron wagged his head. "That's precisely the point. To call attention to the graffiti so we can find out who's responsible."

The driver, however, had not finished. "But once large numbers of the citizens become aware of what the graffiti is actually saying, they may be emboldened to express similar . . . even stronger feelings."

The Baron had been pacing back and forth in front of his desk, but now he stopped in his tracks. In spite of assurance to the contrary, he *hadn't* considered this. How could he have? It was inconceivable that even *one* person could be unhappy with the way he controlled . . . er . . . governed the Metropolis. But that there might be others? Unthinkable! He naturally presumed that everyone was just as happy as he was. Why shouldn't they be? But he had forgotten, once again, what ingrates the citizens of the Metropolis were. Malcontents, complaining about every little thing. Their hours at the factories. Their working conditions. The poor air. The scant supply of food at the open markets. Wah! Wah! Wah! What a bunch of babies!

He had to admit it. Wirm had a point. If he called attention to the graffiti, others might agree with the sentiment it expressed, and then what? They might even feel sympathy for the criminal. Or worse! Sweat popped out on the Baron's forehead and jowls. His heart began to race. What if they . . . ? But it was unthinkable! Yes, it was clear to him now. A reward was a big mistake.

Still, he wasn't going to let Jeriah Wirm get away scot-free. If he were doing his job, the criminal would have been caught by now and the Baron could have gone back to enjoying his life. Now that he thought of it, in fact, the entire situation was Wirm's fault.

"My patience is running out, Wirm," he'd said. "You have until Rosamund's birthday party. That's three days! Three days! If you haven't caught the criminal by then, well . . . tell me, have you ever been to the Terra Nequam? It's lovely this time of year."

Recalling the scene now, the Baron was startled to hear what he thought was that same low growl that Wirm had involuntarily emitted. But then he realized the noise was only the resumption of the commotion outside, the workmen hacking off the limbs of a tree as they prepared to wrench it from the place it had stood, like a sphinx, for centuries.

Chapter 27

Easy as Pie

"Rosie? . . . Rosie?"

Polly tried to keep her voice down, both for her sake and for Rosie's. She also tried to keep the worry out of her voice, though this was becoming increasingly difficult. She would never have said it aloud, but privately, she confessed that Rosie's playfulness had become almost dangerous. Just yesterday, for example, the girl pranced not two feet behind her mother, hands on her hips, mimicking the older Baroness's haughty posture and imperious gait. To make matters worse, she did it directly under the nose of Signora Porchini. Fortunately, the gluttonous tutor was so involved with the almond cake she was devouring that she hadn't noticed.

Now the two girls were playing what was supposed to be a quick game of hide-and-seek before the scheduled arrival of Rosie's mother and the small army of seamstresses, hairdressers, and masters of comportment to whom she had given the task of making Rosie presentable for the ball. Polly searched their adjoined rooms, but she hadn't been able to find her charge. She got down on her hands and knees and looked a final time under Rosie's bed.

"Drat!" she muttered.

She sat on the floor, defeated. She was beginning to think that when she had closed her eyes to count, the younger girl had broken their rule again and run off into other parts of the palace.

She tried again, this time in a stage whisper. "Rosie! Please! Your mother will be here any minute!"

"Oh, all right! But you didn't call 'Ally Ally Oxen Free.'"

Polly looked up.

She knew it was impossible, but the girl's voice seemed to have come from the ceiling. Then she saw it, the ringlet, red as a firecracker.

"Rosie! Come down from there!"

Rosie poked her nose over the edge of the frilly canopy, soaring above the bed like a bank of clouds.

"Gotcha!" The younger girl laughed as she propped her head on her elbows.

"Rosie, please . . ."

"You look like an ant from up here! Ha! Ha!"

"But how . . . ?

"I shinnied up the bedpost. Monkeys can do it. So why can't I? It was easy. Easy as pie."

"Rosie . . ."

"Hey! I'm a poet. Listen! 'Monkeys can do it. Why can't I? It's easy, I thought. Easy as pie!'"

"Rosie, please. Your mother will be here any minute. She's already going to be angry when she sees your—"

"There's nothing wrong with my *nose.* I'm just catching a little cold, that's all."

She gripped the frame of the canopy and did a forward flip over the top. The petticoats and crinolines of the ridiculous dress the Baroness insisted she wear puffed up about her like a parachute. She landed on her toes not three feet in front of her governess.

"But the ball—"

"The only balls I'm interested in are ones I can juggle."

And to show she meant it, she grabbed three enormously expensive crystal spheres her mother had placed on her bedside table as decoration befitting the room of a young baroness.

"Rosie, now don't . . ."

But it was too late. The balls were already whirling through the air in an intricate figure-eight pattern. Polly held her breath. If Rosie should drop one . . .

"I could do this with my eyes closed," Rosie sniffed, tossing the balls even higher and catching them now behind her back. "Red nose and all!"

And then she uttered two words Polly had come to dread: "Watch this!"

She began to twirl, hopping on one foot as she tossed the crystals higher and higher until she resembled nothing so much as a revolving fountain.

Polly put her hands over her eyes but, unable to help herself, peeked through her fingers. One of the balls was headed straight for the leaded window.

"Rosie!" Polly cried out.

The ball was within an inch of crashing through the

windowpane when Rosie snatched it from the air as easily as if it had been a floating seed of waterweed.

"Ha!" she laughed, pointing at Polly, whose face had gone completely white. "Gotcha again! You didn't really think I was going to let one of these go through the window, did you?"

Polly sighed with relief as the girl put all three spheres back on the table.

"My mother would—"

The Baroness Gertrudina's voice shattered the air behind them. "What would your mother do, young lady?"

She filled the doorway, straight and hard as a column of marble. Her battalion of attendants stood at attention behind her.

Experience had taught Polly to think on her feet. This was not the first time the Baroness had surprised them.

"I . . . think what the young Baroness was going to say," she began, "is that . . . her mother would be very pleased with the . . . with the progress she is making." She shot a quick glance at Rosie. "Her curtsy, I mean. Isn't that right, Your Highness? You *are* making progress with your curtsy."

Rosie cleared her throat. "Uh . . . right!"

"Well?"

The impatience in the older woman's voice coalesced into a hard edge, sharp as the blade of an ax.

"Am I going to see this so-called curtsy or not? I haven't got all day."

Rosie spread her skirts, put one foot behind her, tilted her head slightly to the left, and toppled over backward.

"Get up!" the older Baroness shrieked. "Get up at once, you clumsy goat."

It was a source of amazement to Polly that though Rosie could backflip across the room or juggle with her feet, she was totally unable to perform a simple curtsy. Invariably, she teetered to one side or plunged forward into a somersault or wobbled backward, landing on her bottom with a very unladylike thud. Sometimes, Polly wondered if Rosie did it just to annoy her mother. She wouldn't have blamed her. Still, just once, she might have saved them both the scouring sting of Gertrudina's vexation.

"And you!" the older Baroness shouted at Polly. "What good are you? All I have asked is that you teach the girl to perform a simple curtsy. Just one curtsy! What have you been doing in here all day, anyway? Playing hide-and—"

"It isn't Po . . . *Mary's* fault," Rosie interrupted. "It's mine. I slipped. That's all. Don't worry. By the time of the ball, I'll be able to do it perfectly."

"By the time of the ball, indeed!" If Gertrudina hadn't been a baroness, one might have said that she had actually snorted. "Three days! Three days and look at . . . look at . . ." She peered directly into her daughter's face for the first time since she had entered the room. "YOUR NOSE!"

Rosie covered the implicated organ with her hand.

"Oh, *that*," the girl replied, her voice muffled by the screen of her palm. "It's nothing. Just a little redness. I'm catching a cold."

Polly looked on as the loathing that had come over the older Baroness faded to a limp wash of resignation.

Polly nearly felt sorry for the woman. For months now, she had been putting all her energy, as powerful and dangerous as the windstorms that swept the Terra Nequam, into the ball. But unlike those windstorms, her efforts had been without consequence. If anything, they had backfired. Now, with the onset of this cold or whatever it was, Rosie had awakened with a nose the color of a ripe cherry.

The Baroness raised her arms. The swarm of lackeys winced en masse. But rather than administering a communal slap, which no one present doubted she would have been able to pull off, Gertrudina clapped her thin white hands twice. The loud reports echoed through the hall as sharp as gunshots. The attendants scattered.

"I suppose I'll have to send for that abominable quack," the Baroness said, to herself as much as to Polly or Rosie. "Not that he'll be able to do anything with you."

She curled her upper lip and flared her nostrils. It was almost as if she'd been forced to swallow a mouthful of curdled milk. Polly put a protective arm around Rosie's shoulder.

"Keep her in bed until Purgatorn arrives," Gertrudina barked.

She turned on her heel and pulled the door behind her, stopping it abruptly just before the hasp slipped into its catch. It closed with a final, chilling click, more bloodcurdling than if she had slammed the door off its hinges.

Polly did what she could to soften the blow of Gertrudina's anger.

"Well," she said, pulling Rosie even tighter to her, "it was to be expected."

"Now, where was I?" Rosie asked. She pulled away from Polly and moved toward the bedside table. "Oh yes, I was about to show you how I can juggle those crystals while balancing on the back of a chair."

Chapter 28

There Were Limits to Her Loyalty

There were few things about which Polly agreed with the older Baroness, but one of them was her assessment of Dr. Perfidio P. Purgatorn. Not only was he an insufferable windbag, but his treatments more often than not worsened the condition he was supposedly curing. Rosie detested him, too, and with good reason. It was he who originally prescribed the winter baths of coddled cream and iced sunstones to get rid of the freckles, and it was he, too, who suggested that Rosie gargle twice hourly with fermented oil of squid to give her voice a sweeter tone.

But he had been her mother's family physician for three generations, and though Gertrudina thought he was an imbecile, she knew he was discreet, and discretion was something she prized highly, especially when it came to her daughter.

When he arrived later that afternoon, dressed in his black robes and his ridiculous black hat, Polly was reminded, as she always was, of a picture she'd shown Jeremy of a piglike animal, a peccarina. They laughed for days afterward because the text accompanying the picture said that the peccarina's rump gave off a strange, musky odor.

Polly heard the drone of Purgatorn's voice long before she saw the man himself. She brought her hand to her nose as he entered the room.

"Ah, yes, a cold," he was saying to the Baroness.

"Cold is the opposite of hot, Madam.

" 'Hot' is the first syllable of 'Hottentot.'

" 'Tot' is another word for 'child.'

"A child with a cold is often hot.

"Heat is energy.

"It takes energy *to read.*

"The past tense of 'read' is a homophone for 'red.'

"Therefore, Madam, I'm quite afraid that the source of your daughter's red nose lies in the fact that she enjoys *reading*!"

The Baroness made no reply, but from her arched brows and flared nostrils, it was clear that she would like nothing more than to toss the good doctor into a pot of boiling oil.

Both Polly and the Baroness stayed in the hall while Purgatorn examined Rosie. Gertrudina said nothing to Polly, but more than once, Polly caught her staring at her, studying her in a way that made her blood run cold. Occasionally, a high-pitched yelp escaped from Rosie's chamber, a yelp that Polly was certain could only have come from the doctor. At one point, she was sure she heard him say, "Get down from there, you naughty girl!" only to hear Rosie suggest that he come up and get her. Still later, it sounded as if a rough game of tag was taking place inside the room and that heavy furniture was being dragged across the floor.

If the Baroness heard all this, she pretended otherwise, thinking, perhaps, that the examination was the doctor's problem and that she had enough of her own.

An hour. Then two. Gertrudina cleared her throat. She paced. She tapped her foot. She put her hand to her forehead again and again.

"What could be taking him so long?" she uttered.

Polly wisely kept silent. When Gertrudina was in this state, her distress often found its way into her hand.

If she slaps me this time, though, Polly thought, *I'll slap her back. I swear I will.*

But she shared Gertrudina's concern. What *was* taking Purgatorn so long?

As the Baroness checked the massive hall clock for what must have been the thousandth time, the door slowly swung open. A considerably changed Dr. Perfidio Purgatorn emerged. The blood was drained from his usually scarlet jowls. His hat was on backward, and for the first time since he had come into Polly's acquaintance, he seemed at a complete loss for words.

"Well?" the Baroness asked, not caring a whit for this remarkable difference in the doctor's appearance. "Will she be over the cold in time for the ball?"

The doctor opened his mouth as if he was going to speak, but then shut it again, like a catfish that had just been yanked from the river.

"I asked you a question," the Baroness snapped. "Will Rosamund be over the cold in time for the ball or not?" She narrowed her eyes and smiled. "And for your own sake, you'd better give me the right answer. There are limits to my loyalty, Purgatorn."

The doctor drew in a breath and, with a corner of his robe, mopped his brow, now bejeweled with perspiration. He glanced at Polly.

"Perhaps I should have a word with the Baroness in private," he finally managed to say.

"Go to your room," Gertrudina barked at Polly. "You've no business out here!"

Polly desperately wanted to check on Rosie, but she did as the Baroness ordered. To oppose her at any time was perilous, but in this mood, it would be practically suicidal. Once she closed the door, however, she bent down and pressed her ear to the keyhole.

For a moment or two, she could hear only muffled whispers, and then, suddenly, as if Rosie's mother had stumbled barefoot onto a bed of hot coals, she screamed. And roared. And bellowed.

Polly put her hands over her ears and fell away from the door. It hadn't been a scream of pain. She was sure of that.

No, Polly decided, *it's rage. Pure rage.*

And still the Baroness screamed. It echoed through the voluminous halls until Polly was certain it had gotten trapped there, like a ghost, forced to relive its own terror over and over again. But now, oddly, the screaming was punctuated with a series of squeals, like a hog being led to the butcher. Once more, Polly knelt at her door, peeking this time, rather than listening, through the keyhole.

She gasped.

Dr. Perfidio Purgatorn was in the hands of the palace guards. They were dragging him down the stairs, his arms outstretched toward his benefactor.

"Mercy, Madam!" he shrieked. "You knew it was a possibility. I'll tell no one! No one! Your secret is safe."

But Polly saw that the Baroness was unmoved. She stood as cold as stone.

"Get the fool out of my sight," she hissed at the guards. "Take him to the Choir Stall!"

Chapter 29

More Evil than the Devil

Jeremy lifted the patch from his right eye and peeked out from under the stands.

"It's a full house tonight, Daffy," he whispered. "Just like last night. Every single seat is taken!"

Daffodil, wearing a patch identical to Jeremy's, wriggled with excitement. Her pink tongue flicked the air in front of her; she'd already learned not to lick Jeremy's face when he was wearing his makeup. With his yellow eyebrows and his red nose and his curly wig, no one in tonight's audience would guess that Jeremy was not a cloon himself.

He hugged the puppy closer to him. Lexi and Connie had just finished their act, and now Toby and Letitia stood in the center of the performing area. Letitia began by doing some simple spelling.

"Letitia," Toby shouted so that everyone, even those in the highest rows, could hear, "how do you spell 'cow'?"

"'Mother'?"

"'Father'?"

Letitia trotted to the cards, spelling each consecutive word without the slightest hesitation. The crowd applauded appreciatively. Next, Toby increased the difficulty of the questions, asking for words of five and even six syllables. Letitia answered the questions as if she had invented spelling. The crowd applauded a little louder.

Jeremy watched in amazement, less at Letitia's talent—he was used to that—than at the masterful way Toby worked the audience.

"We've got to learn to do that, Daffy," he said to his black and white partner, whose stub of a tail beat against his chest.

Now came the real portion of the act, the part when Toby called on volunteers to quiz the sapient pig. The first volunteer, a woman with a black gateway where her front teeth should have been, asked Letitia a riddle. She sat directly across from where Jeremy and Daffy were waiting.

"What goes up but never comes down?" she shouted.

Letitia trotted over to the "Y." Next to the "O." When she finished, five letters later, she had spelled "Your age." This time, the applause was charged with a new energy, as if a jolt of electricity ran through it. It was accompanied by a volley of spontaneous cheers.

Now Toby chose a thin girl with limp, blond hair and a racking cough. She also tried to ask Letitia a riddle, but her voice was so weak that the man sitting next to her—Jeremy guessed it was her father—took over when the girl was unable to catch her breath.

"Here's what my Magda wanted to ask," he boomed out as he lifted the girl lovingly into his arms. "It's more powerful than God. It's more evil than the devil. The poor have it. The rich need it. If you eat it, you'll die. What is it?"

Before he had finished the question, Letitia was working. "Nothing," she spelled out.

The crowd rocketed to its feet, and the wild applause and cheering were backed up by loud whistling. Toby extended his arm and bowed in the direction of Magda and her father. The volume of the appreciation increased. Daffy tucked her head into the opening of Jeremy's pirate jacket, the one Ba had made for him, but Jeremy enjoyed the noise, adding to it by whistling through his fingers. Bo had taught him to do that.

Eventually, the crowd sat down, eager to see what new way Letitia might amaze them. But the volunteer Toby selected next had an entirely unexpected effect. The boy was sitting outside Jeremy's line of vision, somewhere above where he and Daffodil were waiting to go on. His voice was nasal, as if he had a cold, making it difficult for Jeremy to hear him well. But more unpleasant than the quality of his voice was the derision in his tone.

"Make the pig spell our illustrious Baron's name," he ordered. Jeremy felt he could almost see the sneer on the boy's face. "His *full* name! I'll bet my blue jacket that the sow can't do it!"

An uncomfortable silence fell over the crowd. It was broken by a low murmur and an anonymous catcall.

"Boo!" someone yelled. "Boo!"

And then a chorus of boos.

The person sitting directly over Jeremy identified the volunteer as an officer in the Junior PatPats, adding an expletive that Jeremy had often heard but had never himself dared to repeat. But Toby was an experienced performer. He held up both hands and smiled. The audience quieted.

"Not a problem," Toby said. "Letitia, you heard this here gentleman's challenge. Spell the Baron's full name."

Without the slightest hesitation, Letitia trotted over to "B," formed in that same distinctive hand that Jeremy had never been able to place.

"B!" Toby called out.

The audience settled down, hypnotized by the pig's ability. As always, Toby was clicking the nails of his index finger and thumb together.

"A."

"R."

"O."

"N."

"Baron."

"I."

"G."

"N."

"A."

"T."

"I."

"U."

"S."

"Ignatius!"

The crowd applauded.

"F."

"Y."

"O."

"D."

"O."

"R."

"M."

"A."

"X."

"I."

"M."

"U."

"S."

"Fyodor Maximus!"

The audience cheered. Letitia took a quick bow and continued.

"V."

"O."

"N."

"S."

"T."

"R."

"O."

"M."

"P."

"I."

"E."

Then, almost as if it were an afterthought, Letitia returned to the "E" and, with her trotter, delicately scraped an accent mark in the sawdust floor over it.

"Yes!" Toby shouted. "Baron Ignatius Fyodor Maximus von Strompié!"

Cheering! Whistling! Stamping! Clapping! All for the sapient pig and her master. But from the way Toby kept looking in the direction of the volunteer who had asked the question, Jeremy guessed that the JP was not satisfied. Toby calmed the crowd again and bowed dramatically.

The volunteer spoke, louder than before.

"But that ain't all of his name!"

Jeremy's heart quickened. It almost sounded like . . .

"I told you," the boy jeered at the crowd. "I told all of you, didn't I? The sow can't do it! Somebody ought to make sausage out of her!"

The boy had barely finished when Jeremy saw someone throw a wadded-up program in his direction. The crowd was on its feet now, booing and pointing in the direction of the surly volunteer. Their faces were twisted into masks of anger. It was as if a wizard had waved his wand over the crowd, transforming it from a laughing, relaxed gathering of friends into the first stage of an angry, sneering mob. Instinctively, Jeremy pulled Daffodil closer to him.

Once again, though it took longer this time, Jeremy watched as Toby managed to settle the mob back into their seats.

"Now, now, Ladies and Gents," he called out. "The young gentleman is correct. Letitia, let's finish the job."

Letitia trotted over to the "T" and quickly spelled "the." Then she returned to the "T", starting, Jeremy supposed, that last word in the Baron's full name: Baron Ignatius Fyodor Maximus von Strompié *the Third*. But instead of going to the "H," she trotted over to the "U." The audience was apparently as confused as Jeremy. They looked at each other, raising their eyebrows and scratching their heads. What was Letitia up to? Next, she went to the "R," and finally to the "D"!

"That's it!" Toby shouted. "Baron Ignatius Fyodor Maximus von Strompié . . . the Turd!"

Jeremy gasped. What had Toby allowed Letitia to do? Or had Toby himself directed her? Whatever the answer, Jeremy looked behind him, expecting a squadron of PatPats to come swarming in to carry Toby away, just as they had Mim and Pip. By now, the audience had risen once more. Screaming, cheering, stamping the thin soles of their shoes on the wooden risers. Magda's father threw his hat into the air. A hundred caps rained onto the floor of the tent. Jeremy had never seen anything like it.

As Toby and Letitia continued to bow, the crowd, almost as if it were being directed by an invisible hand, took up a chant.

"Von Strompié the Third? NO! Von Strompié the Turd!"

"Von Strompié the Third? NO! Von Strompié the Turd!"

The crowd was still chanting when Toby and Letitia trotted past Jeremy on their way out.

"Toby!" Jeremy shouted over the noise of the crowd. "What were you thinking? The Baron . . . the PatPats . . ."

"Aw, don't be such a worrywart," Toby shouted back. "Can't ya hear that crowd? I ain't scared of no Baron, neither. He's already done everything to me he can! Now go and do your act. I got 'em warmed up for ya!"

He and Letitia trotted out of the tent.

The crowd still had not completely settled when Watty stepped into the triangle. The hat he was wearing, in the same purple and green silk stripes of his tuxedo, added at least a foot to his height. It never failed—the chanting faded first into an unrecognizable murmur and then to nothing at all.

"Ladies and Gentlemen!" Watty called out. "This evening, you've been *mesmerized* by Gravitas! *Dynamized* by Sylvana! *Harmonized* by Melchior! *Scandalized* by the Dictionary Duo. Now be *rejuvenized* by the antics of Jemmy the Pirate and His Moralizing Pup, Daffodil!"

Watty swept his long arm to where Jeremy and Daffy waited. They ran into the triangle, Jeremy swaggering and juggling the wooden pirate sabers that Bo had carved for him and Daffy running in circles about him on her front paws.

A spontaneous burst of laughter broke out, and Jeremy knew that this performance was going to be their best yet. Each part of the act brought louder, more rambunctious laughter and stronger, more enthusiastic applause. From the corner of his eye, Jeremy saw Bo and Ba watching him from where he and Daffy had stood. They were laughing and clapping, too.

All too soon, the boy and dog reached the finale, the part where Jeremy scanned the audience with the telescope, the part where he looked for Polly.

He climbed the miniature mast. Right on cue, Daffy snapped at his bottom and grabbed the baggy seat of his trousers. She rolled her eyes and shook her head while Jeremy trained the telescope on the section of the audience where Magda and her father were sitting. "Yo! Ho! Ho!" he called out as he began the long, dramatic sweep across the audience.

He allowed his mind to rest for a fraction of a second on each face, as he had done on the previous two nights. There was the old man with the misshapen nose, and the woman next to him, whose features were nearly obscured by the wrinkles of hard work and hunger. There was Magda, gray but smiling, and her father, his eyes not on Jeremy, but on his daughter. There was the man, Bo's age or younger, with the terrible scars, the souvenir of some wasting disease.

Face after face swept by, each one with a story to tell. Each saying, *Look at me! I'm here. In spite of everything, I've made it this far.* And Jeremy did look, taking in each set of features, allowing them to tell their owner's tale. But all the while, his attention was focused on his memory of Polly and the hope that hers would be the next face to be framed by the round lens of his telescope.

When he got to the end of the row, just about where he guessed the volunteer's voice had come from, a face came into view that caused the spyglass to fall away from his eye and very nearly from his hands, they were shaking so badly. For a split second, Daffy looked at her master and then, realizing that something was wrong, distracted the audience from Jeremy's lapse by jumping on her hind legs and spinning in the air like a top.

Jeremy panted, trying to catch his breath. Perspiration poured down his neck and back. His eyes began to sting as tiny rivulets of makeup ran into them, and he thought for a moment that he was going to vomit. *But I have to make sure,* he told himself. *I have to.*

He swallowed hard, fighting the bile that was rising in his throat, and lifted the instrument again.

He focused the telescope once more on the boy in the blue jacket.

Jeremy's lips formed the name, but no sound came out.

"Pickles!" he finally whispered. "Pickles! It's you!"

Chapter 30

Ever Heard That Song Before?

Pickles sat on the edge of his bed, polishing the buttons that ran in parallel rows down the front of his jacket. He took care not to let the yellowish paste rub off on any of the jacket's fine wool and was careful not to tangle the braided cording hanging from the epaulets.

The gold piping and the brass buttons shone bright as a sunrise against the garish blue of the jacket but looked sadly out of place in the miserable surroundings in which they now found themselves. The attic room Pickles rented, up three flights of rickety stairs in one of the most dilapidated houses in the Cudgels, was the cheapest he could find. The peeling wallpaper gave the frightening impression that the walls suffered from a virulent, possibly even contagious, illness, and the one small window, cracked and gray with grime from the factory soot, cast the room in a permanent dusk even on the brightest days.

He could have afforded something less shabby, and in a nicer neighborhood, too, but he was saving up. It was all there in a tin box under the bed—every last pié he had made from the Baron. He wasn't sure what he was saving for, not exactly, but his previous life had taught him to economize. Besides, he *knew* the Cudgels, knew all its narrow alleys and its dark corners. He was comfortable there, could come and go without being seen. If need be, he could slip into one of the dark shadows that functioned almost as the Cudgel's veins and disappear.

He lifted his head and laughed.

"That fool actually paid me to go to the cloon shows," he said aloud. "That's like somebody paying you to have a piece of cake."

He laughed again, thinking how he had jacked up the price of the tickets when he told the Baron what they'd cost. That, plus what he'd charged him for the errand itself, had made him a pretty penny.

He brought the jacket closer to his face and stared at his reflection in the gleaming concave surface of the brass. It was upside down. Satisfied that the jacket looked as commanding as the first day he had donned it—the day after the raids—he took the hanger, the single visible object in the room besides the bed and the jacket itself, and draped the garment carefully over it. He walked to the nail he'd pounded into the cracked plaster, tested it as he always did to make sure it was solid, and hooked the hanger over it.

Then he knelt on all fours at the side of the bed, first looking behind to check for—for what? No one lived in the building besides himself and the landlord, a shriveled, toothless creature too feeble to climb the stairs. Cautiously, he reached under the bed and pulled out a rusty tin box that at one time might have held biscuits. He pried open the lid of the box. His pulse quickened. There it was—the latest note from the Baron—just as he had imagined it, resting like a protective coverlet on top of all his beautiful piés.

He wasn't even sure why he'd saved the note, really. He knew that he liked the feel of the heavy parchment between his fingers. But more simply, he told himself that it might come in useful one day. He picked it up and read.

> Boy,
>   My daughter's birthday ball is coming up. I want to invite a cloon show to ~~entertane~~ ~~intertain~~ entertain my guests. Go to all the cloon establishments and make a ~~detailed~~ ~~detaled~~ ~~deet~~—tell me who has the best show. Our usual ~~arangement.~~ ~~Arrangmint~~ . . . deal.
>   Baron Ignatius Fyodor Maximus von Strompié III

Pickles tightened his lips as he had when he first received the note. The newly developed tic in his left eye began to jitter. Why did the Baron address him as "boy"? He'd told him and that pale freak who was always at his side that his name was Dill, the new name he'd chosen for himself. Dill was a proper name. No more of this Pickles rubbish. He'd told them more than once, too. And yet, the Baron never called him Dill. Not even Pickles. It was always "boy." As if he didn't count, as if he didn't deserve a name.

"And that's why, Mr. Baron von Fancypants," Pickles whispered as he refolded the note and put it back in the box, "I didn't tell you about the kid with the pig and how the two of them stirred up the crowd at that cloon show. You don't deserve to know. Not now. Not until you show me some respect. And when I do tell you, it's going to cost you. It's going to cost you plenty."

He closed the box and shoved it back under his bed.

"Am I interrupting something?"

The hair on the back of Pickles's neck stood at attention. He sprang up and wheeled around in one motion. If there was one thing he hated, it was to have his back to Jeriah Wirm.

"I told you before, Wirm. Knock."

"Oh, but I did knock, boy," Jeriah Wirm rasped. He closed the door behind him. "I knocked that first night, the night of the raids. I knocked at the door of your soul."

"Very funny," Pickles replied.

He hated it when Wirm talked like that. Knocked at the door of his soul. Yeah. Right.

"Don't you want to know what I saw there, boy?" Wirm continued. "Don't you want to know what I saw when I knocked at the door of your soul?"

"Nothing," Pickles said. "You didn't see nothing."

"Correct!" Wirm practically squealed as he clapped his white hands together. "I saw nothing. Your soul was as black as night."

The pale creature chuckled and began circling the room, forcing Pickles to keep his eyes on him.

"What do you want, Wirm?"

"Oh, but I think you know," the pale man whispered. "Our little deal. What was that name now? Oh yes, oh my, yes! Our little deal, *Dill*."

Wirm laughed until a tear the color of milk rolled out of the corner of his pale eye.

"Deal, Dill," he repeated as he circled round and round the room. "Deal, Dill."

The deal Wirm was referring to was the arrangement he had made with Pickles when he first understood that the Baron was going to use the boy for purposes other than that first one, the one where Pickles led them to the closed library where a band of the stray children was living. Wirm had realized instantly that it wouldn't do to have the boy working so closely with the Baron without *his* supervision. What if the boy were to stumble on a clue that led the Baron to the answer of the graffiti problem? It would rob him, Jeriah Wirm, of the reward the Baron had promised. The Commander Generalship. No, it wouldn't do. It wouldn't do at all. So, the night after the raids, he had paid Pickles a visit in this very room.

"You'll tell me everything you see, everything you hear when you're off on one of these errands. You'll be like a camera. You'll record everything in that cunning brain of yours, and then you'll come back and you'll tell it all to me. Every single detail."

"And what if I don't?" Pickles had retorted.

"Hmmmm. What if you don't? A good question. A very good question. Let me think for a moment. What if you don't?"

He'd circled the room, in just the way he was doing now. He began to hum. At first, Pickles thought that Wirm might be losing his mind.

"I wonder if you'll recognize this, boy?" Wirm had

asked, stopping, for the moment, the insane droning. "This little melody, I mean. I wonder if you will."

Then he sang outright. His voice was surprisingly robust.

> *The Baron's digestion!*
> *Oh, what a wonder!*
> *It's the talk of both*
> *Wise men and fools.*
> *When he sits on the pot*
> *You won't hear no thunder*
> *Just the* click-click
> *Of glittering jewels.*
>
> *But I've got a secret*
> *That everyone knows;*
> *I'll share it with you—*
> *Mum's the word!*
> *From the top of his head*
> *To the tips of his toes*
> *The Baron himself*
> *Is a turd.*

"Sound familiar, boy?" he'd asked. "Ever hear that song before? Ever sung it yourself?"

Pickles had turned as white as the creature who stood before him.

"N-no!" he'd stammered, turning away so that Wirm couldn't see his face. "I never heard it before."

"Oh, but I think you have, boy. I think you have. My drivers pick up quite a bit, young puppy. Quite a little bit. And they remember. They remember everything. Just the way I've trained them. Just the way I'll train *you*."

He paused as if he were finished, but just at the moment Pickles began to relax, the little man continued. "I wonder how our Baron will feel when he learns that his favorite little puppy dog is a songbird, too? Now, what are those lyrics again? 'From the top of his head to the tips of his toes, the Baron himself is a—'"

"All right, Wirm!" Pickles had shouted. "I'll do what you say. But you got to pay me."

Pickles always shivered whenever he remembered the way Wirm had lunged at him, grabbing him by the collar of his T-shirt and nearly choking him with it. It was as if his limp white body had transformed itself into a single taut, terrifying muscle.

"What was that?" Wirm had whispered, as if it were he who was being choked. "I didn't quite hear you. What is it I 'got' to do? Tell me again. I want you to." He'd given the collar a twist, tightening it against Pickles's windpipe.

Pickles shook his head. "N-nothing," he'd managed to get out. "I didn't say anything."

Wirm loosened his grip. "I beg your pardon," he'd said. "I must be hearing things."

From that evening on, Pickles told Wirm everything he saw on his errands, everything he heard—or almost everything.

Wirm stopped his circling at last and stood with his back to Pickles, facing the grimy window.

"Now, you went to the cloon shows. Tell me what you saw there."

Pickles began his account with the first show, a small one on the far side of the Metropolis, and ended it with the Living Museum.

"It was the best one," he concluded. "There was a boy there dressed like a pirate with a trick dog. It was funny."

Dogs were of no interest to Wirm. He knew what dog tracks looked like. They were common enough, and the tracks that accompanied the person responsible for the graffiti weren't those of a dog.

"Anything else?" he asked. "Any other animal acts?"

Pickles noted again that whenever Wirm quizzed him about his errands, he always ended by asking if he'd seen any unusual animals. The boy had never been able to discover why, but he knew it must be of some importance.

"Well, there was a kid there with this pig."

He held back, wondering if he should tell Wirm about how the boy and the pig had worked the audience into a frenzy against the Baron. For the moment, he decided not to.

Wirm turned from the window and faced Pickles.

"A pig, you say? What kind of pig?"

"What kind of pig? How should I know? Just a pig. That's all. A big pig, and it was smart, too. It could answer questions."

Wirm began his circling again, this time in the opposite direction. Pickles was starting to feel dizzy.

"Fascinating," Wirm murmured. "A smart pig. I wonder, boy"—he paused—"I just wonder. Would you happen to know what a pig's tracks look like?"

"Pig tracks. Sure, I seen plenty of 'em when the

Baron was throwing one of his shindigs. We used to hang outside the slaughterhouses hoping to take a scrap home."

"Charming," Wirm sneered, conveniently forgetting the story of his own youth. "I don't suppose you could draw one for me? A pig track."

"Draw one?"

"I think you heard me. You can draw, can't you? You can do anything, isn't that right, boy? Isn't that what you told the Baron?"

Pickles looked squarely at Wirm, forgetting, for a moment, his fear of the man. What was the bloodless monster up to now? Oh well, he might as well play along. Maybe he'd learn something about this animal business.

"I can draw. But what with? I don't see paper around here, do you? Not a pen, either."

"Be inventive, boy. That's what you're good at. Draw it in the grime on the window."

Pickles walked to the window. He could feel Wirm's breath, hot as the air of Hades, against the back of his neck. He put his finger to the window, drew a curved line, and then rubbed it out. After several of these false starts, intended only to drive Wirm mad, he drew in earnest.

He might have drawn anything, the track of a zebalo or of a deer; Wirm wouldn't have known the difference. But the boy's ego took hold of him. He'd show Wirm to treat him like a nothing! He'd show Wirm that treachery wasn't his only talent! Why, if he put his mind to it, he could be a great artist! Greater even than Cassopi or whatever his name was. In a matter of seconds, he was done.

"There, Wirm!" he announced, unable to disguise the pride he felt at his handiwork. "That is the spitting image of a track a pig will leave. I hope you're satisfied."

He stood back to admire the way the light shone through the image he had drawn.

"Anything else you want me to draw, Wirm?" Pickles asked. "How about a portrait? Yes, I think I could do you justice in the filth on this window, Wirm."

But when Pickles wheeled around, he discovered that he was talking to himself. Wirm had already left the room, not bothering even to close the door.

Pickles turned back to look at the track he had drawn. It was very much like a child's drawing of a tulip, a tulip with two small leaves protruding on either side. What was so special about the track of a pig that it had caused Wirm to disappear? The corner of his eye caught movement on the street below. Pickles looked down to see Jeriah Wirm dashing away. Wherever he was going, he was in a hurry.

Pickles ran to his jacket and pulled it off the hanger.

"I don't know what you're up to," he said, buttoning his jacket as he ran out the door, "but one thing you can count on, Jeriah Freaky Wirm: I'm going to find out! And I have the feeling that when I do, the terms of our little deal are going to change!"

Chapter 31

No Such Thing as Worry

The letter from Helios commanding the Living Museum to perform at the birthday ball arrived late in the afternoon, just minutes before the first show, on the day after Jeremy saw Pickles in the stands. Bo didn't like it. None of them did. But it was only Toby who refused to go.

"The note is very specific, Toby," Sylvana said. Bo handed her the letter. "'*All* the acts are to perform,'" she read.

Toby was drinking from his tin cup. When he set it back down, beads of water exploded onto the table. He crossed his arms.

"I said I ain't goin', and that's that! Not after what he did to Mim and Pip!"

The others remained silent, not knowing what to say, until Bo spoke from his place at the head of the table.

"I think we'd best let Toby make his own decision."

"But we can't allow him to defy the Baron!" Ba protested. "It isn't safe!"

It was the first time Jeremy had heard her disagree with Bo.

"Ba is right," Lexi said, standing up. "It isn't *safe*!"

The others waited for Lexi to add a string of synonyms, but for once, the verbose man seemed to be at a loss for words. He sat back down beside Connie.

"Sometimes," Bo said—he paused and looked at Toby—"a person has to choose between what is *safe* and what is *right*."

Ba left the table and walked into the tent. In the minutes that followed, the group quickly decided that if Toby's absence came up, Bo would tell the Baron that Toby had been called away to the Petropolis on urgent business.

"I've got a sister there," Sylvana reminded Toby. "You can stay with her until everything blows over."

"But I ain't done nothin' wrong," Toby argued. "Why should I go running off?"

Jeremy spoke at last. "The first day I came to the Living Museum, you told me you were going to look out for me," he said. "How can you if you're in the Choir Stall?"

Toby tilted his head to the side. "You're a sly one, you are, Jeremy," he said at last. "Letitia and me will go to the Petropolis. But only for two weeks. After that, we're comin' back. Back where we belong. Back *home*. Ain't that right, Letitia?"

Letitia oinked her assent. It was settled. Toby and Letitia would leave for the Petropolis before dawn the following morning.

Now, much later, Jeremy was sitting cross-legged in the grass near where he'd first met Sylvana. Daffy lay curled in his lap, dozing. Tonight's audience had been more appreciative than ever, cheering both boy and dog to go far beyond the levels of their previous performances. They'd jumped higher, flipped farther, juggled faster than they thought possible. They were both exhausted. And yet, Jeremy couldn't sleep. That was why he was out in the field. He looked up at the full moon. It had risen the color of a bruised lopeberry, the kind he and Pickles used to find on the sidewalk outside Helios.

"What do you suppose she's thinking, Daffy?" Jeremy asked his black and white companion. "The moon, I mean."

The puppy sighed as if to say that human philosophy was far too complicated for a little dog like her.

Jeremy sighed, too. Only twenty-four hours had passed since he'd seen Pickles in the stands, but that was all the time it had taken for him to feel like a different person. It was as if his heart had slowly somersaulted, flipped around right there in his chest. By the time it came round right, something had fallen out, making room for a whole new way of feeling and understanding.

"I should refuse, too, Daffy," Jeremy said. "But I'm not as brave as Toby. Or as strong."

His thoughts next turned to Pickles. It wasn't only the jacket that had upset him, though that was upsetting enough; it was the boy's crooked half smile and the hard glint flickering in his eyes, as if a bomb had detonated deep inside him. Jeremy thought about the blue jacket and remembered what Pickles had said: "I'd like to have me one of those."

Well, he has it, Jeremy thought. *Was it worth it?*

He understood it all now—why Polly always encouraged him to find new friends among the Parrots, why at the end of the day the red cap always seemed to contain less change than he'd expected, and most terrible of all, why Pickles was absent when the PatPats had stormed the Licreeary.

Now Pickles had found his way to the Living Museum. What did he want there?

Once more, Jeremy looked up into the night sky.

"Polly could be looking at the moon right now, Daffy. Just like we are."

Daffodil stood, put her paws on Jeremy's shoulders, and wagged her tail. He found the spot behind her ears and scratched. She hopped down and snuggled back into his lap. Almost immediately, she began to snore.

Jeremy reached into his pocket and pulled out the slip of paper he'd found pinned to the flap of Toby's tent less than an hour ago.

On a ramble, Jeremy read for what must have been the tenth time.

The words were formed in that same distinctive hand that Toby had used for Letitia's alphabet cards, the one that always made Jeremy think he'd seen it somewhere before. But tonight, this feeling nagged at him. He couldn't escape the sense that the note was trying to tell him something. Something far beyond the mere meaning of its words.

With his fingertip, he began to trace the curlicues on the beginning letter of each word, and as he did, it was almost as if the letters whispered to his finger, and his finger communicated to his wrist, and his wrist to his elbow, his elbow to his shoulder, which finally shouted in Jeremy's ear.

He jumped up, spilling Daffy onto the soft grass. His heart was thumping against his chest. He could barely catch his breath.

"It's Toby, Daffy," he whispered. "'Down with the Baron'—it's Toby who's writing it."

He looked at the note once more. There was no mistaking it. The letters there and the letters on the wall of the house near Tiny's had been formed by the same hand. He felt the contents of his stomach churn, and though the evening was warm, he shivered. Now he understood why Toby had so easily made the decision not to perform at the birthday ball. That risk must have seemed like nothing compared to the risk he was already taking.

Jeremy's legs felt weak; he sat back down. He looked at the note a final time and then ripped it into a fistful of confetti. If he had made the connection, then surely others might, too. He allowed the wind to carry the bits of paper away.

Daffy shook herself, and once more, she crawled into Jeremy's lap. Nuzzling her fuzzy head into the crook of his knee, she sighed mightily, as if there were no such thing as fear, as if there were no such thing as worry.

Chapter 32

What a Moment!

The morning of Rosie's birthday arrived at last. In the afternoon, the Metropolian Opera would perform a six-hour extravaganza based on *The Exalted History of the Family von Strompié.* The opera was to be followed by the ball, which in turn would be followed by the birthday feast. But at the moment, the only part of the day's activities that Rosie cared the slightest bit about was set to begin: the cloon show.

She and Polly were now sitting on a high platform behind an elaborate three-panel screen. Directly across from the platform, and separated from it by the performance area, chairs had been arranged on the plastic grass. A watered-silk banner draped the screen: THE BARONESS ROSAMUND MILLICENT FLORIFICA VON STROMPIÉ! MANY HAPPY RETURNS!

"I can hardly see through this thing," Rosie complained to Polly, gesturing toward the massive screen. She kicked her feet under her. "What's the point of the cloon show if I can't see it?"

"Try staring *through* it," Polly advised. "You have to imagine it isn't there."

Rosie furrowed her brow and squinted.

"Hey!" she shouted. "It works!"

The screen was a work of art, massive and carved from some rare Terra Nequamian wood. Each of the three panels seemed to tell one part of a story. On the first, a magnificent winged dragon held a princess in its claws. In the second, the young woman seemed to transform into a dragon of equal size. In the third, the two dragons were mere dots in the sky as they flew together toward a distant kingdom.

The maker of the screen formed the images by perforating the panels with thousands of tiny holes. It was a marvelous thing. By following Polly's advice, by staring *through* the screen as if it weren't there, the girls could see what was happening on the other side without being seen themselves.

As Rosie squirmed in her chair, snapping her fingers and tapping her toes in anticipation of the arrival of the cloons, Polly looked at the crowd assembled on the opposite side of the synthetic lawn. At the suggestion of Jeriah Wirm, and against the extreme protestations of his wife, the Baron had invited a few of his informers and spies from among the riffraff of the Metropolis.

"It never hurts to throw the dogs a bone," Wirm had said.

There were two chairs in front. These were occupied by the Baron and by Jeriah Wirm himself. Polly had learned the pale creature's name from Rosie, whose impetuous nature helped her in discovering all the palace gossip. Wirm looked especially pleased with himself today. His smile, if it could be called that, was completely unsuitable on that pale face, like an engorged slug crawling across a slice of moonmelon. Polly did her best not to imagine what was making Jeriah Wirm so happy. Whatever it was, she knew it must be horrible.

Behind them sat the invited guests and some of Rosie's tutors. One of these guests was a tall, hard-looking woman dressed in black. She sat just behind the Baron, erect and vigilant as a cobra.

"Who is that?" Polly asked.

Rosie wrinkled her freckled nose. "Her name is Hulda," she answered. "Hulda Harpwitch. She's a holy terror."

Polly rubbed away the goose bumps that had risen on her arms. Behind Harpwitch, she recognized the dance master and, beside him, Signora Porchini, cramming a fruit pie into her mouth.

"I ought to go over there and give Porky Pie a pinch," Rosie announced. "Like she did the poor cook."

She jumped up as if to make good on her threat, but Polly grabbed her hand and pulled gently until she sat back down in her chair.

"Try to remember what your mother said. Under no circumstances are you to go from behind this screen."

Actually, what the Baroness had said to Polly was that if Rosie so much as showed a fingernail beyond that screen, Polly would spend the rest of her days in the sunstone mines. Polly suspected that the only reason Gertrudina allowed Rosie to attend the show at all was the fuss she knew her daughter would put up, and frankly, since Dr. Perfidio Purgatorn's visit that day, the Baroness didn't seem to have the energy to resist.

Yes, Polly thought, *a definite change has come over the Baroness Gertrudina von Strompié.*

The harsh woman was just as cruel as ever, let there be no question about that. But whereas before Purgatorn's examination of Rosie the woman gave the impression that everything—*everything!*—was under her control, it now seemed to Polly that a strain of hysteria had infected the Baroness. Polly saw it in her eyes, which sometimes flared just a little too brightly, like the flame of a candle does immediately before it extinguishes itself. She heard it in the newly strident timbre of the woman's voice when she snapped at the servants. Polly even thought she could smell it, a musky undertone lurking, like a ravening animal in its den, beneath the heavy floral scent the Baroness always wore.

As it was, Polly and Rosie were made to arrive before anybody else, under the protective cover of two black parasols so large that as they walked to the platform earlier that morning, they resembled nothing so much as a double eclipse traveling across the lawn.

"She cannot be *seen!*" the Baroness had barked to Polly before the two girls left the palace to take their seats on the platform. "Do you understand me? No one must *see* her!"

"I don't see what's so wrong," Rosie had remarked. "So my nose is a little red. I have a little cold. Big deal! If you want to know the truth, I kind of like the way I look."

Suddenly, the bright curtains that hung across the lawn parted, and both Polly and Rosie gasped as an impossibly tall man in a purple and green tuxedo strode out into the performing area. The crowd grew silent.

Rosie jumped up from her chair once again.

"Baron von Strompié," the man said. He removed his hat and made an elegant bow in the direction of the Baron. "The Living Museum wishes to thank you for your generosity on this most auspicious of days."

"He certainly doesn't sound like he wishes to thank him," Polly whispered, listening less to Watty's words than to the way he said them.

"Of course he doesn't," Rosie answered. "People never say what they mean to my parents. They don't dare."

Watty now turned toward the screen and bowed once again. This time, he spoke more sincerely.

"And to the young Baroness, may I wish you, on behalf of all of us at the Living Museum, a very happy birthday."

"Thank you!" Rosie hollered from behind the screen. "I'll bet I could jump over you if you gave me the chance!"

"Distinguished Guests!" Watty continued in spite of the nervous laughter that erupted at Rosie's unexpected outburst. "Citizens of the Metropolis! May I present to you our first act. The Dazzling Dictionary Duo!"

And so the show began. One after another, the performers appeared. Lexi and Connie. Melchior. Gravitas. Sylvana. With each act, Rosie's excitement grew—so much so, in fact, that Polly considered having the girl sit in her lap in case Rosie got the idea to jump off the stage and run out into the performing area. But the ruffles and hoops and crinolines that layered them both from head to foot made such an arrangement impossible. Besides, Gertrudina had forced both Rosie and Polly to don identical bonnets with preposterously large brims. Polly's view of the show would have been completely obstructed.

The Baron seemed to be enjoying himself nearly as much as Rosie was. This surprised Polly, since just yesterday afternoon, Rosie had brought back word from Signora Porchini that her father was under the strain of a tremendous difficulty of state, some nonsense about graffiti and a disloyal subject. But watching the Baron now, smiling moronically and tapping his feet, it seemed to Polly that whatever had been troubling the man had been resolved.

Polly also kept her eye on Jeriah Wirm. If the way he kept fidgeting in his seat was any indication, he was no longer taking the same pleasure in the goings-on as he had earlier. He paid no attention whatsoever to the performers, but instead kept his eyes fixed on the curtain. The only time he seemed the least bit interested in what the cloons had to offer was when the tall man who introduced the acts walked into the arena. Then, Wirm sat at attention, clutching his hands and tilting his head toward the man so as not to miss a word. But midway through each introduction, Wirm would scowl and kick the rung of his chair.

He's up to something, Polly thought.

Yes, Jeriah Wirm *was* up to something. He'd been planning it since the moment he had seen the pig track on the window, the one that matched those in his photographs. What a joke! Ha! Ha! The culprit he'd been looking for was just a kid. A kid with a pig!

He could have brought the boy to justice right then, gone to the Living Museum and snatched him out of his tent or whatever they lived in. But Jeriah Wirm, invisible though he almost was, had a little-known flair for the dramatic. He'd decided not to tell the Baron what he'd learned, but to catch him off guard, surprise him by nabbing the boy publicly on the day of the birthday celebrations.

What a triumph it will be! Wirm had chortled when the cloons started their show. *The Baron doesn't suspect a thing. Any minute now, the boy and his little piggy-wiggy will start their act. Who knows? Maybe I'll even let them finish it. But when the time is right, I'll stand and accuse him! Right there! In front of everybody! And then the whole Metropolis will know that it was I who caught the criminal. I! Jeriah Wirm! Not the bleeping Baron Ignatius Fyodor Maximus von Strompié. They'll see who has the brains in the Metropolis. And they'll see whom to watch out for, when I'm Commander General!*

But now, well into the performance, he was wondering if this decision to delay the boy's arrest had been wise.

Where is he? he asked himself as one performer after another finished up and the next was announced. *Where is he?* He had no idea, of course, that Toby had already left for the Petropolis.

Mazeppa had just finished. Watty appeared again.

"And now, Ladies and Gentlemen, our *final* act."

This was it! His moment of glory! Wirm actually jumped up and clapped his hands. The last act! It had to be the kid and the porker!

"Sit down, Wirm," the Baron ordered. "You're making a fool of yourself."

"We conclude our show," Watty continued, "with . . ."

"The boy and the pig!" Wirm called out, unable to contain himself further.

". . . Jemmy the Pirate! Yes! Jemmy the Pirate and His Moralizing Pup, Daffodil!"

Jeriah Wirm, normally white as a sun-bleached bedsheet, turned the color of a grape.

"What?" he shrieked. "No! Where's the—?"

"Wirm!" the Baron snapped. "I told you to sit down!"

"But—"

"Are you trying to make things worse for yourself, you miserable insect?" the Baron whispered. "Three days, Wirm! That's how long I gave you! You failed me! Now sit down!"

Jeriah Wirm, his mouth hanging open like the entrance to a defunct sunstone mine, slumped into his chair.

Jeremy and Daffy ran into the arena, juggling and swaggering as usual. Jeremy made a grand gesture with the telescope. Hulda Harpwitch's eyes widened, but Jeremy hadn't seen her; the Baron had managed to set up the performing area so that when the entertainers faced the larger audience, as Jeremy was doing now, they were looking directly into the sun. Nor did he see Harpwitch crouch forward and whisper into the Baron's ear. Did anyone else? If so, it little mattered, for what happened next caused such a commotion that the morning came to an abrupt and unexpected halt.

The catastrophe might have been prevented if Polly hadn't been watching the pirate cloon so closely. But the instant he appeared with his little black and white dog, she rocketed out of her chair so suddenly that Rosie thought she'd been stung by a bee.

"Polly!" she said. "Where did it get you?"

But Polly didn't answer and instead pressed her face against the screen, staring through it as if she were hypnotized. The rest of the world had disappeared. It was only the little cloon that mattered.

"Jeremy!" she whispered. "Jeremy! It's *you*!"

Rosie sprang out of her chair like a jack-in-the-box.

Who's Jeremy? she wanted to ask. But she never got the chance. It was those hoops her mother had forced her to wear! They caught on the edge of her chair. Rosie threw her arms out, hoping to regain her balance, but this only increased the velocity with which she was thrown forward. She crashed into the screen like a boulder sprung from a catapult.

"Oooops!" the audience heard from behind the massive wooden barrier.

Then, to everyone's utter amazement, the screen began teetering. First backward. Then forward. Then a little farther backward. Then a little farther forward. Backward. Forward. Backward. Forward. Until it made up its mind and toppled off the platform, banging against the hard, artificial lawn with an earsplitting crack.

It was this noise that brought Polly to her senses. She tore her attention away from the pirate cloon and ran to Rosie, who was floundering on the platform like a sea creature tossed by a storm onto a spit of dry land.

Jeremy whirled around to see what had happened behind him. Though he didn't need his telescope, he instinctively raised it to his eye and was struck with the odd sensation that, entirely of its own accord, the telescope was fixing itself on the taller girl even though her face was completely hidden by her bonnet.

The shorter girl—the young Baroness, apparently—was also wearing a bonnet, but it was knocked back just enough for the telescope to allow Jeremy to see what he might not have with the naked eye. At first, he thought he had somehow been turned around and that he'd trained the telescope on some of the entertainers from the Living Museum who emerged from behind the curtain to see what the fuss was.

But he hadn't gotten turned around. The telescope had rested on the Baron's daughter's face. His heart thumped against his rib cage.

Can it be? Jeremy asked himself. *Can the Baroness Rosamund Millicent Florifica von Strompié be a . . . ?*

But before Jeremy could finish his thought, a shriek pierced the air and he was knocked to the ground. It was the Baroness Gertrudina von Strompié, swooping into the performing area, screeching and flapping her arms like a dangerous bird of prey.

Chapter 33

She's a Poet, Too!

Polly, her head bowed, her hands behind her back, stood before the smoldering figure of the Baroness.

"I'm sorry, Madam, I—"

"Sorry?" the Baroness bellowed. "Sorry? You've ruined everything! Thanks to you, I've canceled it all. The opera! The supper! The ball!"

Hey! thought Rosie, who stood next to Polly, the hem of her torn skirt hanging at an unlikely angle. *My mother's a poet, too.*

> *Thanks to you,*
> *I've canceled it all.*
> *The opera! The supper!*
> *The big birthday ball!*

She reminded herself to repeat the rhyme to Polly once her mother left them alone.

The Baroness raised her hand. Before she could bring it across Polly's face, Rosie hopped in front of her companion.

"It's my fault! I was the one who knocked the screen over."

The Baroness lowered her arm in disgust. She couldn't bear to touch her own daughter, even if it was to slap her. She turned her attention back to Polly.

"I won't be sending you to the Terra Nequam, after all," she said, training her eyes directly on Polly's. "Instead, you'll continue to act as companion to that . . . that thing there." She pointed at Rosie. "That's the cruelest punishment I can think of."

She walked over to the bedside table and picked up the three crystal spheres. Then she turned to face Rosie.

"And as for you . . . you monstrous creature, don't you dare to think of Helios as home. Instead, my fine freckled friend, you are about to learn that it has become your prison."

Rosie's mother wasn't making sense. How could the palace with its marble and its chandeliers and its army of servants be a prison?

The Baroness made her way to the door.

"You will never step outside the walls of this chamber again," she hissed. "Neither one of you!"

She slammed the door behind her, but not before she dropped the crystal spheres onto the hard marble threshold, where they shattered, spraying their splinters across the room, sharp missiles of the Baroness's cruelty.

Chapter 34

It Was the Principle that Was Important!

The Baron Ignatius Fyodor Maximus von Strompié III pulled his monogrammed handkerchief from his pocket and wiped the perspiration from his brow, thankful that his wife had left him in peace at last.

To tell the truth, he didn't see what the fuss was about. Rosamund was still a baroness, wasn't she? Her father was still the Baron Ignatius Fyodor Maximus von Strompié III. Nothing was wrong with *him,* so what was the problem? Couldn't Rosamund just wear a veil or something?

He jumped up from his desk. That was it! He wished he'd thought of it when Gertrudina had been in his study screaming like a banshee and throwing everything she could get her hands on. He'd pass a new law. All the women in the Metropolis would wear veils! He congratulated himself on the simplicity of the idea. No one would ever have to see Rosamund's face again, including him and his wife. It was perfect! The Got Ya Covered Proviso. That's what he'd call it!

But even before the final "o" in "Proviso" had

disappeared from his mind, he knew that it would not satisfy Gertrudina. That woman had become absolutely unreasonable!

"You *must* get rid of the cloons, you great idiot!" she'd thundered. "Seize their land! Burn their tents! Pass a law forbidding anyone to even mention the word."

But what about Rosamund? he'd wanted to know. Wasn't she a—?

"Don't you dare!" his wife bellowed, clasping her hands over her ears. "Don't you dare say it! We'll keep her *here,* where no one will ever see her!"

She perched on the edge of the gold brocade chair that only the Baron was permitted to sit in, but he thought perhaps now was not the best time to mention it.

"After a bit, we'll let it be known that Rosamund has a delicate constitution," his wife continued, calmer now. "We'll say the doctor has ordered us to keep her quiet. But she must never be connected to *cloonodium felicitatum!* Never! Not my daughter! Do you hear me? NOT MY DAUGHTER. We'd be the laughingstock of the entire Metropolis!"

Oh well, the Baron thought now. *Why not just do as she asked and get it over with?*

He would send the cloons to the Terra Nequam. And thanks to what that hag Hulda Harpwitch had whispered in his ear, he now had a reason to do it—*two* reasons, when it came right down to it. One, according to Harpwitch, was that the cloons had tried to deceive him. They'd tried to pass off that boy with the dog as a cloon! He'd paid to see real cloons, hadn't he? Not impostors wearing makeup and wigs! (Actually, he hadn't paid at all, but never mind. It was the *principle* of the thing that was important!) To deceive a baron was bad enough—as if such a thing were possible! But there was another reason, too, one that until this business with Rosamund had popped up was even more deserving of the Baron's displeasure.

According to Harpwitch, the boy was actually living with the cloons! The very idea! Why, it wasn't natural! It wasn't right! Anybody could see that. Everyone should stick to his own kind. He'd said that from the very beginning. Everyone should stick to his own kind. Harpwitch had told him that the kid was a no-good troublemaker, but at least he *was* a boy, a *normal* boy! The cloons were freaks! Yes, they were harmless, he had to admit it, but they were freaks nonetheless. Freaks should stay with freaks, and boys should stay with . . . well, whomever they should stay with, it shouldn't be freaks. Of that much, he was certain!

But before he could get to the Weekly Wisdom Wagon Address that would get the ball rolling, he had other business to attend to. He looked at the clock. Any minute now . . . yes! There it was, the revolting tap of Jeriah Wirm on the other side of the door. The Baron had been waiting for this. This was going to be good.

"Enter, Wirm."

Wirm crawled into the room even more abjectly than he had in the past. He practically slithered before the Baron's desk.

"O Most Patient and Forgiving Baronial Person," he began. "Please allow me to explain—"

"Three days, Wirm! That's what I said. Three days! Seventy-six hours."

"Er . . . seventy-two," Wirm whispered. "Three days is seventy-two hours."

The Baron gave his back to the driver and counted on his fingers.

"Whatever, Wirm," he said, turning on his heel. "Seventy-two. Seventy-six. Whatever. It's of no consequence. Not now. You've disappointed me for the last time, you miserable wretch."

He raised his hands over his head and clapped. A squadron of PatPats buzzed into the room from behind one of the paneled doors.

"Wirm," the Baron said, "allow me to introduce the new Commander General of the PatPats."

To Jeriah Wirm's horror, the new CG stepped into the study, wearing the full-length blood-red coat that was reserved for his rank. It was at least three sizes too large. Wirm quivered like a chrysalis waiting for a creature of the night to burst forth and spread its wings.

"You?" he shrieked. "You? But *you* didn't catch the criminal. *I* did. Or I almost did, anyway."

"Maybe I did catch him. Maybe I didn't," the new CG said.

"What's that supposed to mean?" Wirm snarled.

The Commander General didn't respond immediately, but instead took a moment to model the coat for Wirm.

"I really do think that red is my color, don't you?" he asked. With a nod of his head, the PatPats, now under his command, surrounded Jeriah Wirm.

"I know this is hard for you, Wirm," the Baron said. "But think of *me*. It's not easy being a baron, you know."

"I'll get you!" Jeriah Wirm shrieked at the new CG. "I'll get you if it's the last thing I do!"

They dragged him kicking and screaming out of the study.

"Good job, boy," the Baron said to his new Commander General.

"The name is Dill, sir."

The Baron was too pleased with himself to notice the way Pickles looked at him before he disappeared through the panel. If he had, he might have taken pause. But as it was, he had to get to that speech, the one that was the first step in getting rid of the cloons.

He clucked his tongue at the shameful way Jeriah Wirm had comported himself.

That is his problem, the Baron thought as he sat at his desk. *No dignity.*

Then he picked up his gold pen. He cleared his throat.

Birds of a feather . . . , he wrote.

Chapter 35

Peas and Ice Cream!

When the Living Museum returned from Helios, Jeremy knew that Toby and Letitia were safely gone. But he was not resting easy. The emptiness they had left behind filled him with troubling thoughts. He'd kept his recent discovery about Toby quiet. Nor did he mention what he had seen through the telescope at Helios. The red nose. The curly red hair. The twinkling eyes.

Now, late that night, Jeremy lay dreaming, Daffy curled at his feet. It was a disturbing dream, one that involved the Baron's daughter and the taller girl who protected her. Both girls' faces were totally obscured by those enormous bonnets, but the young Baroness's had slipped back just as it had at the birthday performance. Each time Jeremy tried to focus the telescope on her, the telescope moved as if by some mysterious force to the taller girl. Time after time, Jeremy trained the telescope on the young Baroness. Time after time, it moved in his hands to the girl who attended her.

He was about to give up when the taller girl stepped

forward and untied the strings of her bonnet. However, instead of removing the ridiculous hat, she spoke. But something was wrong. Her voice was mechanical and unnaturally loud.

"Birds of a feather—" she screamed.

"—flock together."

Jeremy awakened to the sound of the Wisdom Wagon reverberating all around him. The loudspeaker must have been turned up to its highest volume to have reached him in his bed in the tent.

"Birds of a feather flock together!" it repeated. It was the Baron's voice, giving his Weekly Wisdom Wagon Address.

"Yes, that's what the old saying is, my friends. Birds of a feather flock together. And what is this ancient wisdom telling us? It's simple, really. Very simple. It's telling us that we should stick to our own kind. Barons with barons. Commoners with commoners.

"Imagine, for a moment, what the world would be like if birds of a feather did *not* flock together. If everything were all mixed up. Topsy-turvy. Helter-skelter. Higgledy-piggledy. Imagine *that* kind of world! Why, it would be like . . . like eating peas with ice cream. Nobody eats his peas with his ice cream. And if they did, I'd pass a law. Yes, I'd pass a law making it illegal! Why? Because it's *not normal*! Peas should stick with peas, and ice cream should stick with . . . er . . . ice cream.

"But it has come to my attention, O fellow Metropololians, that certain birds are *not* flocking together, certain—how shall I put it?—*unusual* birds. Certain birds with bright red beaks!

"For years, we—and by 'we,' I mean *me*—have tolerated these . . . uh . . . birds. We felt sorry for them. We pitied them. They are not like you. And certainly, certainly, they are not like *me*! No, my friends, they are not normal, these . . . *cloons*!"

Jeremy sat up, unable to believe what he was hearing.

"But we have allowed them to stay in the Metropolis, hoping they would keep to themselves so that decent citizens, *normal* citizens like you and like me, would not have to be reminded of their freakish existence. But now it seems they are not satisfied to stay among themselves and the other freaky-deaks they draw to them. No!

"It has come to my attention, my dear Metropoleeites, that the cloons have among them . . . a boy. Not a cloon boy. Not a boy with the monstrous red nose of their kind! Not a boy with their hideous deformities! No! A *regular* boy! A *normal* boy!

"Is this right? I leave it to you. IS THIS RIGHT? No! It is not right! This is not birds flocking together. This is peas and ice cream, my friends! PEAS AND ICE CREAM!"

From the way the loudspeaker screeched, it had apparently reached the limits of its ability to handle the volume of the Baron's screaming these last four words.

Jeremy jumped out of bed, his heart racing. Still in his pajamas, he ran to find Bo and Ba. But he was stopped in his tracks by what the Baron said next.

"Who is this poor boy? Who is this unfortunate orphan who was practically snatched from the arms of his loving guardian? His name . . . his name is Jeremy. Jeremy Cabbage!"

Chapter 36

It Doesn't Make Sense

Jeremy found Bo and Ba at the top of the steps, just behind the double doors that served as the entrance to the Living Museum. Sylvana was with them, listening. Next to her, Lexi and Connie held hands, talking quietly to each other. Watty stood on the landing. He'd removed his glasses and was polishing the lenses with his handkerchief.

All the performers of the Living Museum, in fact, were awake, standing singly outside their tents or gathered in small groups. Some of them, like Jeremy, still wore their nightclothes. They shook their heads and looked blankly at each other as they listened in stunned silence to the Baron's address. Jeremy raced up the wooden stairs two at a time, using the railings on either side to propel himself forward. Daffy followed at his heels.

"How did he know?" he panted as Ba opened her arms to him. "How did he know my name?"

"That woman!" Ba answered. "It must have been that horrible woman."

Jeremy hadn't seen Harpwitch at the birthday performance, but "horrible woman" could only mean one thing.

"Harpwitch?" he asked. "She was there?"

Ba nodded. "I saw her whisper something to the Baron when you and Daffy ran on. Oh, I should have known there'd be trouble."

"The fiend," Sylvana said. She curled her upper lip so that all of her gold teeth showed at once.

"Fiend," Lexi repeated. "Demon! Incubus! Succubus! Hellhound!"

"Hush, dear. Hush," Connie said, patting his hand. "There's a child present."

Jeremy bent down to pick up Daffodil.

"But it doesn't make sense," he said. "How did she know it was me? I was wearing my makeup. And my wig. Everybody thought I was a cloon."

"I'm not sure she did recognize *you*," Bo said.

Jeremy thought back to the last day he'd seen Harpwitch, the day Bo and Ba had come to take him away from HHMDUCSC. Suddenly, he understood.

"It was the telescope!" he said. "She recognized the telescope!"

Jeremy was right. It *was* the telescope. The instant Harpwitch spotted the spyglass, she was as certain of who was behind the red nose and black eye patch as she was of her own capacity for mischief.

Jeremy had no way of knowing it, of course, but Harpwitch had been waiting for such an opportunity since the moment he'd walked out of HHMDUCSC with the spyglass. The memory of that day had festered on the skin of her soul like a carbuncle, one that would only be lanced by the sharp edge of revenge. *To love, of course.* That's what the cloon had told her that morning when she asked why they wanted a child. *Well,* she'd thought when she craned forward to whisper into the Baron's ear, *let's see how love helps when I suggest to von Strompié that the cloons are conning him, trying to pass off a normal boy as one of their own.* And, wonder of wonders! She had even been able to tell the Baron the boy's name.

Watty spoke next.

"What shall we do?" he asked.

He returned the glasses to his face, but he kept the handkerchief in his hand, ready, or so it seemed, to wipe the world clean of the spreading stain with which it now seemed to be tarnished.

"Do?" Bo said. "We'll do what we always do. We'll get ready for this evening's performance."

"What is he up to?" Sylvana asked. "The Baron, I mean."

"Any ideas, Jeremy?" Bo asked.

Jeremy shook his head. The only thing he knew for sure was that to have heard his name resting so comfortably on the Baron's tongue was one of the worst shocks of his life. He remembered Polly reading to him that in ancient times in the Terra Nequam, it had been a crime to say another person's name aloud. He and Polly had laughed at such a silly thing. Now it didn't seem so funny.

Throughout the day, the Wisdom Wagons continued to broadcast the speech. By evening, all the residents of the Living Museum were on edge. Even the zebalo, the bovaloo, and the wowwie were shaken. They kicked in their stalls and nipped at Radu, who did his best to keep the great beasts calm. Just before the doors were to be opened to let in the audience for the evening's performance, Bo called all the performers together.

"We've done nothing wrong," he said. "Acting as if we have will only make things worse. Do your best tonight. Your very best. If we're lucky, the whole thing will blow over by tomorrow."

For the first time since the Living Museum reopened, empty seats studded the stands, but the performers vowed not to allow this unsettling change to affect them. Bo said to do their best, and do their best they would. Gravitas even went so far as to wear a blindfold inside the mystery ball, and Lexi and Connie defined fifteen words in less than a minute, practically a record.

But of all the performers, Jeremy had the most difficult time that evening. It was *his* name that the Baron had uttered. The charged silence that preceded his entry into the tent nearly caused him to drop one of the wooden sabers. But this mistake helped him focus his concentration, and in the end, he and Daffy gave an almost flawless performance. They worked together like a single organism, some creature from the Terra Nequam, maybe, part boy, part dog. By the time the finale came, the audience had let go of its initial hesitation and was cheering them on.

The only moment that Jeremy came close to failing was when the time came to scan the audience with the telescope. He very nearly didn't lift the instrument to his eye. Half of him was afraid of what he might see. Pickles. Or worse. But the other half suddenly remembered the girl in the bonnet. It was as if the dream he'd awakened to chose just that moment to come back and haunt him. Why had the telescope returned again and again to the girl?

Daffy pointed her muzzle toward the ceiling and howled, directing the attention away from Jeremy and reminding him to finish their act.

"Thanks, Daffy," he whispered.

He swept the barrel of the telescope over the audience. Nothing. Not Pickles. But not Polly, either.

Finally, the ordeal ended. The boy and his dog ran out of the tent. Jeremy tried not to notice that there had been no calls for encores. Watty bade the crowd a good-night. The show was over; the audience filed out. Everyone breathed a little easier.

"Maybe it will all disappear," Sylvana said to Jeremy as they walked back to their tents. "You know the Baron. One day he passes a law making it illegal to whistle. The next day it's illegal if you don't."

Later, Jeremy lay in his room. With Daffy curled up and snoring on the pillow next to him, his thoughts turned to Toby. He tried to picture him and the intrepid Letitia safe in the Petropolis. He missed his friend, but he was grateful that Toby was not there to experience whatever it was the Baron was up to. There was no telling what he might do.

He missed Polly, too. With all his heart. But oddly, it was the image of the girl in the bonnet that carried him over the bridge from consciousness into a fitful, troubled sleep.

Chapter 37
Topsy-turvyism of the Worst Kind!

When Jeremy awoke the next morning, he knew by the sunlight dappling the interior of the tent that it was much later than he usually slept. He listened intently for the terrible sound of the Baron's voice blaring from a loudspeaker. Though he concentrated, the only sounds were those of the Living Museum beginning a new day—the ringing of the sledges as they hit the iron tent stakes, the braying of the bovaloo, Madame Josephine's vocalizing as she groomed her beard. He stretched and hopped out of bed.

"Come on, Daffy," he called to his pup.

Both he and the dog padded out to the big table, where Ba was serving some kind of crumble with mounds of violet-colored whipped cream.

Everyone but Toby was there. Under normal circumstances, the noise at the table as the group prattled and laughed would have carried to the far edge of the field, but this morning, the only sound was the dull clink of a spoon as it hit the bottom of a bowl. Like Jeremy, everyone seemed to be waiting, listening.

Sylvana made room for Jeremy next to her. Ba handed him his breakfast.

The meal continued this way until Sylvana finally broke the silence.

"The speech started much earlier yesterday," she said. "Maybe it's passed. Maybe the Baron's already moved on to something else."

"I think perhaps he has," Connie asserted.

"I'm certain of it," Lexi agreed. "Confident. Convinced. Completely assured."

Minute after minute passed without the hateful interruption of the loudspeaker. Their spirits began to rise. Watty described the day his parents, who were normal-sized people, removed all the ceilings in their house so that their growing boy could stand up without getting a crick in his neck. Sylvana told the story of how she got her gold teeth, a tale involving a bad landing and a lovesick dentist. Jeremy talked, too. He even dared to imitate Harpwitch when Bo had asked her to open the drawer where the telescope was hidden. They howled when he puffed out his cheeks and hiccuped. As the others talked and laughed, Bo tapped his foot under the table and absentmindedly fiddled with his half-eaten crumble.

Family. The word drifted into Jeremy's consciousness once again. *This is my family.*

"Salt and pepper. Bees and honey. Bread and butter." The Baron's voice blasted through the loudspeaker.

Bo brought his fist down on the table.

"What are these, O Citizens of the Metropolis?" the Baron continued. "I'll tell you what they are. They are things that *go together.* They make us feel happy and complete. They make us feel that everything is in a natural order."

The others looked at one another. Without any kind of visible signal, they joined hands.

"But there are some things, my friends . . . there are some things that do *not* go together. And these do *not* make us feel happy and complete. They do *not* make us feel that everything is in a natural order. Barons and hunger, for example. Commoners and sunstones. Boys and . . . boys and *cloons*!"

"Liar!" Jeremy whispered. "Liar!"

"But, my fellow Metropolesians, we do have a boy being raised by cloons! Right here in our Metropolis! I expect that kind of thing to happen in the Petropolis. But here? Here? I say NO! . . . Never! Not in my Metropolis! It's topsy-turvyism! Topsy-turvyism of the worst kind!

"He is living with them. Our own Jeremy Cabbage, practically kidnapped from his loving guardian, forced to live with cloons. Right under our very noses. He had no choice. And they are teaching him their freakish ways, my friends. They are teaching him to become like them. Yes! That's what they want!

"But is this what *you* want? I think not! I think I know the citizens of my Metropolis, and . . . I . . . think . . . NOT!"

The fact that this last phrase could also be interpreted to mean that he didn't think at all was lost on the Baron.

Apparently, it was also lost on the citizens of the Metropolis. The stands were more than half empty at that night's performance, and the people who did show up were troublemakers, most of whom were under the employ of the Baron.

Jeremy watched from beneath the stands as they booed Lexi and Connie out of the tent, accusing them of cheating and giving them words like "freak" and "kidnappers." Then a man with a ponytail tossed a cinder on Gravitas's spiral so that when the cloon began to propel himself upward, the mystery ball wobbled and fell to the ground with a sickening thud. The man with the ponytail stood and took a bow. The audience laughed and applauded.

Bo instructed Watty to announce that the rest of the show was canceled and to inform the audience that their money for the tickets would be refunded.

"But we don't want a refund!" shouted a woman. "We came to see Jeremy Cabbage!"

Jeremy clutched Daffy to his chest and stepped into the shadows.

"You've got him locked up somewhere!" shouted another. "Where is he?"

"They're probably giving him freak lessons right now! But don't you worry, Jeremy, the Baron will save you. The Baron won't leave you here much longer!"

In the end, Watty had been able to control the audience just enough to get them to leave. But as Bo and Lexi were barring the great double doors, Jeremy heard a terrible noise from the street, the sound of metal caving in on itself. The mob had turned Lemondrop upside down.

Chapter 38

What Would They Have Seen?

The crows at Helios no longer roosted in the trees outside Baron Ignatius Fyodor Maximus von Strompié III's study. The artificial branches left a sticky residue on their feet, and the synthetic leaves soaked up the heat of the sun and turned the crowns of the trees into steaming ovens. But if the birds *were* still roosting at Helios, what would they have seen the night the thugs overturned Lemondrop?

They would have seen the Baron practicing his third and final address, the one that would "seal the deal," as he liked to say to himself. This one he would give in person, right on the steps of the Living Museum itself! What a clever baron he was!

They would have seen the Baroness Gertrudina pacing in her chambers, too, weeping with fury in a way not at all befitting a baroness. *Why,* the crows might have said to each other in their alien, cacophonous tongue, *she isn't even bothering to wipe her aristocratic nose!*

They would have seen a boy in a blood-red coat

moving in to Jeriah Wirm's old hidey-hole in the basement of Helios. From the pocket of his coat, he removed a handful of photographs and tossed them back onto the table from where he had stolen them. He would have to do something about those rats.

Finally, the crows would have seen two figures scrabbling down a rope flung from a high window on the second floor. The smaller of the two, in a dress and bonnet, was as nimble as a monkey and scrambled down the braided strips of brocade cloth as if she had been doing it all her life. The other, dressed identically to her companion, struggled.

But there were no crows to see such things. They had all flown west, to the spare forests of the Terra Nequam, and the house kept its secrets like a beggar who has seen many disturbing things in his life on the streets but has lost the voice that could tell them.

Chapter 39

He Kept a Steadfast Heart

The morning after the Baron's second address, the one that caused the citizens to attack Lemondrop, Jeremy was sitting in his familiar spot at the edge of the field. He had risen long before the others. He and Daffy had come there to think while it was still quiet, before the Baron began blasting more of the hateful lies that Jeremy felt were certain to come.

He yawned, having slept poorly because of the dream. It had come again last night, playing over and over in his head. In the grass, the white X where Sylvana had made her perfect landing had faded until it had almost disappeared.

"It seems like *everything* could disappear, Daffy," Jeremy said.

The sun was just beginning to peek through the morning clouds when Jeremy looked up to see Watty running toward him at full tilt. The tall man was barefoot and still wearing his nightshirt, a billowing affair made of shining blue silk. He resembled nothing less than a tidal wave rushing straight toward where

Jeremy and Daffodil sat. Watty was upon them almost before the boy had spotted him.

"You have a visitor," he said breathlessly.

Jeremy was sure his ears had played a trick on him. *A visitor?* he was about to repeat, but before he could, Watty swooped him up and threw him over his shoulder. He turned around and took off in the direction from which he had come, carrying Jeremy fireman-style as effortlessly as if he were a bag of turnips.

"Hey!" Jeremy shouted. "What gives?"

Daffy ran after them, wagging and barking and trying to catch the hem of Watty's nightdress in her teeth.

"It's Toby, isn't it, Watty?" Jeremy yelled, bouncing softly on Watty's shoulder. "Toby's come back early!"

Of course! That had to be it! Toby! His heart began to race at the anticipation of seeing his friend. It was dangerous for Toby to have returned, yes, but with the Baron's current mischief, it was dangerous for all of them now. He looked forward to seeing Toby in the flesh and to feeling the bone-shaking slap in the small of his back or the heart-stopping jab in the ribs, gestures that he had come to recognize as signs of Toby's unwavering affection. Letitia would be there, too. Big, beautiful, sapient Letitia. Whatever happened, they would all be together.

"Come on, Watty!" Jeremy shouted. "Tell me! It *is* Toby, isn't it? It *has* to be!"

But Watty was concentrating all his energy on getting Jeremy to this mysterious visitor as soon as possible. He continued to run without a word of explanation.

Toby's arrival was the only thing Jeremy could

think of that would make Watty act so strangely, and his friend was certainly the only visitor he could imagine. But then his mood shifted suddenly, and for the first time since Watty had hoisted him over his shoulder, he fought to get down.

"It's not *her,* is it?" he cried out. "It's not Harpwitch?"

This seemed unlikely to the boy, and yet, his short life had already taught him that unlikely things happen all the time. Besides, Harpwitch seemed to have developed the terrifying habit of reappearing in his life at unexpected times, like an infection that returns no matter how many times it is treated.

He struggled, kicking his legs and arching his back. Finally, Watty reached the tree by the tent, turned around, and set Jeremy down. Both man and boy were panting. Jeremy looked ahead of him. They were all there, lined up in front of him: Bo, Ba, Sylvana, Lexi, Connie. All of them, like Watty, still in their nightclothes.

"What's going on?" Jeremy asked. "Where's Toby? Where's Letitia? It isn't Harpwitch, is it?"

As if on cue, the others stepped aside, revealing the figure who waited behind them. For a moment, Jeremy stood stock-still, unable to breathe, afraid even to bat an eyelash.

I must be dreaming, he thought.

He blinked.

Once.

Twice.

Three times.

Each time, he expected the figure to disappear. But each time he opened his eyes, the figure stood solidly before him, as real as Daffy's wet nose nuzzling his calf or the rough bark of the tree.

"Polly?" Jeremy whispered. "Polly?"

"Aren't you even going to say hello?" Polly laughed.

That was what he needed. That was what he needed all along. To hear her voice. To hear Polly's voice. She held out her arms. He ran to her, wrapping his arms around her. He practically knocked her over.

"Polly," he said. "It's you!"

"Yes, Jeremy," the girl answered, holding him close. "It's me."

Eventually, Jeremy released his grip and stepped back so that he could see Polly's face. He took in each of her features: her mouth, her nose, her eyes. He promised himself that he would never forget them again. Then he hugged her once more, needing to feel a final time that she was real, that she was here.

The others formed a protective circle around them. Someone handed Polly the preposterous bonnet, which had fallen to the ground behind her.

"You were the girl in the bonnet?" Jeremy shouted.

She pulled Jeremy to her. "Yes," she said. "Did you think that makeup and a wig could disguise you from me? I can't tell you the relief I felt when I saw you. Just to know that you were safe."

She looked at Bo and Ba. "And happy," she added.

"I knew it!" Jeremy beamed. "The telescope *did* find you! I could feel it, pulling toward you that day."

But suddenly, a furrow began to work its way across his brow. The smile faded. He looked down at Daffy, running circles around his feet. He stepped back, away from Polly.

"You recognized me," he said, "but I didn't recognize you."

"So?"

"So don't you see? During all the time we were apart, I was sure that I would find you, that I would find you and rescue you. Just like the heroes we read about in the Licreeary."

For a moment, Polly said nothing. Then she placed her hands on Jeremy's cheeks and gently tilted his head until he was looking directly into her face.

"You kept a steadfast heart, Jeremy," she finally answered. "That's heroic enough for me."

"Polly," Jeremy whispered.

"Anyway," the girl teased, "I hope you don't want *all* the glory. I do hope you'll give me a little credit for our reunion."

"And don't forget about me!"

They turned. Rosie stood in the door of the tent.

"So it's true!" Jeremy said, looking at the bright red nose. "What I saw through the telescope, I mean. You're . . ."

"Yes!" she shouted happily. "I'm a cloon!"

There could be no doubt about it. The full effects of *cloonodium felicitatum* were now completely apparent in Rosie's face.

"I was the one who braided the curtains into ropes and taught Polly how to climb down them," she said. "If it weren't for me, we might still be locked up in that room."

Rosie backflipped toward Polly and Jeremy.

"After the disaster at the birthday celebration," Polly explained, "Rosie's mother locked us in our rooms. Yesterday, the day passed without a soul knocking on our door, even to deliver a meal."

"She was starving us!" Rosie interrupted. "My own mother was starving us!"

"We had no choice," continued Polly. "We had to leave. And so . . . and so last night, we escaped."

"Ah," Lexi interrupted, unable to contain himself. "In other words, you fled. You decamped. You absconded."

"Yes," Polly responded, smiling at the blue man, happy to show off the vocabulary she had acquired from years of living in the Licreeary. "We made a departure. An exodus. A hegira."

"Oh, happy day!" Lexi declared. "A girl after my own heart!"

"You should have seen me climbing down those curtains, Jeremy," Polly continued. "I think you would have been quite proud."

She looked once more at Bo and Ba.

"This was the only place I could think of to come. I . . . I hope it's all right."

Ba reached out to Polly and took her hand. "You'll find none of the Baroness's cruelty here," she said. "And there'll be no more worrying about where your next meal might come from, either. Or where you're going to sleep. All of that is over, dear girl. This is your home now."

Ba turned to Rosie. "Yours, too, Missy. If you'd like it to be."

"I'm never going back to Helios," Rosie declared. "Never! This is where I belong!"

"She reminds me of you, Ba," Bo whispered to his wife. "She really does!"

It was still very early in the morning. Ba went inside the tent to prepare breakfast. Polly wanted to help, but Ba wouldn't hear of it.

"There will be plenty of time for that later," she said. "For now, you just sit tight."

And sit tight they did, talking and laughing right through lunch. Polly told Jeremy all about her life at Helios, and Jeremy told Polly about Harpwitch, Tiny, the Parsepins, all of it. Rosie spent the day with Ba. By the time everyone regrouped at the table for dinner, they were starving again. Ba had outdone herself, serving a steaming mound of something she called Gelled Wiggy. Rosie asked for seconds.

After dessert, Bo quieted everyone down. He turned to Polly.

"I don't have to tell you how happy we are that you are here," he began. He winked at Rosie. "*Both* of you. Almost as happy as Jeremy, I expect."

"Hear! Hear!" Watty seconded. The table broke into a welcoming applause and a round of cheers.

"But it's only fair to tell you," Bo continued, "that we seem to be in some difficulty at the moment. The Baron . . ." He looked at Rosie. "Your father appears to be planning to, well, we're not sure what he is planning."

"Beats me," Rosie said, shrugging her shoulders. "The only thing I know is that when Polly and I were sitting at the window, we heard the servants whispering that he was locked up in his study working on some big speech he's planning to give."

This news might have been enough to dampen the high spirits of the celebrants, but Ba raised a glass.

"Let's think of that tomorrow," she suggested. "Tonight, we have something to be happy about."

Once more, the group broke into a round of cheers and toasts.

Jeremy was sitting next to Polly, one hand on the table, one hand resting on the bench. He agreed with Ba. Toby was safe! Polly was here! Everything was perfect. At least for tonight. Occasionally, he would touch Polly's arm, as if he needed reassurance that she wasn't an apparition.

He was just about to propose a toast himself, to Toby and Polly and Rosie, to all of them, but as he raised his glass, he felt something brush against his leg. At first, he thought it might have been Daffy. But it couldn't be. The dog was snoozing comfortably in Polly's lap.

There it was again! He looked down.

"Letitia!" he cried out.

Chapter 40

She's Not Only a Cloon! She's a Genius!

It was a wonder, really, that Jeremy recognized the sapient pig, she was so changed. She'd lost at least fifty pounds, and her skin, normally as pink and healthy as a newborn baby's, was bruised and filthy. Her brass nose ring, too, which Toby always kept polished to a bright sheen, was so badly scratched it looked as if it had gone through a great deal just to stay in Letitia's snout. But most distressing of all was the expression in the great pig's eyes. The intelligence was there—that would never go—but the confidence was gone. It had been replaced with the kind of sadness that only a five-hundred-pound pig can convey.

"Letitia!" Jeremy repeated.

She oinked softly, as if to say, *Yes, it's me, but just barely.*

By now, the others had jumped up from the table and were gathered around Letitia, who slumped on her haunches, too tired, it seemed, to stand.

"Toby must be on his way back!" Sylvana said. "He must not have made it to the Petropolis."

"He would never leave Letitia!" Connie confirmed.

The two went to search for the boy, expecting at any minute to see him open the doors and descend the stairs. But they soon returned to the table with disturbing news.

"He's not here," Sylvana reported. "We've looked everywhere. He's not here."

Jeremy had taken one of Ba's napkins and was gently wiping some of the dirt from Letitia's face. Until then, Jeremy didn't know that pigs could cry, but there was no mistaking it. A single tear formed in the corner of Letitia's eye and rolled slowly down her jowl. He patted her head softly while Daffy licked away the salty track left by the tear.

"There, there, Letitia," Jeremy said softly. "Don't worry. You're home now."

The instant Ba had seen Letitia, she jumped up from the table and ran into the tent. Now she returned with a platter piled high with lopeberry corncakes soaked in syrup and topped with a mound of pink whipped cream. This was the great pig's favorite dish. But Letitia simply turned her head away. This caused everyone's heart to break.

"Letitia," Jeremy said, kneeling in front of the pig so that he could look into her eyes. "Where's Toby?"

At the sound of her master's name, Letitia squealed pathetically.

"She's trying to tell us," Watty said. "She's trying to tell us where he is."

Bo left his place at the head of the table and stood next to where Jeremy was kneeling.

"Yes," he said. "But who among us can understand her?"

Rosie spoke next, and what she said bound her to the group as if she had been at the Living Museum all her life instead of just one day.

"What about the cards?" she asked. "Isn't that the famous pig who answers questions?"

"Rosie!" Jeremy shouted. "You're not only a cloon! You're a genius!"

He handed the napkin to Polly and ran toward Toby's tent.

Some girls might have been reluctant to approach a pig who weighed perhaps five times as much as they, but Polly was not one of those. Without the slightest hesitation, she knelt by Letitia and dabbed the napkin in the bowl of warm water that Ba had brought from the tent. Letitia seemed to trust the girl immediately and grunted softly each time Polly applied the napkin to her skin.

"Don't worry, Letitia," Polly whispered, carefully swabbing a nasty scrape on the pig's left ear. "Everything is going to be fine."

Jeremy returned a few minutes later with the stack of cards. As the others gathered around him, he dealt them onto the grass in two concentric arcs, just as he had seen Toby do. When all the cards were dealt, Jeremy stared at the two arched rows of letters, spread one above the other on the grass like a double rainbow. It was impossible for him not to think of the first time he'd seen those letters on the graffiti house in Tiny's neighborhood. It seemed a very, very long time ago.

"You ask her, Jeremy," Sylvana said. "Letitia is most likely to answer if you're the one who asks."

He didn't need to be told twice.

"Letitia," he said, trying to imitate Toby's tone and inflection. "Where's Toby?"

As if she had been waiting for this since the moment of her arrival, Letitia ran to the cards, looking almost like her old self. But when she got to the first row, she hesitated, turning first to the "A" but then moving away before she had actually selected it. She did the same thing with the "B," then the "C."

"She seems confused," Sylvana said. "Ask her again, Jeremy."

"Letitia," Jeremy asked, "where's Toby?"

Once more, Letitia moved among the cards. Once more, she moved from one to another without actually making a choice.

Jeremy's heart sank.

So it's true, he thought. *She isn't sapient, after all. Toby was signaling her, telling her which card to choose by clicking his nails. She's just a trick pig.*

Letitia looked back at Jeremy as if to say, *Help me!* But there was no help to be had. She stopped and drooped her noble head as she released what could only have been an immense sigh of porcine sorrow.

"Let's not humiliate her any further," Bo said. "We'll have to try something else."

With heavy hearts, the group turned their backs on the cards and began to walk toward the table, Jeremy with them.

"It's all right, Letitia," he said. "You did your best."

But Letitia was not about to be put off by Jeremy's sympathy. She grabbed the hem of his shorts between her teeth and pulled him back toward the cards. Jeremy struggled to keep his balance against the force of the pig's tugging.

"What's gotten into her?" Watty asked.

"I think she wants to try again," Jeremy said.

This time, Letitia trained her expressive eyes on Jeremy's. She oinked, then nudged Jeremy's hand with her snout. She did it again. And again and again and again, until Jeremy thought he understood what she was trying to say.

"Okay, Letty," he said. "I'll try it."

He moved back in front of the cards.

"Letitia," he asked a third time. "Where's Toby?"

He clicked his nails. Letitia's ears stood at attention. Had she actually grinned at Jeremy? She ran to the cards. There was no hesitation now. She went directly to the "I."

"So that's it," Jeremy said as he continued to click. "Toby wasn't giving her the answers. The noise calms her down, helps her concentrate."

Letitia ran from one card to another.

Polly produced a small pad of paper and a pencil from the pocket of her dress. She wrote down each letter that Letitia selected. When she was done, Letitia ran back to where Jeremy was standing and sat down, panting.

"You're a fabulous pig, Letitia," Bo said, patting her on the head.

The others cheered and clapped.

"Polly dear," Ba said at last. "I'm afraid I lost track. Could you read back to us what Letitia has spelled?"

Polly read out the letters.

"I-N-C-A-R-C-E-R-A-T-E-D," she answered. "Incarcerated."

Connie was already searching for the word. She found it just over Lexi's belly button.

"Incarcerated," she read simply. "Adjective. *Imprisoned.*"

The group fell silent.

"That can only mean one thing," Bo said at last.

Jeremy exhaled and said what everybody was thinking.

"Toby is in the Choir Stall."

Chapter 41

It Wasn't the Flying that Frightened Him

Though so much had occurred, Jeremy and the others had not forgotten about the Baron or what he might be planning. And from what Rosie had said earlier, he hadn't forgotten about them, either. Surely more trouble was on the way, and after what had happened to Gravitas and to Lemondrop, it was of a kind that frightened even the bravest among them. But the thought of Toby suffering in the Choir Stall was unbearable. The biggest difficulty, of course, was how to get over the high wall that surrounded the terrible prison.

"It's too tall," Watty lamented. "Even for me."

"But it's not for *me*!" Sylvana showed all her gold teeth.

Her plan was a daring one. She would position her cannon in the empty lot across from the dreaded prison and shoot herself over the wall.

"But how will you get out?" Polly asked.

"The warden at the Choir Stall is a horror," Rosie piped up. "But offer him enough money and he'll hand you the keys himself."

Watty brightened at this information and ran off at a quick pace toward his tent. Sylvana set to work calculating angles and deciding how much gunpowder she would need.

"Too much and I'll overshoot my mark," she muttered as she scribbled down equations on the tabletop with a piece of chalk. "Too little and I'll fly smack into the wall."

In spite of the immense difficulty of the plan, Toby's friends grew more and more hopeful.

"It just might work," Bo said with increasing optimism. "It just might work."

But at the last minute, an obstacle presented itself that nearly defeated them.

"My cannon!" Sylvana wailed. "It's still at Helios! The Baroness kicked us out so quickly I didn't have a chance to retrieve it."

"Surely you have a spare, Sylvana," Ba suggested.

But Sylvana shook her head. "Just the Junior Phuse 2300," she replied.

"Well?"

"It's too small. I used it as a kid. I'd never fit in it now."

Jeremy stepped forward. "But I will," he said.

Silence descended on the group as each person realized the terrible risk Jeremy was taking by suggesting such a thing. They had all heard Sylvana's hair-raising stories about her early years, and they recalled with vivid detail the descriptions of the broken legs and bandaged head. The chances of Jeremy's pulling off a first flight without coming to serious harm were slim indeed. But only Ba protested, and then, very little.

"No, Jeremy," she argued, putting her gloved hand to her mouth. "I can't permit it. The dangers of human cannonballing are—"

"Sometimes," Jeremy interrupted, suddenly sounding much older than his years, "a person has to choose between what is *safe* and what is *right.*"

"Well, Jeremy," Polly said later, "it looks like you're going to get a chance at being a hero again."

Jeremy shook his head. "Not a hero," he replied. "Just a friend."

By the next morning, they were ready. The problem of how to get out of the Choir Stall had been quickly solved the day before when Watty showed up with a size 37 shoe box. It contained his life savings. "If the jailer is as greedy as Rosie says, this ought to help."

Piés flowed to the table from every tent. Madame Josephine, Gravitas, Melchior. No one held back, not even Radu, who was known to be something of a penny-pincher. He arrived carrying a feed bag filled to the brim with piés.

"I been saving up for rainy day," he'd said, emptying the bag onto the table. "Well, looks like raining now. Pouring, in matter a fact."

Jeremy stuffed the money into a rucksack. Polly made a contribution, too, though not of a monetary kind.

"From what I hear about Toby," she'd said, handing Jeremy a package tied up neatly in brown paper, "he won't like it much, but it will help to keep him safe until you get him back to the Living Museum."

After a great deal of discussion, and a long, though unsuccessful, argument from Rosie centering on how useful she would be on such a venture, it was finally decided that Sylvana and Jeremy would venture out alone. With the current atmosphere in the Metropolis, the less attention they drew to themselves, the safer it was for everybody.

It was hard, naturally, for Jeremy to say good-bye to Polly after having just reunited with her. But Polly made it easier by reminding Jeremy of a story they'd read together in the old days at the Licreeary.

"Just think, Jeremy," she said. "You'll be like Icarus." She straightened the straps of the rucksack, which had become twisted when Jeremy had hoisted it onto his back. "Just don't fly too close to the sun the way he did."

"I won't, Polly," he replied, remembering the way the boy's wax wings had melted and sent him plummeting into the ocean below. He didn't say it—he didn't want to alarm Polly—but it wasn't the flying that frightened him. It was the landing.

"You'll be here when I get back, won't you?" he asked.

"Don't you worry," Polly said. "I'll be waiting right here."

Just before he and Sylvana set out, Jeremy picked up Daffodil and put her in Rosie's arms. They were standing with Bo and Ba on the landing at the top of the steps.

"Take good care of her," he said.

It wasn't clear, though, to whom he was giving these instructions. Was it to Rosie? Or the pup?

Bo closed the door behind them.

Chapter 42

Tuck and Roll

Though the Phuse 2300 was a junior model, it was still plenty heavy to wheel over the crumbling pavement of the Metropolis streets. Connie had suggested disguising the cannon as a vegetable stand on its way to the open markets. A clever idea since it decreased the chance of the plan's being discovered, but it also came with the disadvantage of making the transport of the cannon even more awkward. Still, as difficult as the journey to the Choir Stall was, it was not nearly as rattling as what Jeremy and Sylvana discovered once they were outside the walls of the Living Museum.

The first time he saw it, he thought his imagination was playing a cruel joke. The second time, he knew it was not his imagination, but as real as the Junior Phuse 2300 itself. The third time, his stomach roiled. For a moment, he thought he might be sick.

SAVE JEREMY CABBAGE!

On walls. On sidewalks. On the street itself. Scrawled everywhere he looked, in fact.

SAVE JEREMY CABBAGE!

With chalk. With paint. In every conceivable medium. On every conceivable surface.

SAVE JEREMY CABBAGE!

Big. Small. In block letters. In flourishing calligraphy. In all the colors of the rainbow. Sometimes, it was even misspelled, leaving out the second "e" in "Jeremy" or starting "Cabbage" with a "K." But in letters white as snow or red as blood, clumsily printed or in swooping cursive, spelled phonetically or following the rules, the message was always the same:

SAVE JEREMY CABBAGE!

"It's nonsense, Jeremy," Sylvana counseled. "Don't even look at it."

Sylvana knew this advice was impossible to follow, but she wanted to say something comforting to Jeremy, especially because the power of the three words was exaggerated by another oddity. The streets were completely deserted. Though the hour was still very early, Jeremy and Sylvana should have been passing workers shuffling their way to the early shifts in the factories. They looked up and down every cross street. Not a soul was to be found.

Neither of them said it, but both automatically connected the eerie, empty streets to the recent turn of events the Baron had set in motion. They still didn't understand what exactly the foolish man was up to, but they couldn't help but think that whatever his plan was, it seemed to be working.

"Where is everybody?" Jeremy finally asked.

"I don't know," the Wuman Cannonball answered.

"But let's look on the bright side. It makes wheeling this thing a lot easier."

An hour later, they arrived, perspiring and heart-sick, at the empty lot across from the Choir Stall.

Tuck and roll. Tuck and roll. Tuck and roll.

Jeremy repeated these words over and over again as he squirmed inside the tight, dark barrel of the Junior Phuse 2300.

"That's all you have to remember, Jeremy," Sylvana told him. "When you land, tuck and roll. Don't try to do anything fancy like land on your feet. Just tuck and roll before you hit the ground and you should be all right."

Before he hit the ground? Neither of them said what both were thinking: Tucking and rolling just might work on a grassy field, but what was on the other side of the wall? The Choir Stall was not known for its lush landscaping or its verdant fields. But this was no time for second thoughts. Toby was inside the Choir Stall. Jeremy was nestled in the barrel of the 2300. It was now or never.

"Ready?" he heard Sylvana ask through the earplugs she'd handed him earlier.

"Ready," Jeremy shouted back. He closed his eyes.

"One. Two."

Tuck and roll. Tuck and roll. Tuck and . . .

"Three!"

BOOOOOOOOOOOOOOOOOOOOOOOOOOOOOM!

The sensation of being shot from a cannon was one that Jeremy would never forget. He tried to describe it whenever he told the story of Toby's rescue, but he felt he never got it right. Sometimes, he would say it was like riding a tornado. Other times, he said it was like the entire universe had suddenly gasped for breath.

He opened his eyes. Below him, the Metropolis spread out in all directions. He was struck with the sensation that it was nothing but a toy, a model set up on a tabletop for a wealthy child to play with. He tried to look for the Living Museum, but the dizzying speed at which he traveled turned everything below him into a blurry brown and gray streak. Sylvana had warned him about this.

"Try to focus on something," she'd said, "or else you'll get airsick. And believe me, you don't want *that* to happen when you're spinning like a pinwheel fifty feet above the ground."

He was at the apex of his flight now.

I wish Polly could see me, he thought. *I'm flying! I'm like Icarus!*

He sailed over the wall without the slightest difficulty. He was starting even to enjoy it, and he told himself to remember it all—the way the wind felt against his face, the lovely silence of flight—so that he could tell Polly what it was like. But before he knew what was happening, he began to feel himself falling.

Moving far too fast to make a judgment about his landing, he closed his eyes once again. Falling faster now, he brought his knees up and pulled his head forward so that his chin was tucked firmly against his chest.

Tuck and roll. Tuck and roll. Tuck and roll. Tuck and . . . Oooooooooof!

It was over. Just like that. For a moment, he lay still, not daring to move, not sure, really, if he was alive. The wind had been knocked completely out of him, and a peculiar sensation of numbness lay over him. But slowly, his lungs began to expand, at first just a millimeter or two, but with each short breath, more and more life-giving oxygen flowed into him until a tingling sensation began to bubble in his fingers and toes, then his hands and feet, and finally throughout his entire body.

My nose itches, he thought.

He opened his eyes and brushed away the frilly green leaves of a carrot.

From that day forward, no matter what difficulty he was in, Jeremy Cabbage considered himself to be the luckiest boy on earth. He'd landed in the one soft patch of ground in the entire compound, an eight-by-eight-foot garden where the jailer grew some spindly vegetables. The rest was a mass of pavement and stone. If he'd landed six inches to the left— Well, it was best not to think about that.

He stood up and brushed himself off, making sure that nothing was broken. Already, he could feel his bottom lip swelling where it had knocked against one of the rocks that outlined the garden. He spat out a bit of blood and, with it, something small, hard, and white.

Hands at his side, he surveyed the scene before him. He was in a courtyard. Behind him was the wall he had just flown over. On the other three sides, the Choir Stall loomed over him seven stories high. The color of sand and pockmarked with the scars of time, the walls were lined with tiny windows and, over each window, a series of iron bars. It was like an immense walled city from the ancient past. His heart sank. How would he ever find Toby?

"Jeremy!"

His name echoed off the wall to his right.

"Jeremy!" he heard again.

At first, he thought that maybe the knock he'd received when he landed was causing him to hallucinate. But when Toby called out the third time, Jeremy knew it was no mistake.

"I'm over here. To the left. Look up!"

Jeremy turned around.

"On the second floor!"

Squinting, Jeremy trained his eyes on the long row of windows that paralleled the ground two stories above. Halfway down the row, he saw his friend's face pressed against the bars.

"Toby!" Jeremy called out. "It's me!"

"Yeah! I can see that! I heard the cannon! The door is at the end of the wall, Jeremy. Hurry! Before guards catch you."

In a flash, Jeremy spotted the door and ran to it. Rusted and pitted, the iron door was immensely heavy, but Jeremy had not been shot from a cannon to be defeated by a door. He put both hands on the handle and pulled with every ounce of his strength. Sweat broke out on his forehead. He found himself thinking about

Tiny and how he had pulled her up onto that first step of her porch.

Where is she now? he wondered.

With a long, painful squeak, the door slowly opened. Jeremy found himself peering into the end of a long, dark corridor. He wasn't prepared for the terrible stench that met him, nor for the sounds of the prisoners moaning and crying for help, the dreadful "singing" for which the Choir Stall had been named.

Jeremy hesitated for the tiniest fraction of a moment. Then, putting his hand over his mouth and nose, he stepped over the threshold and ran full throttle into the Choir Stall.

Chapter 43

Save Jeremy Cabbage!

Sylvana's heart had climbed all the way up her throat when Jeremy shot out of the Junior Phuse 2300. She hadn't liked the way he was listing to the right. If the flight was longer, he might miss the Choir Stall altogether, so it was with a certain amount of relief that she saw him sail over the wall and disappear behind it.

"Tuck and roll, Jeremy," she'd whispered, crossing her fingers. "Tuck and roll."

She waited, motionless, wondering what the silence that followed could mean. They hadn't talked at all about what would happen if one of the guards spotted him. What would have been the sense of it? Once he was behind that wall, he was on his own.

Sylvana waited a few more minutes, listening for the clanging of alarms or the wail of a siren, but once she was convinced no alarms would ring, she covered the 2300 with brush, as they had planned, disguising it as just another piece of junk littering the Metropolis.

"Good girl!" she whispered, giving the cannon a final pat.

They'd also decided that the safest thing was for Sylvana to return immediately to the Living Museum. The Wuman Cannonball was not happy about this and had argued strongly against it. But Bo had remained unmoved.

"If Jeremy is discovered," he'd said, "they'll suspect he had help and will send out the PatPats to find his accomplice. No, you come back to us the moment you're certain that Jeremy is over the wall. It's probably a good idea to take a different route home, too. Just in case."

Now, as Sylvana made her back way to the Living Museum, she was dismayed to see that the same graffiti appeared in these neighborhoods with just as much frequency and variety as it had in the ones through which she and Jeremy had traveled earlier.

"Save Jeremy Cabbage, my gold teeth!" she muttered. "It's us who need saving. From the Baron!"

These sentiments, along with her worry for Jeremy and Toby, so enveloped her it took her some time to realize that, unlike earlier that morning, she was not alone. The streets were teeming with pedestrians. Men. Women. Boys. Girls. And nearly everyone carried a bag or a basket of one kind or another. Sylvana noticed something else peculiar, too. They were all moving in the same direction as she was.

Sylvana willed the goose bumps that were forcing themselves onto her forearms to disappear. She approached a woman to her right. The woman, who moved with a slight limp, carried a dirty, torn basket over a frail arm. Her thin gray hair and deeply wrinkled face made it impossible to guess her age.

"Excuse me," Sylvana said. "Can you tell me where everyone was earlier this morning? The streets were empty."

"We was all sleepin' in," the woman replied, showing her total lack of teeth. "Didn't you hear? The Baron declared a holiday."

Sylvana's constitution was as stable as a sailor's, but her stomach suddenly flip-flopped.

"Holiday? What holiday?"

"For that little feller them cloons has captured," the woman answered. "Jeremy Cabbage Day. That's what the Baron's callin' it. That's where we're all goin' right now."

"Going where?" Sylvana asked. She wasn't at all sure that she wanted to hear the answer.

"To the Livin' Museum. That's where they got 'im. That boy, I mean. Jeremy Cabbage. The Baron's givin' a big speech there later. We're all supposed to go and hear it." She paused for a moment and then punctuated her explanation with three words. "Save Jeremy Cabbage!" she added.

Sylvana tried to ignore this and instead looked down at the basket the woman was carrying. It was filled with rotting tomatoes.

"What are those for?" she asked.

"The Baron said we was supposed to bring 'em. If them cloons wants red noses, we'll give 'em red noses. That's what he said." She pointed to a group of Junior PatPats roughhousing across the street. "They got baskets, too," she added. "But it ain't just tomatoes that's in 'em."

Chapter 44

Instead, He Smiled

It was taking Jeremy longer than he would have liked to find Toby's cell. The unlit stairwell was black as pitch, and in his haste, he accidentally passed the entrance to the second floor and ran to the third. He only realized his mistake when a prisoner, who'd watched the scene in the courtyard from his cell, corrected him.

"Hey, you! Flyboy!" the man shouted. "You're too far up. He's right below you. Go and get him. Get your buddy out of this hellhole."

Jeremy thanked the man and ran back down the long corridor, lined on both sides with doors identical to the one the man had called from. Twice, he had to swerve to avoid colliding with one of the rats that scurried from piles of rubbish littering the Choir Stall. But once he was on the second floor, he had no difficulty finding Toby's cell. By now, news of the attempted escape had spread throughout the prison like a flash fire.

"You're almost there, boy," one prisoner called out as he dashed by. "Don't give up now."

"Watch your step there," another cautioned. "The floor is slippery with . . ."

"Just three more doors!"

And he was there! Gulping for breath, he pulled back the iron bolt and swung the door open. The corridor rang with applause and cheers.

"I knew you'd come for me, Jeremy!" Toby cried out. "It was Letty, wasn't it? She told you where I was! Good ol' Letty!"

Jeremy grabbed his friend and hugged him. "Let's get out of here," he said.

Toby grabbed his hat and stepped over the threshold of the cell, but Jeremy stopped him. He reached into his rucksack and pulled out the package that Polly had contributed to the effort.

"Put this on!" Jeremy said, ripping off the brown paper.

Toby looked at Jeremy as if he had just walked through a wall.

"What?" he balked. "Have you gone nutters? I ain't puttin' on no dress!"

"It'll be safer for both of us," Jeremy explained. "Once we're out of here, the PatPats will be everywhere looking for us."

"I said I ain't wearin' a dress!"

But as Toby pushed the dress back toward Jeremy, a pié, which had caught on one of the buttons, floated to the floor, landing almost on Toby's boots. He picked it up.

"What's this?" he asked.

Jeremy opened the rucksack and showed him the stash the Living Museum had collected.

"From Watty," he said. "From Watty and Lexi and Connie and Madame Josephine and . . . and everybody."

It took a moment for Toby to realize what the money meant.

"You mean . . . ?"

Jeremy nodded. "Even Radu," he said.

Was it the bad air inside the Choir Stall that caused Toby's eyes to water? No matter. He grabbed the dress from Jeremy's hands and threw it on over his shoulders. He put the bonnet on, too, giving Jeremy his hat to store in the rucksack.

"Okay," he said. "I'm ready. Let's go."

The two boys stepped out into the hallway, Jeremy in the same clothes he wore when he flew over the Choir Stall's wall, Toby in a dress and bonnet. Though he looked as awkward in the ruffles and hoops as a wrestler in a tutu, the dress fit him surprisingly well. It was the same one Polly had worn at the birthday ball and the one in which she'd escaped. Anyone who didn't know better might have thought it was Polly herself.

Jeremy couldn't help it. "You look very pretty," he teased.

"Don't you dare never tell nobody about this," Toby warned, accidentally stepping on the hem and ripping off a scallop of lace.

When he was searching for Toby, it had been hard for Jeremy to ignore the cries for help that had echoed against the filthy walls of the Choir Stall. Now it suddenly occurred to him that since Toby was free, or almost, perhaps he didn't have to. He looked at Toby. Toby looked back. Though the brim of the bonnet partially hid his expression, both boys knew what they had to do.

Without a word between them, they ran down the corridor, Jeremy on one side, Toby on the other, flinging back one bolt after another. One by one, the prisoners began to emerge, dazed, unable to believe what was happening.

Those who could walk on their own helped those who couldn't, and those who could run followed Jeremy and Toby to the floors above. In a matter of minutes, the entire population of the Choir Stall, led by Jeremy and Toby, was rushing toward the main gate. Old men. Young women. Even children. Different as they were from each other, all of them had fallen under the merciless baton of the PatPats and their spies. They cascaded toward the gate like a great river about to overflow its banks.

Dr. Perfidio Purgatorn, a changed man, was carried along with the rest.

"I warned the Baroness," he muttered to himself as he hobbled along. "I told her years ago that her family carried the gene. Just because she and her mother and grandmother had been spared didn't mean her daughter would be. Luck doesn't last forever."

He turned to the prisoner next to him, a young man in his twenties. "Am I free?" Purgatorn asked. "Has she changed her mind?"

"We're all free!" the young man answered.

The warden, a horrid man with a patch over his left eye, heard the commotion and ran to the alarm. As the clanging jarred the air over his head, Jeremy expected a throng of guards to come rushing toward them. But no guards were to be seen. Like the rest of the population, they had been given the day off to attend the rally at the Living Museum. Only the jailer remained.

The man lifted his eye patch as if to make sure that what he was seeing was real. Corrupt but not stupid, he ducked back into his apartment as the huge crush of prisoners approached the gate.

Together, Toby and Jeremy lifted the heavy iron bar that locked the gates. The doors swung open. They were free. The river of prisoners behind them flooded the streets. Some were laughing. Some were crying. Some were cheering. Some were silent. All of them were filled with wonder at the knowledge that it was a boy who had defied the great Baron Ignatius Fyodor Maximus von Strompié III and set them free.

Eventually, the great river began to disperse, first into tributaries and then into single streamlets as the newly released prisoners found their way to the roads and alleys that would lead them home.

"You did it, Jeremy!" Toby shouted, clapping him on the back with a tremendous wallop. "You did it!"

Much later, when strangers asked about his gold tooth, the replacement for the one that had broken off during his landing, Jeremy refused to explain. Instead, he smiled, letting the tooth glint in the sunlight like a medal, which, in a way, it was.

Chapter 45

He Looked Good in a Dress

"You were right, Jeremy!" Toby said. "About that night I riled up the audience against the Baron, I mean."

The two would have walked side by side, but the skirt of Polly's dress took up most of the space on the crumbling sidewalk and forced Jeremy to proceed a little ahead of his friend. He had no trouble hearing Toby, though; the brim of the bonnet worked exceptionally well as a megaphone.

"It was that Junior PatPat who did me in. Letty and me was just about to leave the gate and head out toward the Petropolis. Before I knew what was happenin', I was surrounded by a bunch of them JP devils. They was bein' directed by that boy who asked Letitia to spell the Baron's name.

"I didn't stand a chance. There was too many of 'em. All hollerin' and screamin' like demons. But I gave a couple of 'em what for. You can bet on that. It broke— *arrgh!* These hoopy things is tryin' to kill me! I don't know how girls do it, Jeremy. I swear I don't."

Jeremy bit his lower lip to keep from laughing as Toby grabbed fistfuls of Polly's dress and yanked it violently up to his knees to prevent his boots getting tangled yet again in its crinolines.

"Anyway, like I was sayin' . . . ," Toby continued, once he worked out a system for dealing with the treacherous underskirts. "It broke my heart to see the way they took off after Letty, chasin' her down the street and her squealin' like that. She's okay now, though, isn't she, Jeremy? They didn't hurt her or nothin'?"

"She's perfect," Jeremy reassured his friend. "A scratch here and there, a little thinner, maybe, but in a day or two, she'll be back to her old self. You'll see."

A long, slow sniff escaped from the bonnet.

"Poor Letty," Toby said. "And the whole time, that kid laughin' like a creature from the Terra Nequam."

As he listened to Toby, Jeremy prodded the stub of his broken tooth with his tongue. All along, since identifying Pickles that night, part of him had been holding back, looking for ways to give Pickles the benefit of the doubt, but after listening to Toby, his misgivings were confirmed beyond any question.

The boys turned a corner.

"He used to be a friend of mine," Jeremy said quietly.

Toby stopped. He shoved back the bonnet. "You're kiddin' me!"

"I wish I were. It was Pickles."

They continued walking.

"You'd better put the bonnet back on," Jeremy cautioned. "There are a lot of people on the street."

Toby did as his friend asked. They moved in silence for a few minutes before Toby picked up the conversation.

"You mean that boy who was one of them Parrots?

Is that the one you're talkin' about? Who used to live with you and Polly in the Licree . . . Licara . . ."

"Licreeary," Jeremy corrected. "Yes. That's the one."

"Well," Toby responded after they'd proceeded farther down the block, "I never did like the sound of that rascal. Course, I didn't say nothin' on account of he was your friend. Anyway, don't you worry nothin' about that. You got a *new* friend now." He rested his arm on Jeremy's shoulders.

"Yes," Jeremy replied, allowing the solid weight of Toby's arm to comfort him. "I guess I do." He took another step. "Even if he *does* look good in a dress," he added.

"Hey!" Toby removed his arm and gave Jeremy a good-natured punch. "I warned you about that!"

Toby had been vague about the reason for his arrest, allowing Jeremy to believe that it was because he'd turned the audience against the Baron that night. Jeremy, of course, thought he knew the real reason, but he said nothing. What was to be gained by forcing Toby to admit he was responsible for the graffiti about the Baron? In the end, it would only cause him to relive once again the dreadful reasons for it. Instead, Jeremy turned the conversation to all that had occurred since: the disaster at the birthday celebration, his reunion with Polly, the surprising news about Rosie. This last was too much for Toby.

"You mean she's a *cloon*?" he shouted.

Several pedestrians turned their heads toward the two boys.

"Full-fledged," Jeremy whispered. "Try to keep your voice down."

"Well, I'll be a wowwie's nephew!" Toby whispered, shaking his head so that the strings of the bonnet swayed wildly under his chin. "The Baron's own daughter!"

The bonnet so limited Toby's vision that he hadn't seen the new graffiti that had taken over the Metropolis since his arrest. But it was there nonetheless, just as before. It would have been impossible, though, not to have become aware of the number of fellow travelers, which increased exponentially with each block they passed.

"Say," said Toby, "where are all these people headed? It's almost like they're goin' the same place we are."

Jeremy didn't reply, afraid to say aloud what he suspected. The two boys moved along in silence now. The crowd of people had grown so thick that it was almost certain their conversation would have been overheard. The pedestrians, like Jeremy and Toby, also walked without speaking. It was like traveling with a vast congregation of sleepwalkers, and the closer they got to the Living Museum, the quieter the somnambulists became.

Finally, Jeremy and Toby rounded the corner that led to home.

"What the—?"

But Toby stopped himself and whistled instead. The street in front of the Living Museum was a sea of heads. It seemed to the boys that the entire population of the Metropolis had gathered there.

Chapter 46

But Why Didn't They Try?

Jeremy stood on his tiptoes and saw over the crowd that a high platform had been erected on the street directly in front of the Living Museum. The platform was hung with bunting in the official colors of the von Strompié family, royal blue and peach puff. He reached for his telescope, then remembered that he'd left the spyglass in Polly's care. It would almost certainly have been destroyed in his escapade as a human cannonball, but he missed the instrument now.

Though he was too far away to recognize with any surety who they might be, three people sat on the platform. One of them, he was almost certain, was the Baron himself, but the others—two women, he thought—were in the shadow cast by the same magnificent screen that had toppled during the birthday celebration. The screen now provided a backdrop for the platform party. Jeremy could not see the flash of red behind it, nor the pair of eyes that peered out through the perforations, watching the crowd like a grizzly bear scrutinizing a river teeming with fish.

Jeremy and Toby realized that it would be impossible to get inside the Living Museum now.

"Let's try to get as close to the steps as we can," Jeremy whispered.

Toby nodded. They began to make their way toward the front of the crowd. With just the slightest pressure from Jeremy's hand, the crowd parted like a living organism responding to an outside stimulus. It cleared the way ahead for the boys and closed behind them once they had passed. Though thousands of people were gathered there, the only sounds were the rasping coughs as prevalent in the Metropolis as birdsong might have been elsewhere.

There was something eerily familiar to Jeremy about the silence of so many people. As he and Toby moved through the mob, he found himself thinking back to the fire at Tiny's. The flame's unstoppable will to gobble up everything in its path was undeniably the most frightening thing he had ever seen. But even more chilling, he realized now, had been the response of the people whose houses were being destroyed. They'd simply stood there, silent, like Tiny, their arms dangling helplessly at their sides or crossed tightly against their chests. No one had tried to organize a bucket brigade. No one had tried to beat the flames down with shovels or blankets. Jeremy knew that fighting the fire might not have done anything to prevent what had happened. *But why didn't they try?* he thought.

A man whose face was darkened with soot stepped aside to make room for him. In spite of the heat generated by so many bodies pressed shoulder to shoulder, there was something in the man's empty expression that caused a chill to run down Jeremy's spine, and he suddenly realized what living under the Baron's control had done to the citizens of the Metropolis.

It's destroyed their will, he told himself. *It's destroyed the belief that they can do anything to stop whatever fate puts in their way.*

This seemed more destructive to Jeremy than even the fire.

He glanced back at Toby, tramping through the crowd behind him. Toby *had* exercised a choice; he *had* fought back.

But, Jeremy thought, *he put himself in terrible danger to do it.*

And what of Pickles? He had made yet another choice.

Are these the only alternatives for citizens of the Metropolis? Jeremy asked himself. Would everyone eventually have to choose between heroism, like Toby, or treachery, like Pickles?

Jeremy stepped around a boy standing with the help of wooden crutches and looked up into the faces of the adults closest to him. He was hoping to find the glimmer of an answer, another choice. But he saw nothing. Only the vacant stares of the citizens of the Metropolis as they waited to be told what to do next.

They were nearing the front of the crowd now. He turned his gaze to the top of the steps, toward the double doors that led to the Living Museum. Bo and Ba. Watty. Sylvana. Lexi and Connie. All of them were waiting on the other side of those doors. They were gathered there on the landing, looking through the key-hole, listening, and wondering what to do. And they were frightened, not just for themselves, but for him and for Toby. Polly was on that landing, too. He was sure of it. And Rosie.

Everybody I care about is behind those doors, he thought. *Everybody except Toby, and he's right behind me. So what if they are cloons and giants? So what if they are oddballs with gold teeth and tattoos? They're my family.*

By the time they reached the front of the crowd, Jeremy felt much less helpless than when he and Toby had rounded the corner to find the population of the Metropolis gathered outside their home. He was for-ever connected to the people on the other side of those doors, and nothing could change that. As Toby sidled up next to him, he took a deep breath, ready for any-thing that might happen.

They were standing behind the thick gold cording that had been set up to separate the platform from the masses.

"Well, if it ain't the Big Man hisself," Toby said.

The Baron Ignatius Fyodor Maximus von Strompié III was perched six feet above them on a gold and red velvet chair. Now Jeremy could also identify the two women. One was the Baroness Gertrudina. She sat stiffly, looking straight ahead and holding a handkerchief to her nose. Beside her, smiling as if she had just been elected President of the World, sat Hulda Harpwitch.

Chapter 47

A Frock of Fleaks

The Baron looked out on the crowd and shifted uncomfortably. He was disappointed. After all, today was a special day. It wasn't that often that he appeared before his people. Couldn't they have dressed a little better? Did they think it was pleasant for him to have to look out on such a raggedy shamble as was gathered before him now? Well, it was true, he supposed—some people just didn't have any consideration for others.

Still, he had to admit there was very little to complain about at present. The deranged brat responsible for the graffiti about him had been captured and was now locked away in the Choir Stall. Ha! Just a boy apparently. More proof that the citizens of the Metropolis needed tighter controls.

He had gotten rid of that smart-alecky Jeriah Wirm, too, and, even better, the new Commander General of the PatPats was turning out to be positively ferocious in his administration of justice. The Baron was still in awe of the way the boy had tricked the Chief Driver, stealing the photographs and putting two and two together in order to snag the graffiti whelp. Well, it served Wirm right! He should have told *him* about the animal tracks! At any rate, no need to fret about it anymore. The CG was stationed behind the screen even now, keeping an eye out for troublemakers.

And today, finally, he would be getting the Baroness Gertrudina off his back about this cloon nonsense. He'd practically had to bribe her to accompany him to this event, though. He convinced her only by telling her that he needed her presence to set a good example for other wives and mothers in the Metropolis.

Rosamund should be here, too, he thought. *The citizens of the Metropolis could learn something about what a good family looks like. Maybe then their own filthy brats wouldn't go around feeling free to paint dangerous slogans all over the place.*

But then he remembered why Rosamund was absent. He shrugged. Oh well. He hadn't seen her since the day of the ruinous birthday party, and when he'd asked about her, Gertrudina was uncharacteristically mild in her response. Instead of the usual hysterical sermon on her daughter's failings, she'd only smiled vaguely and muttered, "Rosamund is being taken care of."

Well, women were mysterious. And that included Hulda Harpwitch. She'd never said what she had against the Cabbage boy, but whatever it was, he was glad for it. He would introduce her as the guardian from whom the cloons had snatched the boy away. Then, once the citizens were good and worked up, he would give his speech, the one in which he would announce the new law banning the cloons and their hangers-on.

He smiled to himself, recalling how pleased he'd been when he came up with the name of the law. It was one of his best. The Freedom from Freaks Act. *He* would get something out of it, too. That was the best part. The land on which the cloons had built the Living Museum. Perhaps he'd build a new palace there. Heli-also, he might call it. Or Helios East. He looked up toward the sun. Were they east? he wondered. He'd never been very good with directions.

"Can't we get this started?" Gertrudina hissed from behind him. "I'm practically fainting from the smell."

"I suppose you're right, dear. But don't forget. Patience is a virtue."

His wife groaned. He stood up.

"Happy Jeremy Cabbage Day!" he yelled into the microphone.

Silence.

"Happy Jeremy Cabbage Day!" he repeated.

"Happy Jeremy Cabbage Day," a few of the citizens called back.

"I said," the Baron shouted, "Happy Jeremy Cabbage Day!"

This time, the mob understood what it was to do.

"Happy Jeremy Cabbage Day!" they repeated in unison.

Under the bonnet, Toby's eyes grew as large as bowls.

"What's goin' on, Jeremy?" he said. "You got a whole holiday named after you now?"

"Yes," the Baron continued. "I said Happy Jeremy

Cabbage Day. But is Jeremy Cabbage happy? How could he be, dear friends, himself a normal boy, locked up with a flock of freaks? How could he be?"

The Baron paused, waiting for this turn of phrase to take its full effect on the citizens of the Metropolis. Flock of freaks. He loved that. He'd thought of it himself.

"Now," he continued, "with your permission, I'd like to introduce someone to you. Someone very special. Someone, too, whose heart has been broken by this very same frock of fleaks . . . er . . . I mean, flick of frooks . . ." Scattered chuckles from the crowd. The Baron reminded himself not to veer from his prepared speech again. "She's a *good* woman," he continued. "A woman with a heart of gold."

Hulda Harpwitch stood and walked slowly toward the microphone. Her earlier smile was now twisted into a mask of tragedy.

"Miss Hulda Harpwitch," the Baron announced. The microphone screeched. "It was in her loving care that Jeremy Cabbage was thriving before the cloons snatched him away to teach him their dark, twisted ways. It was she who was instilling the virtues of the Metropolis into his heart, and it is she who pines for the poor boy to this very day and longs to have him back at her side."

As the last words echoed over the heads of the crowd, Jeremy ducked and scooted under the cording.

"Help me up," he said to Toby.

Toby was sure he had misheard his friend. "What?"

"I'm going up there," Jeremy said.

"But—"

"Do it!" Jeremy shouted. "Now!"

Chapter 48

Down with the Baron!

Toby followed Jeremy and folded his hands into a stirrup. In less than a second, Jeremy was standing on the platform. Harpwitch stopped in her tracks and hiccuped. The Baron raised his arm. He had no idea who this little ruffian was and was about to take the back of his hand to him. Before he could, Jeremy reached the microphone.

"My name is Jeremy Cabbage," he said.

A slow wave of excitement rippled through the crowd. The Baron put his arm down.

"Happy Jeremy Cabbage Day!" Jeremy shouted.

"Happy Jeremy Cabbage Day!" the crowd roared back.

"What the Baron said is true!" Jeremy exclaimed once the mob had quieted. "I live with cloons."

Scattered boos and cries of "Freaks!" punctuated the air.

"You see," the Baron said, elbowing his way back to the microphone, "I told you so."

"And the reason," Jeremy continued, ignoring the

Baron and pointing to Harpwitch, "is because she *sold* me! She sold me like I was one of those poor dogs she tortures."

A dark murmur went through the crowd. Harpwitch's face turned whiter than Jeriah Wirm's.

"Three times! Am I right, Miss Harpwitch? Isn't that the rule? Three strikes and you're out? You remember that, don't you?"

"Don't listen to him!" Harpwitch shouted between the hiccups that were taking complete control of her. "The boy's mind has been twisted by the cloons. He's lying!"

The crowd came to attention in one mass. Things were finally getting interesting. But who to believe? It might easily have gone against Jeremy, except for what happened next.

"She's the liar!" a familiar voice called out. "And I got the ding-dong papers to prove it. Alls I got to do is find 'em!"

Jeremy peered into the crowd. "Tiny?" he asked into the microphone. "Tiny? Is that you?"

"How ya doin', Cole Slaw?" Tiny shouted from her place a few rows back.

The beehive bobbed above the crowd like a single black cloud as Tiny weaved her way to the front. Jeremy couldn't believe his eyes. She was *twice* as fat.

"After that ding-dong fire, I gave up smoking," the large woman explained from her place in the front row. She shoved a bar of chocolate into her mouth with her right hand and deftly unwrapped another with her left. "That's when I discovered chocolate."

"Now see here!" the Baron sputtered. "I've come here today to—"

"You're doin' great up there, Cole Slaw," Tiny interrupted. "In fact, I'm gonna come right up there and give you a big old hug. For old times' sake." She waddled her way to the steps at the side of the platform. "While you're up there, how about sayin' something about that there Squatters' Law?"

"Now see here!" the Baron shouted again. "I passed that law to protect—"

"You passed that law to steal our property, you varmint," Toby retorted. "And don't you try to say different."

The crowd rumbled in agreement.

"No," the Baron insisted. "That isn't right. I . . ."

By now, Tiny was on the platform and was enveloping Jeremy in a smothering hug. Toby, still in Polly's dress and bonnet, hopped on the platform beside them. The Baroness Gertrudina, mistaking him for Polly herself, jumped out of her seat like a wild bovaloo.

"You wicked girl!" she shrieked. "You wicked, wicked girl!"

Toby had just enough time to put up his arms to protect himself from the blows Gertrudina was landing on him.

"I ain't wicked," he yelled. "And I ain't no girl!"

"Where is she?" the woman bellowed. "Where is she?"

"I don't know who you're talkin' about," Toby hollered.

"You know exactly who I'm talking about!" Gertrudina screamed. "You've brought Rosamund here, haven't you? You've brought that . . . monster here! Where is she? WHERE IS SHE?"

"I'm right here." Rosie flipped onto the platform. "And you're wrong about him bringing me here. I came by myself."

Rosie was not alone. The minute they'd heard Jeremy's voice over the microphone, the entire population of the Living Museum had thrown open the double doors and run down the stairs to his aid. Some jumped onto the platform, some took the stairs. Jeremy looked around him. They were all together at last. Nobody missing. Nobody in the Choir Stall. He had never felt happier. Or more courageous.

"I'd like you to meet my family!" he shouted into the microphone.

He took Bo's and Ba's hands. "My mother and father!"

He gestured to Polly and Rosie and Sylvana. "My sisters!"

He pointed to Toby. "My brother!"

He made a sweeping gesture toward Lexi and Connie and Watty and all the others. "My aunts and uncles and cousins!"

The crowd at first seemed stalled in a confused silence. How could this ragtag group of outcasts be called *anybody's* family, let alone a normal boy's? But Jeremy's courage overwhelmed even the most doubtful. A small group somewhere near the center of the mob began to applaud, only a smattering at first, no more than a spark. But the spark caught, and as individuals began to feel the infectious joy of sharing in another's happiness—some for the first time—the clapping spread from person to person. Finally, the entire crowd was caught up in a mighty cacophony of applause and cheering. Some were whistling. Others were stomping their feet, and at the edges of the crowd there were even those who entered into impromptu dances, kicking up their heels and swinging each other by the arm. All this for Jeremy and the oddball inhabitants of the Living Museum.

Rosie made her way to the microphone. "They're my family, too," Rosie shouted. "At least, I *think* they are."

Watty picked her up and put her on his shoulders. The Baroness shrieked and fainted dead away.

"Hey!" someone shouted from the crowd. "Ain't that the Baron's daughter?"

"It is!" another shouted. "And she's a *cloon!*"

"Yes!" Rosie answered, smiling. "I am! Isn't it terrific?"

"But he was going to ban the cloons today. Everybody knows that."

"What kind of a man would ban his own daughter?"

"No," the Baron tried to defend himself. "Of course I wasn't. I was just going to ban the others. I mean . . ."

"Oh, so you were going to send all the other cloons to the Terra Nequam but protect *her,* then? Is that what you were up to? You probably just wanted their land."

"Yes," the Baron answered. "I mean . . . no . . . I mean . . . they're freaks!"

"You're callin' your own flesh and blood a freak?"

"Boy!" the Baron shouted to the screen. "Boy! Dill! Do something."

But the Commander General knew there was nothing to be done. It was over. Anyone could see that. Besides, he was tired of jumping every time the Baron snapped his fingers. He'd saved up quite a lot of piés now, and what he hadn't saved he'd stolen.

You're a little late with that Dill business, Pickles thought. Though he had to admit, he was disappointed. He had been looking forward to seeing the expressions on Jeremy's and Polly's faces when they discovered that he—Pickles!—was the Commander General of the PatPats.

Oh well, he said to himself. *That's the way the cookie crumbles. You win some, you lose some.*

Without another thought, he jumped down from the back of the platform and disappeared into the crowd. The red coat lay in a crumpled heap on the floor.

In the meantime, the citizens of the Metropolis were growing angrier.

"You was tryin' to make us believe the cloons was bad. And you near did it, too."

"They *are* bad!" the Baron shouted. "They're freaks."

"You're the freak!" someone shouted right back. "Your own daughter is a cloon, and just look what you were planning to do."

"That ain't the only thing, neither!"

"What about our hours at the factories?"

"And our wages?"

"What about all them laws?"

"And the Wisdom Wagons?"

"What about the libraries?"

Jeremy balled his hands into fists, not from anxiety

this time, but from anger at all the Baron had done, at all he had tried to do. The anger shaped itself into four words. Indecipherable at first, they hooked together like railroad cars loaded with heavy, dangerous freight. They raced along the track running unobstructed from his heart to his mind until he could see them as clearly as if they were printed on a sign in front of him.

"Down with the Baron!" he shouted into the microphone.

Chapter 49

Tuck and Roll, Redux

"Down with the Baron!"

The words were sweet in his mouth. Sweet and strong. Toby joined him this time.

"Down with the Baron!"

The crowd rose up in a mighty chorus. *"Down with the Baron! Down with the Baron!"*

The Baron Ignatius Fyodor Maximus von Strompié III tried to back away, but he couldn't avoid the tomato. It hit him squarely on the nose. Harpwitch took one, too.

The tomatoes couldn't have weighed much, but those few extra ounces made all the difference. The platform had been erected hastily and was designed to hold the weight of four people, not the multitude that was on it now. It swayed dangerously.

"Cole Slaw?" Tiny called out.

The floorboards groaned.

"Jeremy?" Toby yelled.

The joists cracked and splintered.

"Polly?" Jeremy hollered.

The support posts buckled.

"Everybody?" Sylvana shouted. "TUCK AND ROLL!"

Chapter 50

There Were Other Changes, Too

Six weeks had passed since Jeremy Cabbage Day, and most of the injuries Jeremy and the others received when the platform buckled were already healed. Jeremy's arm was out of its sling now, and he was finally able to finish the family portrait he had painted on the panel in his room. The likeness of Polly was surprisingly accurate, but most people mistook the bonnet that lay at her feet for an armadillo. Rosie was included in the portrait now, too; she stood on her head next to him, just in front of Bo. And there was another addition as well, one that took up nearly all the room left on the panel.

"Good thing the Baron broke my fall," Tiny said. "I coulda really hurt myself."

"Well, we couldn't have that, Tiny," Bo responded. "You wouldn't be ready for your performance tonight."

"Yes, Tiny," Ba added. "You're getting quite famous."

"Famous!" Lexi said, though the effect was somewhat muffled since he was speaking through a mouthful of the delicious lopeberry crumble that Polly had made. "Noted. Celebrated. Eminent."

"Yes, dear," Connie said, patting her husband's arm affectionately. "We know."

Audiences at the Living Museum were better than ever now, and the newest act—Tiny: The Colossal Collector—was proving to be a sensation. It came to Jeremy the evening after the platform fell when they were both recuperating on the cots that Ba had set up under the tree. (Tiny was actually on three cots that Bo had strapped together.)

"I gave up smokin'," she informed Jeremy through the chocolate bar she had just jammed into her mouth. "But I didn't give up savin'."

The act was constructed along the lines of Lexi and Connie's. On three brightly painted carts, the bovaloo, zebalo, and wowwie hauled everything Tiny had saved since the fire into the Performance Tent.

The audience was instructed to call out the name of an object—a batterball racket, for example, or a used ticket to the Wheel of Heaven—and Tiny would produce it. Actually, it was Polly who produced it. She'd taken on the task of organizing Tiny's collection so the woman never found herself in the same situation she had with the deed. The audience was as entranced by Polly's charm as they were by Tiny's size.

As for the Baron, well, things were changing in the Metropolis. It was amazing what a couple of tomatoes could do. Every day, the study at Helios was packed with Deputations for Decent Domiciles, Committees for Clean Air, Workers for Fair Wages, Laborers for Libraries. One after another, they came.

"The PatPats have completely deserted me," the Baron whined to his wife. "The cowards! If I'd known it was going to come to this, I never even would have become a baron. It's not fair! There's even talk of . . . an election!"

But Gertrudina had slipped into another world. Her only interest now was the size and color of her own nose.

"It's getting redder, isn't it?" she asked her husband a thousand times a day. "Did it change shape when I was sleeping? It looks rounder, doesn't it? Doesn't it?"

There were other changes, too. Harpwitch's Home for Mean Dogs, Ugly Cats, and Strey Children had mysteriously burned to the ground. The dogs had escaped, but the wooden box full of piés was reduced, like the rest, to a mound of ashes. Harpwitch appealed to the Baron for help, and because of her loyalty, he did what he could: He gave her a job in the factories.

Polly brought the bowl of crumble to the table and set it in front of Toby.

"I brought another serving for Letitia, too," the girl said.

It almost sounded as if Letitia giggled.

Jeremy couldn't help but notice the way Polly had begun to blush every time she was around Toby. It made him feel so happy that he sometimes blushed, too. And they weren't the only ones turning red.

Watty stood up. He cleared his throat and turned a shade of crimson very like the circles of color that had appeared on Rosie's cheeks.

"I . . . I mean, *we*"—he looked at Tiny—"have an announcement."

The group settled. Watty was growing redder by the moment.

"Miss Tiny and I," he continued, "have made a momentous decision."

"Awww, Wattikins," Tiny said. "Just say it out, direct-like."

She stood up beside the gentle giant. "This here tall drink of water and me are gonna get hitched," she said, grabbing the man's hand. "Yessir! We're gonna tie the ding-dong knot! I knew it the minute I saw him. It was love at first sight."

"Yes, it was, Tinykins," Watty said, looking with love through his spectacles at his large bride-to-be. "For me, too."

Sylvana was the first to raise her glass. "Here's to the happy couple!" she shouted.

Jeremy scratched Daffy's ears with one hand, and with the other, he pounded on the table, adding to the cheers and whistles from the dinner party. His new gold tooth glowed warmly in the candlelight.

Rosie hopped up and jumped over the table.

"The tallest man in the Metropolis married to the fattest woman!" she shouted. "Hooray! Hooray for Tiny! Hooray for Watty! Hooray for the Living Museum! Hooray! Hooray! Hooray!"

Jeremy looked across the table at Polly and Toby, who were cheering and shouting out their congratulations along with the others.

The tallest man in the Metropolis married to the fattest woman? he thought. *Why not, Daffy? After all, everybody deserves to be as happy as we are, right?*

The little dog wagged her tail and barked, as if she were agreeing, as if she were shouting out a radical new idea to the wide, wide world: *Yes! Yes! Everybody deserves to be happy!*